What's
Not
Mine

What's Not Mine

Nora Decter

a novel

For every book sold, 1% of the cover price will be donated to Sunshine House, a resource and drop-in center in Winnipeg with the only mobile overdose prevention service in the province.

This book is also available as a Global Certified Accessible™ (GCA) ebook. ECW Press's ebooks are screen reader friendly and are built to meet the needs of those who are unable to read standard print due to blindness, low vision, dyslexia, or a physical disability.

Purchase the print edition and receive the ebook free. For details, go to ecwpress.com/ebook.

Published by ECW Press
665 Gerrard Street East
Toronto, Ontario, Canada M4M 1Y2
416-694-3348 / info@ecwpress.com

Editor for the Press: Jen Knoch
Copy editor: Crissy Calhoun
Cover design: Jo Walker
Front cover photograph: © zodebala (iStockPhoto)

LIBRARY AND ARCHIVES CANADA CATALOGUING IN PUBLICATION

Title: What's not mine : a novel / Nora Decter.

Names: Decter, Nora, 1986- author.

Identifiers: Canadiana (print) 20230561551 | Canadiana (ebook) 202305615X

ISBN 978-1-77041-764-9 (softcover)
ISBN 978-1-77852-288-8 (ePub)
ISBN 978-1-77852-289-5 (PDF)

Subjects: LCGFT: Novels.

Classification: LCC PS8607.E423 W53 2024 | DDC C813/.6—dc23

This book is funded in part by the Government of Canada. *Ce livre est financé en partie par le gouvernement du Canada.* We acknowledge the support of the Canada Council for the Arts. *Nous remercions le Conseil des arts du Canada de son soutien.* We acknowledge the funding support of the Ontario Arts Council (OAC), an agency of the Government of Ontario. We also acknowledge the support of the Government of Ontario through the Ontario Book Publishing Tax Credit, and through Ontario Creates.

ONTARIO CREATES

ONTARIO ARTS COUNCIL
CONSEIL DES ARTS DE L'ONTARIO
an Ontario government agency
un organisme du gouvernement de l'Ontario

Canada Council for the Arts   Conseil des arts du Canada

Canada

PRINTED AND BOUND IN CANADA

PRINTING: MARQUIS   5 4 3 2 1

MIX
Paper from responsible sources
FSC   FSC® C103567
www.fsc.org

For Nic

1.

It's well past midnight when who should text me but the mystery dick pic man who's been burning up my phone with his unsolicited appendage for the last couple months.

The text comes in, announcing itself with a ding, as I pull on my shorts and get ready to leave Someboy's apartment. Townhouse, Someboy would say, if he could hear me think that.

A dick pic, just for me. Yippee.

Tonight's effort is a strange head-on shot, like up the barrel of a gun. Judging by the state of the floors, this clandestine photo shoot was staged in a gas station bathroom, though it seems carefully cropped to highlight the matter at hand. For months now, about as long as I've been seeing Someboy, I've been getting these texts. Dick pics sent from an unknown number, probably someone leftover from last year when I was messing around on apps. I know for a fact it's not Someboy because I got one while I was with him, proving his innocence; we were at the bar and neither his dick nor his phone was out at the time. But even before that, I knew. They weren't his style, too covert. The texts Someboy sends me are direct, punctuation-less. Come over come out tonight when are you off work—

Another ding, another dick pic. I try to black out my screen before he can see, but my fingers aren't fast enough.

What's that?

A rare question mark from him.

He takes the phone from my hand, and for a second it's like we're friends and he's grabbing it to pore over like Steph would, marveling at the mating rituals of our species. But he's not my friend. Neither was Steph.

What a creep, he says, tossing my phone onto the bed.

That's the consensus, I reply, and it makes me feel good to do so. Say what I want to even when he disapproves. The insolence!

He gets up out of bed, gets his jeans from the floor, and puts them back on. I'll walk you home, he says.

Well, this is a twist. And startled by the turn, I bow to his whim. Never have we ever walked anywhere except out of the bar, back to his place, into his room.

The lights are all off in the kitchen and front hall, the room-mates upstairs in their beds. We go out onto the street. It's quiet but for crickets and the forever wail of trucks on the big highway that butts up against the edge of town a few blocks from here.

Let's go, he says.

I lead us to the end of his block and turn up Fifth before offering, casual as can be, That was just some rando who texts me dick pics sometimes. I don't even know who it is.

He gives me a look. Bria, he says, you could get fifty thousand dick pics a day and I wouldn't care.

All right then. The air around us is body temp: inside, outside, day or night, the heat's been steady for weeks, and despite just leaving Someboy's overly air-conditioned abode, I start sweating.

So, where is this place, he says briskly.

It's, like, a fifteen-minute walk, I answer, lying a little, not wanting him to know how far I go to get to him. He knows I live with my aunt and cousins, knows it's a relatively new thing, but even that strikes too juvenile a note to touch on more than briefly, so we don't. Don't do details, don't do plans, just follow the pattern we've been making for months. You don't have to take me the whole way, I add.

I know, he says, words tinged with something. I don't get a chance to figure it out, though, because then he stops abruptly, having walked right into a tangle of silken caterpillar threads dangling from the tree above us.

He recoils, swearing, and tries to shake them off, genuinely grossed out. They are disgusting, especially if you didn't grow up dealing with them.

Let me, I say, swiping at the air to catch the strings that are invisible in the dark. One of our many plagues in Beauchamp, the caterpillars are especially bad this year, eating the branches bare and shitting all over our cars before dropping their fat brown worm bodies down on silk threads to lay their eggs. When we get home, we take pleasure, my cousin Ainsley and I, in picking them off our clothes, out of our hair, and feeding them to the cats. Worst is when they get stuck to my lip gloss at night. It's harder to dodge them in the dark.

I free Someboy, and he pats his body over, checking for worms. They're tricky: you want to get them off you to avoid the shock of disgust a couple hours later when one crawls, somehow hairy and yet also clammy and cool, onto the skin at the back of your neck. But you also don't want to search so hard you crush their fragile bodies into your clothes. Hence the gentle pat procedure.

Wait, I say, pulling him into the relative illumination of a streetlight. He has a worm on his shoulder, inching its way up towards his collar. I pluck it off and fling it away.

Thanks, he says. And with the same look of resentful determination he wore when he insisted on walking me home, he takes my hand.

Yikes. That's the feeling in my stomach when he holds my hand. Yikes.

So where are we going? he asks again.

This way, I say, pointing in the direction of most of Beauchamp. I start forward again, swinging our conjoined hands in the manner of little girls skipping down the sidewalk. It works: he drops it.

Then he takes my hand again. That's when I start to think maybe I've wandered into some kind of pissing contest. Never does Someboy walk me home or even to his door. Generally speaking, I get up and go and he lies there as he pleases, and it pleases me too. To make my own moves.

Fucking Dick Pic Man. He never shows his face, but the dick in his hand casts a long shadow. I won't hear from him for a week, and then I'll get three in a row: car dick, bedside dick, bathroom sink dick. Sometimes he throws a filter on it. A bedroom scene cast in moody blues. An outdoor, oversaturated dick picnic in the park. I try to decipher them, like they're a visual language, pornographic pictographs. Who is this? I wrote back the first time. He answered right away with an arty aerial shot in black and white, jeans dropped low enough to reveal a badly tattooed tiger head on his thigh. Ugly tattoo, ya perv, I replied, and nothing more, until a week later he texted me a shot where he was brandishing his dick with great urgency, like a hose at a three-alarm fire.

I should block him, but I don't know. Not that many people text me these days.

I don't even understand dick pics really. Dicks, disembodied, seem too thin-skinned to me, like what's inside is straining to get out. It puts me in mind of aliens tumbling out of chest cavities—

I thought your aunt lived in an apartment, Someboy says loudly.

His words jump-start my eyes, and I see suddenly that we're standing on the grass in front of my house. Mine. Not my aunt Tash's place, with her boyfriend and my cousins, where I've been staying since I couldn't stay here anymore. Dad's house, where I'm not supposed to go.

She does, I say quickly. And, happy to have a hold of him now, I pull him off down the sidewalk, hoping he can't feel my heart pounding in my fingers while I think of an excuse. But nothing brilliant comes. Sorry, I say, guess I zoned out.

He's looking back at the house, not paying attention to me at all, and that's when I do the thing I finally regret. It's not the breaking of the rule, set by Tash and enforced by Ains, to never go to the house. (When I needed to get my stuff after Steph overdosed, I had to describe to Tash where the object I wanted was, and she'd retrieve it for me, hustling to get out of there fast, like it was a nuclear disaster site.) It's not whatever rift might have been caused by the dick pics, or the fact that even now he's looking back at the house with an intensity that makes me feel loose in my body, like I could waft away.

Here's what I regret: I look back too, and see, blazing from the kitchen window, a light. As if someone had just walked in the back door and flicked it on before taking off their shoes.

As if someone got up for a glass of water in the middle of the night and left it on. As if someone is in there, but not me.

When I go inside the house, I'm careful. Leave everything exactly as it was. Would never leave a light on.

I walk Someboy back the extra blocks I've brought us silently, thinking about the light. It'll be all I can think about now.

I wouldn't be able to do this if Someboy was really from Beauchamp—he moved here a couple years ago because of his ex, who's since moved away. He'd wonder why we took this route, overshooting a shorter path by almost a mile.

Someboy kisses me goodbye at the corner of Tash's apartment complex, tongue in my mouth, and then he's gone, crossing the street diagonally as if to get away from me as quickly as possible. Leaves me to make my way up the block to the courtyard entrance to Paradise Gardens so that, even after all of this, I still have the feeling I'm being dismissed.

~~~

My dad started working down by the border for some bikers maybe six months ago? Not your ideal employers, but it wasn't like I could give him my open and honest critique. I wasn't even supposed to acknowledge the very real change in his demeanor—I'd have been punished for clocking the shift in his phone use and schedule, for eavesdropping on more than one occasion, for having a brain and a pulse and for paying attention.

So, for a while he sends money. Money transfers that arrived on my phone or Steph's with no message attached, just a security question whose answer was my name.

And then he stops sending, and we figure, Sure, that's about right.

I didn't have to tell Steph he wasn't coming back anytime soon. She knew. She was good like that.

I'm nothing if not highly adaptable, she bragged the first day she came home in the uniform she had to wear at the gas station. It was just black pants and a black polo shirt with the company's red logo on the pocket, but it looked way wrong on her. Usually she wore pajamas, flannel ones in pastels or long nightshirts with flowers and teddy bears on them, the kind of thing I'd never seen on an adult before. Or else she'd be done up, red lipstick and hairspray, tight outfits and knee-high boots. Never before in between, until Dad disappearing necessitated the gas station. The work clothes didn't dull her though. She seemed unbothered by employment in a way I had never witnessed. Sinking into the couch eagerly afterwards, her things spread out on the table within reach. Smokes, lighter, ashtray, phone. A Big Gulp from the gas station and her purse, with its stash of pills.

Your parental units have failed you, Bria, Steph once said to me, but you yourself are not to blame.

Aren't you sort of a parental unit? I asked. She was, ostensibly, my dad's girlfriend and for a few months my equally ostensible guardian.

Exactly, she said.

For a couple of months, we were fine without him. She worked a few days a week and I had my part-time burger bucks, and he seemed to be paying the mortgage and bills on time, or someone was. There was no one to hassle me to keep up with school, I had my own thing going on at night, and soon I met Someboy.

~~~~

13

Sometimes I have the power and sometimes Someboy has it. Sometimes he knows and sometimes I know and sometimes no one knows anything. Those are the best times. When we cackle and splash drinks on ourselves and the ground, and it's not a dance or a fight. And no one is listening, and no one is watching. It stays light late, and the radio is on playing some great song, and the wind rips like an ocean through your hair until it gets like a dream you're trying to hold onto.

That's how it is with us sometimes.

~~~~

Ains and I sleep close for comfort. Technically there's an inflatable mattress for me, but it took up all the floor space and always deflated by morning. We share her bed instead, and sometime during the night she'll scoot closer and I'll toss an arm around her and she'll slip her thumb overtop of mine. We're not cuddly in the daytime, and it's not like dancing all over each other at parties like girls do. It's like we're babies in the womb, sharing our whole world. We sleep close because it's cold at night, comparatively. And it calms down my heart, and it calms hers down too.

Emily and Doug's room is next to ours and they often end up in with us, arms and legs tangled up like wires.

I sneak in smoothly after Someboy drops me, hopping down onto the recessed balcony of my aunt Tash's first-floor apartment, half above ground and half below, then coming in through Ains's bedroom window. Tash's room is right next to the front door, so this is the surest way to avoid detection. I'm practiced at this point, removing the screen silently, everything just so, one leg over and then the other, used to the jab of the windowsill in my crotch by now.

Ains doesn't stir when I lay down beside her, holding my breath as I lower my weight onto the bed as gently and evenly as possible. I could go to the Olympics for competitive quietness. I'm that good. When there's no sign of her waking, I start breathing again, trying to slow mine to match hers.

This summer has had the longest days I remember. Days when the sun won't go down, days that refuse to budge. Tash tried to fill them for me, taking the kids out of day care and getting us to babysit instead, which you'd think combined with our evening shifts at Burger Shack would make me tired, and I am, but not enough.

I'm still awake, thinking about the light, when I hear the door to Ains's bedroom open. Assuming one of the kids can't sleep, I throw back the covers to let them crawl in without bothering to look. But then nothing happens. So, I unglue my eyes (didn't take my makeup off) and let the blanket drop. The door is open but empty. No one's there.

2.

How does it start? Like this: I'm seeing somebody. Someboy. He has me in his phone under new thing. Not even capitalized. That's all right, though, because I put him in mine under Someboy. As in, someday Someboy might need a more distinguishing moniker, but not yet. Not now. No.

I meet Someboy at the bar. All Stars. I go there when my teeth have that feeling—they need something to sink into. I have this thing now where I need out at night. In the day we stay in. Undercover. Playing with children. Safe with my mind full up of what I want and none of the other stuff.

Someboy says the more sex you have, the more you need it, so I wouldn't understand and should just let him. Someboy says a lot of things. What he doesn't know is I do understand. I've done more than he will ever know, and I've seen all kinds of things without even trying. I am seeing Someboy, and Someboy sees me the way I want him to. Sees me show up with the night all over me, not asking for shit, not answering for it either. Sees me show up easy, eat pizza afterwards, and head home giving away nothing of myself, because I know him like he thinks he knows me. I know better than better. I know best.

Someboy mutters nonsense in his sleep. I stay up late to read into it. Sometimes he says the strangest things in a pleading tone. Cheeseballs, he begs of me. Sometimes he's upset and says no like you say it to make someone stop. I mutter back whatever words I feel like saying. Credenza. Will you, or won't you? Béchamel. I like words. Saying them and not saying them. Using them to get things. Like what I want.

What? says Someboy, stirring.

Shhh, I go.

Because of the lay of the land and the way our township works, you see strangers all the time, but also word gets around. Words matter. The ones you put on a person can change who they are. Or who they think they are. Which is what counts.

~~~

It's the sound of my birth control alarm that wakes me in the morning, a police siren ringtone I downloaded for its sense of urgency. But it can't be morning because it's set to go off every day at noon.

Oh shit. I roll over and reach towards the floor where I leave my phone at night as the sirens wail. Swiping blindly at the screen, I turn off the alarm.

Now the apartment is quiet, but outside the open window Paradise Gardens is hopping: a cacophony of kids coming and going, families eating lunch on balconies, and further off, the chlorine-soaked splashing of the pool. Another goddamn beautiful day, I gather.

Moving doesn't feel good, but I do it anyway, finding the pack of birth control pills in my purse and swallowing today's. Then pop a pill from the small ibuprofen bottle I keep in there too, for good measure. Rake my hair into a knot and get dressed in a bathing suit, T-shirt, and shorts. The kids and Ains will be at the pool already, so there's no time to spare, even as nausea greens me.

Ains's room feels at wrong angles, and the hallway is also askew. I fill up my water bottle from the bathroom tap, the coldest water in the apartment, and chug from it until surely I've replenished whatever was depleted last night. What did we do last night? I remember, with a pang, Someboy seeing the dick pics on my phone. Then remember the detour to Dad's house (pang) and the light someone left on (pang).

On second thought, don't think of last night. But do feel better having hydrated.

In the kitchen, I do a quick plunder of the fridge, packing some fruit and yogurt for my breakfast and grabbing a couple Popsicles as peace offerings for the kids. The cats, Ursula and Princess Sprinkles, swarm my legs, winding and circling as they work for their breakfast. Or lunch, I guess. Stooping to pet them, I run my hands over Ursula's black fur, her slim body, and then Princess Sprinkles, who is fluffy and gray, enjoying their soft fur on my skin for a minute before I give them what they want.

I'm getting myself together to leave when a pair of legs in black jeans comes into view on the grass beyond the balcony, lumbering down the makeshift milk-crate stairs we've set up for easier access—it's Rick, who isn't as smooth at pulling off this method of entry as some. He's Tash's boyfriend and he's been here for a few weeks since getting surgery for his carpal tunnel. He claims to need the whole summer off work to recover and focus on physio so moved in here so he could sublet his place to save on rent. I'm not really here, if you know what I mean, but I also am, since May, when Tash officially became my guardian.

Afternoon, Bria, he says, making a point of the time.

Hey, Rick, I reply, ignoring the dig. As if he's one to talk. He's spending his summer of gainful unemployment cutting the sleeves off all his T-shirts and working towards his deltoid goals at the gym.

I continue on my way out the apartment. Rick calls after me. I turn. What?

Forget something? he asks.

I've been forced into action so quickly—it wasn't five minutes ago I woke to my alarm—that for a second my brain is as blank as the July sun that's streaming in the sliding door I'm about to walk through. He points at the kitchen counter, where my phone rests.

Oh, I say. Walk back across the room and pick it up. Thanks.

Rick and I have a mutually agreed upon vibe where we both think the other is sponging off Tash and make lots of fun, barely veiled comments to that effect. It's hard to take his jabs seriously, since I'm an actual teenager on summer vacation, not to mention I'm family, whereas he's just a rebound from after Tash's breakup last year with Derrick, Emily and Doug's dad. A rebound with some staying power, I suppose.

I climb up onto the lawn that borders the parking lot and walk across the grass feeling minorly victorious for not checking my phone before pocketing it. An ease settles into me, a feeling of what's right. I'll wait for Someboy to text me. I can stay in for a few nights. I am capable of that. And the light was just that. A light. Tash probably left it on when she went to get clothes for me. No big deal.

~~~

Paradise Gardens is owned by Jeff and Cindy Jerome, who according to Dad got rich exploiting temporary foreign workers on their down-home industrial family farm before going into real estate. All I know is as a kid I would have died to live at Paradise, used to whine about it hard to Dad whenever we'd drive by, which was often since it's on the main road that leads out of town.

Jeff and Cindy built this place in the '80s, an era whose influence on the Beauchamp aesthetic cannot be underestimated. Metal bands, microwave cuisine, misogyny, perms. Flames painted on the sides of trucks. These things are eternal in Beauchamp. Despite vast geographical differences, the Jeromes were inspired by the vacation communities of Florida and thought they could attract short-term renters in the summer season since we have the river right in town and the lake a twenty-minute drive away. It's kind of worked? Every summer there's a small influx of people from the city who come out for a week or two, but the veneer of tourism in Beauchamp is thin.

Dad says Jeff and Cindy are slumlords with more money than anyone in Beauchamp and also that they're assholes. But they're assholes who sponsor all the sports teams at school and who wait as long as possible before evicting tenants who don't pay rent, so like most things Dad says I take it with some salt.

Two months of the year, the pool is open from 10 to 4. Ains and I have a system, taking turns watching Doug and Emily while the other gets an hour of free time. Ains usually spends hers working out on the beach volleyball court with Mark if he's available, whereas I multitask, napping and working on my tan at the same time. It's Ains's job to wake me up before I burn.

~~~~

Bria! Emily shouts as I unlock the metal gate to the pool grounds. She comes towards me as fast as she's allowed to on the wet pavement, quick withholding little steps.

Walk, Ains calls out to remind her anyway. Emily slows to a comically exaggerated tiptoe. She's four, and though she still has some baby pudge, her bones are starting to stretch out and declare themselves.

I present her with a Popsicle. Quick, before they melt, I say, opening it for her and giving her a kiss on the head.

Emily's goodwill is extra appreciated as I brace myself for Ains's reception. She is one of the worst people in the world to have mad at you. Bitch goes cold. Walls right up. Luckily, I am uniquely qualified to unwind her.

It's medium crowded, the kiddie pool populated by a gaggle of kids, parents orbiting around paying varying amounts of attention. There's no lifeguard, but Mark, the building manager, takes it upon himself to hang around most of the day pseudo-supervising. Mark is Cindy and Jeff's loser adult son. Well, he's like twenty-five or something. Too old to have so little of a life, in my opinion. For a guy who's probably rich, Mark spends a weird amount of time at the pool watching over things. He even has a special chair raised up on stilts and accessible by ladder that you aren't allowed to call a lifeguard chair for legal reasons.

Mark is over by the deep end now, watching kids on the dolphin slide and chatting up one of the moms. Emily and I join Ains, who is set up on a deck chair near the kiddie pool, reapplying sunscreen to Doug's back. Sorry, I say, as we approach. Sorry, sorry, sorry.

Whatever, Ains says, hands moving across Doug's skin. Her face is unfathomable, eyes hidden behind the reflective wraparound sunglasses she got for practicing outside this summer. Red fading to yellow, sleek like a superhero's mask, or a radioactive sunset.

She releases Doug, and he heads straight for me, hugging my knees before I can bend to embrace him. I love this baby boy. Ains was a bit bummed about him initially—didn't want to have to share everything with yet another kid—but I think some babies know they need to be easy to love, so that's how they come out. Doug's like that, a cuddly sweet boy with blue-black eyes, the color of the deep lake outside town.

I sit down in the chair next to Ains and help Doug unwrap his Popsicle. I'll watch them now, I say. Go practice with Mark if you want.

She looks over to where Mark stands by the deep end. He's busy, she says. Maybe later.

Mark coached volleyball at the middle school we went to. He was Ains's coach when she first got into playing, and he started helping her train again when they moved into Paradise after Tash and Derrick broke up.

Ains will wait around all day without asking, hoping Mark will offer. Hey, Mark, I yell, good and loud, so that he turns to look immediately, along with everyone else on the pool deck. Can you train my cousin for a bit? I ask.

Don't, she says darkly.

Mark shouts back, Sure, and waves Ains over without hesitation. And she goes, barely glancing back at us when I repeat that I'll take care of the kids.

I watch her walk over to him, legs long and tan in her black spandex booty shorts, the rest of her hidden under an oversized white T-shirt from a tournament. Ains has been mad all the time at everything, for a while now. We work evenings at Burger Shack together, but she wanted to apply to volleyball camps and shit, maybe go away for a few months. At least go visit her dad and his side of the family in Hollow Water, the reservation about three hours north of Beauchamp where he's from. I would be mad about everything that's happened lately too, if it wasn't to my benefit to be another way about it. So, I try to be that way. The way that'll keep getting me by.

The kids eat their Popsicles, and we watch as Ains spikes the ball over the net, smacking it into the earth over and over. Soon Emily's mouth is ringed in red, her hands dripping. Should we go wash up? I ask her.

Yeah! she says, as if it's a much more exciting invite than a trip to the changing room bathroom.

Come on, Doug, I say, you too. I scoop him up onto my hip, shouldering the diaper bag in case we need it while we're in there. Doug is two and already almost toilet-trained but not fail-safe yet.

We head off, Emily's hand in mine. I love tending to my little cousins. Not because I'm supposed to, or because it makes Tash and Ains any less on my case, but because nothing feels so good as burying my head in the sand of their sweetness.

When we get back, I try to make eye contact with Ains, who is still running drills with Mark on the beach volleyball court on the far side of the pool fence, hoping she'll notice this responsible behavior and further forgive and forget my fuckups. She's oblivious to everything but the ball though.

Let's practice our floats, I tell Emily and Doug. The kiddie pool is donut-shaped, with a raised platform in the middle and a palm tree fountain that's supposed to cascade around the outer ring of the pool. Instead, it spews water weakly, occasionally shooting out a killer jet of water that makes the kids scream and lunge out of the way.

I lead Emily and Doug over to some open water in the shallows beneath the palm tree. Okay, I say, on the count of three, lay back, spread your arms and legs out wide, and float.

On three, the kids roll onto their backs and make starfish with their bodies. I keep one hand under Doug's butt to help him stay afloat.

Excellent form, I say, lying back to join them. Close my eyes to the sun, which beats down with annoying persistence. Nary a cloud in the sky all summer, just an indecent amount of blue, except for when the wind blows smoke from the fires our way.

This summer has been so strange I almost don't notice the weather, but it's been fucked up too, like everything else. No rain, just day after day of heat, drying out the fields and the yards. You can feel the dust in your teeth, eyes, hair, everything. Nobody dares complain much since our winters are so long, but summer here has its downside too. Every year it seems some new plague rolls in. The mosquitos came first this year: they were so bad in May the streets of Beauchamp were fogged at night, trucks driving slowly up and down every block aiming pesticide guns at our ditches and yards. That didn't stop the bugs from swarming every time you'd step outside, their numbers soaring as they thrived off the blood of our town. Next came the aphids, sapsuckers who filled the trees, invisible from the ground but whose shit blanketed everything below in a sticky coating that glued your sneakers to the sidewalk with every step. Cars parked overnight on a well-treed street would need their windshields power-washed in the morning, so thick was the lacquer of aphid shit that you couldn't see through it. The aphids dropped off when the tree worms invaded later in June, eating the branches clean of leaves before descending to the ground on their silken strings. The bears don't have enough to eat, not enough space left to roam, so they've come out of the forest into the fields, right into town. Mostly they stick to the dump, feasting on human garbage. Ains and I go out there sometimes when we've got a ride and watch them with the windows rolled up against both the smell and the bears, who are rangy and thin. The other day, the cashier at Valu Lots was telling the lady in front of us that one of the stock boys saw a bear out by the dumpsters. It just looked at him, she said, as if the bear was a shifty character and not a hungry animal. I'm careful when I take the trash out at work now.

~~~

After we swim, the kids and I find Ains bumping the volley-ball behind the building by herself, the insides of her forearms bright. Bump. The ball soars into the sky, arching forward just so much that she has to take a half step to match it. Same hit, same height, same arc up into the sky. Her control of the ball is so tight it's soothing to watch, like it could never fall.

You okay? I ask.

She doesn't answer but bumps the ball slightly out of range, forcing her to hustle a few steps over to make the next hit.

Ains?

I'm fine, she says, hitting the ball straight up again, back in control.

Okay, I say, we'll wait till you're done.

I lead the kids to a spot on the grass about ten feet from Ains, and we plop down. Sweat runs down the side of Ains's face, but she doesn't wipe it away, too engrossed in whatever personal best she's trying to break. Most consecutive ball hits in a summer afternoon, maybe?

Ains believes in the gospel of volleyball and good grades getting her out of here. I have to tell her all the time that a bus ticket to the city is forty bucks; she could swing that plus first and last month's rent off her burger bucks easy by the time she graduates next year. But she wants more than that. She wants people to respect her just by looking at her, not to assume she's teen mom trash and tsk when she's alone with her brother and sister at Walmart. Ains's dad is Ojibwa, and though she says that's why people stare at her in stores like she's stealing, I think she looks like her background could be anything. Plus, people stare at me in stores because they think I'm stealing all the time, and I'm white. Probably people stare at her because she's gorgeous, but she would never believe that. I'd kill to be beautiful and not know it. That's the dream. Instead, I'm reasonably hot and well aware of it.

Bored of waiting, Emily starts dancing like one of those big bendy balloon men in parking lots, dipping at the knee and pumping her arms erratically. Usually, it makes Ains and everyone laugh, but not right now. Emily keeps it up anyway, watching her angry sister until it's more than she can take. She runs over, and Ains, without breaking eye contact with the sky, catches the ball, flattens her arms into a ramp, and rolls it down slow enough for Emily to grab.

Look, I say, I'm sorry I slept in. Sorry you had to do everything. Again. I suck.

Breathing a bit heavy, Ains puts her hands on her hips and looks in my direction. I still haven't seen her eyes today.

Em tried to wake you up earlier, she says. You were, like, dead to the world.

Sorry, I say, the word slipping out automatically. I've said it so many times lately it's starting to feel like a mantra. I stayed out kinda late, I say as explanation.

I know, she says. And then adds, I got in a fight with Mom this morning.

Blessed be. An opening. About what? I ask, trying not to sound too eager.

Ains shrugs, suddenly looking so tired. The usual, she says, as if that says it all. For a frozen moment, I think the usual might be me. But then she goes on: I just get mad she expects so much from us, yet Rick can do whatever he wants all day.

I hear her hesitation around the word *us* but take it as a good sign that she includes me anyway. I don't even think I've ever seen him clear a dish, I offer.

I know! she replies, exasperation animating her again.

I thought to be a social worker you had to, like, make good life choices, I say, trying to ingratiate myself.

Common misconception, says Ains flatly.

Tash went back to school for social work a few years ago, bartending at the golf course in Durham until she finally graduated last year. That's where she and Rick met. He was the sous chef there until carpal tunnel took him down. She got a job right away and now she's never home, always stressed, and when she is home, she clings to the little kids and talks nonstop about apprehension rates and child trafficking.

Emily has lost interest in the volleyball—now she and Doug are pulling handfuls of dandelions and crabgrass from the ground and sprinkling them around with swooshing magic sounds. I pick up the volleyball from where she's abandoned it. Fake toss to Ains. Wanna practice? I ask her.

She nods. Surprised and willing to forgive me at least that much because I never offer to set for her, even though she always asks. That beautiful nod releases me, finally, from this morning's misery, and I get goofy.

Hey, Em and Doug—wanna see how good your sister is at volleyball? I ask, doing some lunges and dancing around to loosen up and make them laugh before we focus in on our drills. Ains will get mad again if I don't do it right. I need the peace of my cousins to soothe me. Need them close to keep everything else out.

I set the ball high like Ains taught me. She smacks it back towards me, hard.

~~~

Then there's the other thing about this summer, or this year overall, I guess, and that's the fact that people keep dying. Well, not always permanently. But it's clear there is poison in the well. Which is to say the drug supply.

Every few seasons the trend shifts. This year pills are in fashion. Pressed ones, fake Percs that are actually fentanyl. Which is strong. To make you feel good, but it's too strong, so you feel so good you forget to breathe.

First there were the boys. Anthony Macdonald, son of someone Tash knows, ODed in his car in the parking lot behind the church on Fifth Street on a Tuesday night in February. He was blue by the time the custodian found him, and not from the cold. Then Tyler Fournier and Mike Bell on the same night, separately, in early spring. It hit the news then, and everyone at school started talking about it, having heard detailed accounts from older brothers and sisters who knew the guys. They brought in a public health nurse from the city who did a talk in the school gym about the dangers of fentanyl. How these pills weren't like the Percocets and Oxys that people were used to, that they had higher concentrations because they weren't professionally manufactured, so you never really knew how much you were taking. Or what you were taking. She showed us one of the kits they were handing out at the drugstore to reverse overdoses, and we all got one to take home. Then a couple from Durham died, two real estate agents with their faces on benches who'd wanted to cut loose one weekend with some

28

MDMA; it wasn't what they thought it was. That was the peak, everyone talked about nothing else, and then it died down. Like maybe the pills weren't so strong anymore or else their users had figured out how to take them safely. Then Steph happened.

~~~~

Only when it's time to gather up our pool stuff and head back inside do I finally let myself check my phone.

Nothing.

No big deal, I tell myself, tucking it back into my bag. To be expected, even.

As we trek across the parking lot to the apartment, Ains falls into step beside me, and I feel a bit better. She knows, sometimes, what I need and when.

Rick's out when we get home. Praise the lord, another miracle. I deal with our wet towels, Ains starts some pasta for an early dinner, and the kids watch videos on YouTube until Tash gets home and it's time to get ready for work.

After she's dropped her bags, kissed Emily, and picked up Doug, Tash turns to me. You, she says. I need to talk to you about something.

Okay, I sing cheerfully, leaving the room. Time to pack up my Burger Shack outfit.

Tash follows me into Ains's bedroom. Holding Doug close, she stands between me and the door.

Folding my uniform carefully, I stuff it in my backpack.

Straight home after work tonight, says Tash.

Sure, I say. My eyes meet Ains's eagerly as she appears in the doorway behind her mom. Bria, says Ains, we better get going.

Both of you, says Tash, I want to talk to both of you later. She steps out of my way though, and we leave together, Ains and I.

This time of summer always scares me. You can only savor the pure freedom from school, from winter, for so long before it starts to creep in like a shadow at the corner of your eye. Our granny had this thing where her retinas started detaching. She'd have to watch for dark spots closing in at the edges of her vision. It's like that.

3.

The next day I get a call from a ghost. Just kidding. It's from Dad. Turns out he's in jail. They got him out on Highway 9, routine traffic stop. At least, that's the story he tells me in half sentences—they found some drugs in the car, not much though. So, it's not good news, but it could be worse?

But why didn't you call? I ask once he's got that out. My voice sounds whiny even to me, and I can feel him rise to the provocation before he says a word. Makes me feel like I'm playing a role in a sitcom I've come to resent but can't quit because, because, because.

I did call, he says.

Who? You sure as shit didn't call me.

I called Steph, he says. And Dave. Tash. My lawyer.

It's loud on his end as he lists the names off, a cavernous roar behind his familiar voice, the snap crackle pop of his smoker's lungs. We were at the pool when the call came in from a weird number, and I knew. Mouthed the word *Dad* at Ains, and she took over watching the kids. I walked to the edge of the pool deck, next to the fence, as Mark eyed me from the elevation of his not-a-lifeguard chair. Everywhere you go, pervs. Pretty much. I remember driving by Paradise and thinking it was so glamorous and Mark was so hot—he was always hanging around shirtless and sunburned, mowing the lawn or drinking beers with buds. Now I can't believe I thought he was such a rock star. I wonder what else will turn to crap when I get old enough to see it.

Hello? says Dad. Bria?

Did you reach her? I ask. Steph, I mean.

Yeah, he says, as if to say, Why wouldn't he?

Though I suddenly wanted to drown myself in the conveniently located pool, I persist. How is she?

She's good. Better. He takes a sucky-in breath, like he's smoking something that needs air to keep burning.

That's good, I say. Nothing in me moves.

Guess I fucked that up, he says.

I guess, I say and hold tight to the fence.

How're things there?

Well, I've been at Tash's, thanks for asking.

I know. I sent her some money.

I thought bikers killed you.

Don't be silly, he says. But we both know I'm not. Be good, he added.

You too, I tell him.

The only real takeaway is that I have seconds of spaghetti at dinner and load on so much parmesan Tash starts in about how she's not made of money. And now I know Dad's not dead too, I guess.

~~~

The night I met Someboy was like all my nights, except for what came after. Ever since Dad left me with Steph, I've lived like this. And when she left too, I lived this even more.

It was early May, a couple of weeks before Steph's overdose. I never invited Ains along on these nights; she wouldn't have come even if I did. And it was better that way. I didn't have to worry about her, and she didn't worry about me either. Or at least not much.

He gave me glances at first. His hair was a little long, a lot greasy. Blue T-shirt, tattoos, strangle hold on a bottle of Standard. Then his eyes started to stay a little longer, until we were a sure thing. He was talking to two guys at a high-top table by the doors, and I knew I only had to wait for him to need another drink before he'd come to me.

Till then I talked to Dave when he wasn't busy. Dave is Dad's best friend, and that's how come I can go to All Stars without too much trouble.

I told you, Bria, I haven't heard anything, Dave said, pausing as he unloaded glasses from the dishwasher and coming over to my spot at the bar.

Whoa, man. Presumptuous much. Relax. I smiled, looked cute.

He glared. The wonderful thing about Dave is I have shit on him and he has shit on me. So, we can really trust each other. He never gives me what I order: always Coke with no rum, ginger without the rye, straight cran. But that's okay. We both know I'll find someone to order my drinks for me.

I don't go to All Stars to see if he's heard anything from Dad anymore, but a couple of months ago, maybe I did. Now it's truly just for kicks, to ease the night away, run down the hours when everyone is asleep.

What do you want, why are you here, Bria? Dave intoned.

My, my, someone's real bitchy tonight, I thought. But I was outwardly demure. I'll take a Tom Collins please, I said, all manners.

He gave me a ginger ale. Thanks, barkeep, I said flatly.

Drink it and move on out of here, he said, or begged more like. I'll call you when I hear something from your dad.

I'd say I don't even care about my dad, or where he is, or what the hell he's up to, but one breath later it wouldn't be true. So instead I picked up my drink from the coaster Dave had put it on and swung my stool around to face the room.

Someboy was watching. Good. I chanced a move. Turned back to the bar, giving him all my angles, sipped long on my straw, and hopped off the stool. Hey, Dave, watch my drink while I smoke? I asked.

Can't be too careful nowadays, said Ron, who basically lives on his stool at the bar.

Too true, Ron, I said.

Dave waved a towel in my direction and grumbled agreement.

I moved across the floor of the bar liquid smooth and powerful, feeling my pockets for my pack. I put anger-mystery-intrigue in my step. I love this more than almost anything. Walking across the bar, eyes on me.

Outside, across the parking lot, past the old guy coughing up his last lung and the couple making out against the wall, cigarettes held away to keep from crushing them between their grinding bodies. I lit one of my own. Took a drag. Don't love smoking, but they're a useful prop. The sound of the bar grew and then became muffled again. There was the slick friction of a lighter flick. Him.

Turned like I was dragging my feet. Like it was the last thing I'd ever wanna do.

Hey, he said. Have I seen you here before?

The line cheered me. I shrugged maybe, maybe not.

He smiled, taking in my body parts.

It's not me that's easy. I'm something else. I'm hard.

———

Two hours later, Someboy was saying he sees special in me. And it was true. I am.

I let him think things he wants to think. That are less than true, more than a lie.

He wasn't holding liquor well by then, and I was more than ready to get out of there. But he wanted to stay, so I had to wait it out.

At some point I took my jacket off, and he whistled like, Oh shit a bomb is dropping.

What?

He gestured. At my chest. Sorry, he said, but your body is sick.

I looked down, shrugged. Yeah, I said. I guess it is.

I almost had the hang of him. A snob, he said outrageous, offensive things; countered with a compliment. Negged me all night long, but I saw past it. Cut him down in return and saw that was right. Got his attention good. He used big words, but stumbled over them, too eager to impress or maybe it was just the booze. Or whatever he was doing in the bathroom, unless that was just a cold I was clocking. Maybe I was being judgmental. Maybe he was cute. He is. So, there's that.

Ha! He laughed at my answer, loud, and I could see he wanted to be the one to introduce me to that information. You're hilarious, he said.

What? I shrugged again, conscious of how the motion accentuated things. I'm still getting used to them, I said, about my boobs. They're pretty new.

This is where he could've asked me how old I am. I'd have explained all my ages, and he could have chosen how to be about it. But he didn't ask, and I duly noted it.

His friends eyed me as if he did this often, like they were a bit embarrassed. But not for me. I was fine. For him.

And it's true he was reaching. Too try-hard. Every story aimed at me, jokes to tear his friends down. I got bored-annoyed and wanted to dance.

Breanna, he said, breaking into my thoughts. Yoo-hoo, he said, snapping fingers in front of my face and laughing too hard at himself. Or me.

It's Bria, I told him. In my head I thought, I don't need you, and tried to project that the right amount.

What? he asked. It was loud in there, and he wasn't expecting me to answer back.

My name. It's Bria. Bria-Michelle Powers.

He laughed like it was funny. In some ways, it was.

At 2 a.m. the lights came full on, and I winced at seeing Someboy's face so clearly. He blinked at me, and I tossed my hair and arched my spine as I saw the question forming in his red wolf eyes.

A rooster only crows when it can see the light, I said.

Who's that a quote from again? Someboy asked.

Me, I said, and he kissed me.

~~~

Actually, Muhammed Ali said it. I got it from the wall hanging in our living room. Steph was big into cross-stitching inspirational quotes, started after she got the job at the gas station, after Dad split.

How old are you anyway? I asked Steph the first week Dad brought her home, after he'd taken off again but before I'd opened my mind to my new chaperone.

First of all, she said, that's a bit rude. Second of all—

It's not rude. That's a very standard question.

Age is just a number, babe. I'm not that easy to pin down— I'm a lot of different ages. It depends on the time of day, year. Circumstance.

I snorted.

You haven't heard the phrase *eternal age* before? She gathered her long hair onto one shoulder and pet it like a small animal. My last job was at a carpet store, she continued. But I've done lots of things. Call centers. Fast food. Sales. Bars. This carpet gig was good though. Real high-end place. I sold carpets to millionaires.

She went on about carpets for long enough I thought she'd forgotten about the age thing, but then she circled back around.

So, when I'm at work I could be twenty-two or thirty-seven or fifty-nine, depending, see? When I met your dad, I was seventeen—

Ew.

No, you know what I mean. I felt young, and like . . . She stopped and flailed in the air in search of an expression expressive enough. Like, bold and bright. You must know how he can make you feel. She looked at me, checking.

I had to admit that made her less suspect. She understood Dad. She wasn't just under his spell; she was aware of it, and that made her more credible. I found out after the overdose, that really she was twenty-five.

As for me, if I had to tell you the truth, I'd say I'm five hundred in my heart, twenty-one in my head, and old-soul ageless everywhere else. Fifteen for real though. Sixteen in a few weeks.

4.

Dave looks like a teddy bear, and whenever I hear him swear or say something off-color, it sounds wrong, feels gross. He projects a deeply harmless vibe, all curly haired, soft-bellied squishiness, but he is Dad's best friend, so. Not that innocent.

Later that same day Dad calls me, Dave comes into Burger Shack and orders a Fat Boy. Ains is on her thirty-minute, which is fine. I go in the back to make it, dropping a fresh basket of fries and throwing bacon on the grill even though he didn't pay the extra charge.

Dave waits for his food at one of the picnic tables adjacent to the parking lot. I keep an eye on him while I cook, wondering what his angle is. He's our only customer apart from this family that's been nursing their meal outside for the last three hours. I suspect they're on a long-distance road trip and might be angling to spend the night in the Burger Shack parking lot. Their huge RV is parked diagonally across three spots and a dog jumped out the back when they stopped, spinning in circles with excitement to be free, even if it's only free enough to roam the narrow bit of grass surrounding Burger Shack's picnic tables. The kids chase each other around screaming, blue-raspberry tongues dark in their mouths, while the parents smoke and eat simultaneously. I don't mind because it drives off other customers like magic.

You want a Coke or something? I ask, putting the tray in front of Dave.

Nah, he says, unwrapping the burger from its foil. Thanks.

Who's running the bar? I ask. He is literally never not there.

I got someone to cover for me. I'm on my way in now.

Now I'm more than suspicious. Dave's bar staff is part-time, and he mostly only lets them stand next to him while he pours drinks. Sometimes they get to clear glasses. Dave inherited All Stars from his mom, Glenda, who kept it going after his dad died. Glenda was famous for her natural flair for insults and covert kindnesses to drunks. She used to water down Ron's whiskey and switch it to apple juice with the foresight of a prophet, cutting him off before anything could go wrong. Or more wrong than it already was. She quietly reminded drunks to take their insulin and helped them do their taxes. She'd give me slices of orange and lime to eat when I came in with Dad, let me play with the satellite radio that soundtracked the bar, switching between stations every ten seconds until someone snapped at me to stop.

You working alone tonight? Dave asks. Where's your sidekick?

Ains isn't my sidekick. We're partners in crime, I reply.

He laughs, but I couldn't be more serious.

She's on her break out back.

Dave takes a big bite, and chili oozes out from between the bun. He looks a bit embarrassed as he wipes his chin with a napkin.

I guess Dad talked to you, I say, staring at that family, who've now set up lawn chairs and are watching TV on a tablet.

Dave nods. There's an orange chili cast to his chin. So, he called you?

Yeah, you fuckhead.

He winces. I can be harsh, it's true. It's a quality I don't know if I should cherish or cut down at its roots.

You could have told me, I say.

He didn't want you to know, Bria.

I glare. Know what?

Dave swallows, like I am the most difficult damn pill. All he said was that he'd been arrested, and he asked me to get some money to Tash. And to keep an eye on you.

Oh great, I say, voice raised, my eyes rolling out of my head. Eyes on me, money to Tash. Never mind, I'm not mad after all.

Dave looks over at those awful people, as if I care what they might overhear. I sink down onto the picnic table bench, my back to Dave. Tash knows, Steph knows, Dave knows. Everyone knows where my dad is, but me.

When I turn back around to him, Dave has downed most of his meal in the last minute. Even now, as I fume, his hands move steadily between his mouth and the pool of smooth red in a white folded cup, dipping fries and tossing them back. Dip, toss. Dip, toss.

Do you know what he was arrested for? I ask.

Asking direct questions like this is not done, not to my dad, not about my dad, and Dave looks appropriately uncomfortable as he chews, swallows. He pushes the tray slightly away and wipes his hands with a fresh napkin before answering. I'm not sure.

Dave is better trained by my dad than I am. Bullshit, I say.

Hey, it's true. I don't have the whole story either. I only know what he told me.

Why'd you even come here then? I ask.

41

He sighs long and hard. I look to the sky to keep from crying.

That guy I've seen you around with lately, Dave says.

What? I ask. The one word comes out rough.

Are you guys . . . involved?

Ha, I say. Involved? Really, Dave?

I mean are you, like, dating?

Yeah, I say, standing up. So?

Dave draws back slightly, holds up his hands. Easy, Bria. I'm just asking.

I glare at him.

Faced with my anger, Dave retreats a little from his line of questioning. That guy's a real dirtbag, you know, he offers more gently. You should stay away from him.

Well, I'm surrounded by them, I say. Dirtbags. I guess I'm used to it.

You don't really know him, Bria.

Anger tumbles out. That's bullshit. He's told me everything about his life and we spend practically every night together and I know all his friends and his roommates, so you can fuck right off, *Dave*, and stop telling me what I do and don't know. Fuck off with the macho hypocrisy—

Jesus, Bria, Dave says edgily. Calm down. I'm trying to look out for you.

I consider this claim. Did you tell Dad? I ask.

No, he says. I didn't tell your dad.

A car pulls into the parking lot and two guys amble out, heading into the Shack without noticing me. I can see through the windows that Ains isn't back from break yet.

Shouldn't you? asks Dave.

I don't move to go in after them. But after a few long beats, I do.

Carl, the Burger Shack owner, fired me once, but I just came back the next day for my shift, and he didn't say anything further about it. Now he only schedules me with Ains. We told him we'd work any night this summer if he booked us together. And he did. It's not so bad. We take care of the kids in the daytime, and at five thirty we report to Burger Shack where we remain until close, then head back home and I get ready to go out. To see what I can find.

~~~

Ains comes back from her break when I'm done serving the dudes and starting to tear down for the night. Sweep or mop? I ask her.

You sweep, she says, because it's the job she likes better and she's a martyr that way.

I start throwing chairs up on tables fast as I can, so they bounce around before settling. The fourth one teeters and then falls, whacking me in the shin. Ow. I gasp out loud in pain. Bend down to examine the spot. It broke the skin.

What, you're in so much of a hurry to go see that old man you have to literally throw the chairs at the tables? Ains snaps.

She never really forgave me for the other night. Staying out, sleeping in. She doesn't understand how it feels when we get home from work. How I can't just go to bed. He's not that old, I say.

She laughs, a little mean, and places a chair gently, responsibly even, on the table in front of her. Um, yeah. He is.

Shit, she really is mad. And it makes me slow down for a minute. But no, I'm pissed. Fuck this. I say what's been hanging in the air between us for weeks. For all time maybe.

What did you say? Her cheeks are flaming now.

I said you're just jealous because I've got somebody. I let the words drop and I'm about to add something about Cole, who

43

Ains used to have a mad crush on and doesn't talk to anymore, but then she looks at me like this is really it: the moment I finally, fully disappoint her.

Quickly, she composes herself. Do you though? she asks mildly and goes back to tabling chairs.

Do I what though? I wonder, confused until I put it together with what I said. She doesn't think Someboy is really into me, either, just like Dave.

I grab the broom from where it rests against the wall beside the garbage can and wait for her to turn back, say more, dig into this fight so we can be together in that, at least. But she finishes with the chairs and goes to count the till, a job that is always hers and never mine, because accuracy is not my strong suit. I sweep the restaurant floor feeling unsatisfied. Denied an ending other than her question.

~~~

My dad is one of those snake men who can talk and charm and sell anyone anything anytime. Anywhere. Anyway. From him I learned how to:

a) Gouge their eyes out if they come for you
b) Key a car for maximum impact
c) Take the temperature of the room with my teeth
d) Talk a beautiful blue streak
e) Roll a joint using a page from the Bible or other household objects
f) Slice a hot dog so it explodes into an octopus when you hold it to the fire

And very little else.

In the early days of Steph staying with us, she told me my youth was a commodity and its value was dropping fast. She said every day that went by I was getting closer to death. She said not many women are beautiful enough to truly make a living off it, but that my looks will still come in handy. She said it's like a life skill, something to have in your toolbox, an asset, but you also need to figure out how to survive. That's why you need to get a car, as soon as you can. A woman's car is her freedom, Bria, she'd say, though she was carless herself as far as I could tell.

She showed up with Dad after one of his stints out of town. Ains and I had been making the most of it: he'd left me fifty bucks for food and told me he'd be back the next day, texting to extend it another and another. We spent most of the money the first night at Shoppers on nail polish and hair dye, then ate food we grifted from Burger Shack for every meal, going over to Ains's place when we craved some variety.

It was late, after midnight, when I heard voices at the door. We were under blankets on the couch watching movies, half conked on some weed we'd scored from this guy Shane who hangs around the hockey rink selling grams to kids at an insane markup. The door opened and cold air invaded the room, carrying Dad's smell of laundry and cigarettes. I would never realize how much I was waiting for him until he'd come home. Then the relief would surprise me so I wouldn't rush to him. I would scan the house in my mind for anything I'd done or left lying around that would get me in trouble though. So, I guess relief and a bit of paranoia.

The remnants of the weed were on the coffee table beside me, and I slid a pizza box over top of them as someone came in the door behind Dad. A woman.

Told you they'd still be up, she said. I adjusted my clothes and pushed off the blankets, smoothing my hair, newly bleached blond the night before. The woman smiled at me and Ains before bending to pull off her boots. They were low heeled and leather and came up to her knees. I wanted them immediately. So, this was why he'd been gone for so many days in row.

Hey, kid, Dad greeted me, not mentioning my hair. He looked cheerfully strung out. Red-faced and handsome.

You said you weren't going to be back until tomorrow, I said. That'd been the last update I got earlier, while I was giving Ains her makeover. Thank goodness we'd already cleaned up from doing my hair, a tense ordeal involving a bleach kit and about ten ruined towels. I had grand plans to dye Ains's hair pink, but she balked at the idea of bleach after watching me endure a burning scalp to lighten my dishwater-brown hair. Ains's hair is a deep walnut color, so it came out sort of faintly pinkish toned, like meat cooked medium well. Still, she looked different and good—I did cat eyeliner and curled her hair and she insisted on checking the progress in the mirror every two seconds, even though I cooed at her to trust me. When I was done, she looked like the older sex kitten version of herself, but she wiped it off before I could even take a picture. Now she was quiet at the other end of the couch.

You must be Bria, the woman said. Dad wound an arm around her and tried to use his hand on her butt to guide her down the hall. But she resisted. She had long thick hair tossed over one shoulder, her eyes big and probably beautiful when they weren't so bleary.

Who the hell are you? I said.

Her smile seemed practiced, like a cheerleader. Or a cult leader. I'm your new stepmom, she said.

Dad laughed and succeeded in dragging her away.

Ains and I looked at each other and turned the movie up.

The way she delivered the line about being my new stepmom was half sarcastic, half like we were in on the same joke. The same way I meant it later when I'd call her that instead of Steph.

Anyway, that was how she came, and she almost never left.

~~~

Someboy left home at sixteen because he had to, because his stepfather figure kicked him out and, that time, his mom didn't invite him back in. He's older than his roommates, than everyone. Thirty-one, I found out when he left his wallet open one night at the bar and I pretended to fawn over his ID picture. You look so good in this, I said. No one looks good in those things. You look like Clint Eastwood.

Ha, he said, no, I don't. Do you even know who Clint Eastwood is?

He isn't working right now, something about his lung collapsing. When he does work, he's an artist slash brick layer, but for now, disability and old debts people periodically pay off to him seem to fund his lifestyle. Someboy's roommates are named Chris and Steve. Chris is quiet and not home much because he's training to be an electrician. They call him the Scientist, I don't know why; maybe because he beats them all at video games and built an ATV in his dad's garage from scratch. Steve is easiest to talk to—like Someboy, he's also home all day and tends to do whatever Someboy tells him to with his time. Let's go to the casino or the hardware store or the hill behind the church where kids toboggan out onto the river in winter, the highest point for ages, and see as far as we can. Let's order pizza or make a proper Sunday dinner or lace the keg with MDMA. Steve is always down. He works nights at Valu Lots stocking shelves. Brings home damaged goods, dented cans, and slightly expired frozen meals. The townhouse used to belong to Someboy and his ex, but he got it when they broke up somehow. I get the feeling the rent he charges Chris and Steve covers the whole place, that he's not paying for anything. His art form's photography, or it was— there are a couple of old Canons on a shelf in the bedroom—but the few framed prints of his that are hung around the main floor of the townhouse are old, from a time before Beauchamp, when he was young and lived in the city and roamed the streets taking snapshots of train yards, people waiting for the bus, an old lady wheeling her grocery cart home. I should photograph you, he said, hand under my chin, appraising me from every angle the first night we were together. But then he never brought it up again, and I never saw him take a picture of anything else, either, though sometimes he points out the light.

Someboy tells me things about himself that I realize are his classic go-to, heavy hitter stories. His canon. About his mom's bad boyfriends and his asshole father, some cold absent man he hasn't spoken to in years. About how he was homeless in high school after the fight with his mom's boyfriend, but he also talks about living with his buddy Phil when they were both seventeen so I don't think that part lasted as long as he makes it sound. He's good at making things sound terrible or wonderful, best or worst, and that's what it's like being with him too.

He doesn't ask me questions about my life, but he is all over my body, talks about it all the time. Exalts in it, sings its praises to pretty much anyone. After a while I realize he has been listening though, because he starts telling people things about me, prepackaged stories like the ones he tells about himself. They are half true, half lie, and I am equally split in how they make me feel. Sometimes I'm so seen it's like he's shone the perfect light

48

on me, I'm a rock star, I'm an ingenue. But then just as easily I feel suffocated by it too.

Bria was selling weed at eleven, little entrepreneur.

Bria's mom is a junkie, so she knows.

Bria is a sexual being, you can tell by looking at her. She exudes stripper pole.

Bria has the same measurements as Audrey Hepburn, but with perfect tits.

Bria doesn't do drugs. Just weed and blow.

That's true, I'll confirm after whatever he says, and everyone laughs. He likes to show me things. Movies, music, ways of being. Every pair of shoes and boots has a story. Tells me not to drink vodka because it makes me annoying, tells me to wear my hair down and to lay off the bleach, tells me to wear the black jeans and not the ones with all the holes because they make me look cheap. That's what I was wearing when we met, I say. You liked them well enough then.

Sometimes he'll land a kiss on my cheek, say you're so fucking pretty, disarm me with some sweetness. Come here, he'll say. I want to show you something.

Makes me lie down, put headphones on, the big heavy ones he keeps in a special zippered case and says are the best money can buy. Commands me: Close your eyes, listen. And it's some loud sad song I've never heard before, and I go calm inside the cavern he and his headphones make around me.

～～～

After the fight with Ains, I decide to go directly to his place, without going home to shower first. I have the shorts and tank top I wore to work in my bag (I don't walk the streets in my Burger Shack outfit, thank you very much), and I scrub my pits out in the bathroom sink before we lock up. I'll smell a bit deep-fried but, in my experience, boys don't mind that much.

Ains tugs on the door after locking it and then walks off towards home. The tug is to try to cement in her brain that the door is truly locked. She doesn't trust herself, or me, and many times has insisted we circle back to double-check we haven't somehow messed it up.

I keep my eyes on Ains until she turns the corner out of sight. Was that a falter in her step when she noticed the lack of me beside her?

I take a drag on the root beer float I made myself before we cleaned the ice cream machine and search traffic for yet another sign. Adding ice cream makes it a complete meal, I'd wanted to say to Ains, but she was too mad at me.

Since we're not currently fraternizing, Ains and I got our close done in record time. It's just after 10. I texted him at 9 and know he's never more than an arm's reach from his phone, so he must be ignoring me. I do some quick text math. It's been two days since the weird walk home. My plan was to text him on the third day: I figured one day was a given, two days was chill, but waiting three days would show true mystique. Still, a forty-eight-hour texting buffer wasn't bad.

Fuck this shit, I think, rising from the picnic table, its wood spongey and gross from the damp heat. I went over four nights last week, sacrificing sleep, sacrificing a lot of things because he begged me; he can offer me sanctuary now when I need it.

And fuck Ains too, for making me feel bad about it. I'm just trying to feel okay in the midst of so much shit. I don't need her of all people judging me.

Fuck everyone, actually. All of them. Fuck Tash for lying to me. Fuck Rick for being a lazy slob. Fuck my dad for fucking off in the first place. Fuck Steph for not knowing her limits. And fuck my mom for obvious fucking reasons.

The light changes, and I cross. Decide to swing by Dad's on the way to Someboy's. To give him a little more time to answer me. To give myself some time to think. Or unthink, as it were.

It's dusk enough now that even from up the block I can see that it's not on anymore. The light. I don't need to get closer to confirm it, just keep walking towards Someboy's, he who hath still not answered my text.

Go back over my catalog of grudges in brand-new detail, tending to them like you poke at a fire to give it some air. Stomp along hungry for someone to cross me, but all I encounter is the night air, still warm enough to make me sweat, and the stupid dangling worms popping juicy under my feet, their cool wet clutch sometimes kissing my arm or cheek. Fuck them too. I leave it till the front porch to pick them off.

But when I get to his door, I think I burned too bright, peaked too soon. My rage has lost its edge. All the good things I was going to say slip away, and I can't remember any of my lines. I pat my head for worms, then my clothes, finding a fat one clinging to the back of my shoulder. For having such fragile bodies, they can really latch on, and the trick, again, is to pry them off without squishing them in between your fingers.

Worm-free, I knock, truly nervous now. He still hasn't replied.

Steve answers the door, swinging it as wide open as his arms are to welcome me. It's plain he's surprised though. I rush to rearrange my face to be friendlier.

He's in his room, Steve says in the pause after we say hi.

Cool, I say, perching on the arm of the couch and trying to act like I have permission to be there. Whatcha watching? I ask. Steve has a movie paused on the big screen in the living room, looks like he was smoking a joint and having a beer by himself when I knocked.

Magnolia, he says, sitting down on the couch. Ever seen it?

No, I say. What's it about?

I don't know, man, he says, leaning forward to grab a lighter from the table. But it's weird and good, he adds. Come watch if you wanna. He pats the couch beside him, one finger on the remote's play button.

I'm bowled over by how much more I want to join Steve and watch a movie than I want to find out what awaits me down the hall with Someboy. But what comes out of my mouth is the opposite. I should see it from the beginning, I say, standing up.

Cool, says Steve. He hits play, and I go down the hall to Someboy's room, which is prime real estate right off the kitchen, with his own bathroom too. He can stay in there a long time without leaving.

I rap my knuckles on the door and open it when he says, Yeah.

Hi.

Hey, he says. On his bed, on his phone, in the dark. Barely looks up to see me.

You get my text? I step into the room and close the door. Sit down next to him, but not too next to him. He's fully dressed, even has his boots on. Looks tired, needs a shave, seems older, bigger, in every way. Maybe it's this light. Or this dark, rather. In the strange glow of his phone, my bare legs and arms are blueish white, and time feels alien.

He hasn't moved, so I sit there beside him with that peculiar feeling rushing through me. Fast but slow. Old but new. I shouldn't have come I guess, but he's been texting me all the time for weeks, asking and begging for me to come by after work.

Until the other night. Still, I thought it would be fine. Maybe that's the thing. I presumed. He doesn't want me running over here with my teenaged problems.

Well then, I'll have to make him forget that I'm a teenager. Not that he's asked.

There was music playing in the room when I came in, but now it's stopped. I go to his computer to pick out something. Standing up and moving is a relief, but even this is a test: if I pick the right thing, maybe it'll break this spell, make things okay again.

No dancing monkey routines, Steph always said, but she did them for Dad all the time. Was totally different when he came home. Or different in key ways. I suppose we all tailor who we are to who we need to be.

This thought is ringing like a gong through me as I sit back down beside him. He tosses his phone aside finally, and before the screen can go dark, in that same strange light and without preamble, he turns to me.

Turns me over. Hands and knees. He tells me what to do. As if I don't know. But I want him to say those things, and if I don't, it's easy to play something better in my head. Besides, at some point during, I usually tear off who I am and put on someone else instead. And then it's easy! The mattress digs in where I whacked my leg on the chair earlier, and there's not enough softness between the coils of metal under the sheets and my bones, but still. Nothing really hurts. He buries his face in my back, and I open my eyes to see his phone, right there in front of me on the bed. It's alight with a new message on the home screen. I can read it without trying.

Can't wait to see you tomorrow, it says. From someone named new thing.

Excuse me?

We don't have plans tomorrow.

We never plan for tomorrows.

He's literally fucking me and fucking me over at the same time. The irony of this would be overwhelming, but thankfully it's over.

I spend a few minutes in the bathroom cleaning up, composing. When I return to the room the bed is disheveled, and Someboy is gone. I hear voices in the kitchen, through the closed door, him and Steve. Are they talking about tomorrow? He gets closer, and I hear him say, clear as day, I'm gonna shower. Gotta rinse the sex off.

The door opens and he goes straight into the bathroom. I stay still until the shower goes and then I need to, need to know. The shape of the passcode for his phone is a zigzag swiping motion—I pay attention when he's on his phone, which is always—and I get it on the second try. Look for my name, new thing, in his messages, scanning down the column of names in his inbox and there I am, with a thud. Bria, second from the top, and right above me new thing. A new new thing.

My mind keeps spinning out when suddenly the shower stops. I don't know what to do, but then something occurs to me, and I hurry to my purse. Shake a pill into my palm and then back to bed.

He comes in as my throat is still trying to muscle down the pill without water. Stops and watches me. On instinct, I pretend to sleep, wondering all the while if he'll make me get up, go home, but then he lays down on the other side of the bed.

For a long time, we don't touch, before eventually an arm lands on my ribs. By his breathing, I can tell he's asleep.

Not me though. I lay awake all night till morning.

5.

But even morning won't release me. Someboy sleeps on and on without stirring, and I just lie here waiting for something to happen to get him to start his day. Keeps not happening though, so I learn all the cracks in the walls. There's one that looks like a mountain range, undulating against a backdrop of sky, and one the exact shape of a stuffed narwhal I had as a kid. Dad brought it back for me from the zoo in the city. I loved their unicorn tusks and how a group of narwhals is called a blessing. And then I'm thinking about global warming and how the narwhals are doing in a warming Arctic Ocean and I come back around the corner to sad. Back to examining the walls and trying to find beauty in his room. Trying to find something to fill my mind with other than the ugly shit it wants to think.

My brain's relentless though. It's a real bitch. Now I see the hills and valleys of the dump outside Beauchamp in the ceiling, dotted with the rumps of grazing bears. And from there I'm thinking about the time when I was nine and the city cops came out and excavated the dump looking for the body of a woman who'd gone missing. They spent weeks digging through the compacted trash before they found her. But it wasn't the woman they were looking for. By some sick turn, it was another murdered woman entirely.

When Dad and my mom broke up, first she went to the city, then after a couple cycles of rehab and relapse, she moved away with her then-boyfriend, this French tree planter dude named Guy. She'd call me from Guy's cell phone sometimes, until she didn't.

Even though I knew this, that she was far away from Beauchamp, it was easy to imagine her dead. It felt like a mental exercise that was good for me. Like an earthquake or a fire drill. In any case, I couldn't stop. I became convinced it was her they'd found, and no one could convince me otherwise because I didn't breathe it out loud. I didn't dare to. Her recent communications had been texts, emails, a card she sent on my birthday last year with only one line written on it: "Happy birthday to my girl, love Mom." But anyone could write that on a card. I didn't have anything real of her to hold on to, just texts she sent Dad, emails Tash printed off for me. I didn't even have her phone number at that point.

I waited weeks for them to come get me, tell me it was her. In class at school, I sat at my desk, ears attuned for the steps of the principal in the hallway, come to take me away. Not that I wanted it to be her, but I wanted my worry for her to finally manifest, instead of being a ghost only I could see. At home I watched the news from a corner of the couch, curled into, around myself, waiting for them to say her name.

When they did say the name of the woman they'd found and it wasn't Mom's, it released something in me, the opposite of relief, because there was no end to it; it would just go on and on, I knew. Unless I stopped it. And I've tried to. I told Ains about this old fear, confessed it when we were talking in the dark during a sleepover a few years after it happened. She, of course, pointed out the obvious thing I'd overlooked: the woman they'd found in the dump, and the one they'd been looking for originally, were both Indigenous. She pointed it out gently, but I felt chastised: this was not my tragedy. I'd been foolish in my fear, as in everything else.

Someboy mumbles something incomprehensible but definitive in his sleep, like he's settling a dream debate. That's when I get up, quick and quiet, and go to his bathroom, grabbing my bag along the way. Shake one more pill out of my little bottle, but only one. And I go back to bed feeling free of what was binding me.

~~~

You know, Bria, Steph told me once, you'll have many loves in your life. And you'll come to know what it feels like for something to end. You meet a man and share a few hours or days or weeks with him, and then you'll look away and back and find it gone. What you thought was there. And the trick in those moments, when the room shifts and something vital vanishes, is to find the door and walk through it. No looking back.

You have to listen for it. You're just bopping along and then one day something mundane pierces the veil. Missing your mother's birthday. Having to go back to work after the weekend. Needing to scrape together money before something bad happens. Or maybe you just sense that he is tired of the way your naked body looks and wants to see another. He's tired of the way you fuck and wants to fuck another. Whatever it is between you will weaken and thin, and it's up to you to stay attuned to the quality of air in the room. You'll know when things are over if you pay enough attention.

At that particular moment, she was drinking gin and tonics and snorting pills off the living room table. This is the exact right combination for this conversation, she said, when I eyed it questioningly. She wasn't a mystery; she told me all about herself. She talked all the time—to the TV, to an empty room, to me.

Hand jobs are highly underrated, she'd say. You can get a long way on a hand job.

I wanted to hate her, but once she moved in, she was impossible to ignore or resist. Apart from Ains, I hadn't had such good company in years, or ever. I liked the house noisy. I liked coming home to her.

~~~

One night back in June, about a month after Steph overdosed and I moved in with Tash, I was out for a walk when I passed a small house that buzzed with the sounds of a party. I didn't know the house, or the street, or the people, but I went inside.

It felt like life would always be like that. Something you could go out looking for and find.

It was another thing Steph taught me. How to navigate a room in which you don't know anyone, a room you have no reason to be in. It was about reaching out and putting yourself in other people's path with no fear of rejection. That was the most important part: to not want anyone to like you. To not need it. Who gives a shit, devil-may-care type of thing. It's just about finding the kitchen, finding out what the supply of booze is like, and who won't notice if you siphon off some of their bottle of Grant's or empty the dregs of a box of wine into a glass.

Emboldened as I was by her brand of advice, and out walking to keep ahead of thoughts I didn't want to think, many of which were about her anyway, I pulled the screen door open and walked in as if I may as well have owned the place.

The living room was full of people I didn't expressly know, but there was something familiar enough about them: they were exactly the same as everyone else I knew but maybe a few years older, one social scene removed from any I'd ever encountered.

I took off my backpack and reached inside for the beer I'd taken before sneaking out of Tash's, left over from a party Ains and I had gone to the night before, the big grad party thrown at the end of every school year at a house outside town.

I cracked the beer, even though it was warm and there might have been something more refreshing on offer in the kitchen, and held it in front of me like a prop, proof that I belonged there. Then I walked through rooms, taking the pulse of the party. It was quieter than the grad party, which hadn't even peaked by the time Rick, at Tash's orders, picked us up at 12:30, way out at the end of the driveway so no one would see us get in the truck with a dad type. When we left, there were still vehicles pulling up with six or seven drunk kids spilling out of them like degenerate clown cars.

This party, though, consisted of twenty or thirty people spread out between several rooms and the backyard, but the music was loud enough I didn't have to worry about talking. I nodded at a dude sunk deep into the couch who was rolling joints on a textbook like he was part of a production line, a small but growing pile of blunts beside him, next to it a heap of broken-up weed waiting to be rolled.

In the kitchen, a girl sat on the counter with a guy pressed up in front of her, pinning her there as they whispered to each other.

Hey, said the girl, leaning around the boy to look at me. She had very beautiful hair that spread across her narrow shoulders in loose waves, expensively colored many shades of blonde. You wanna buy some down?

Someone laughed. Two guys stood over the kitchen table spread with booze, surveying their options. One of them, a tall skinny guy in a basketball jersey with a face so pockmarked by acne it looked like a topographical map, seized a bottle of Captain Morgan and poured three fingers into a plastic cup. As he poured, he said, You don't sell that shit, Kelsey. Stop pretending to be all gangster.

I'm good, thanks, I said smoothly, though it wasn't an offer made in kindness, I could tell. The guy in front of Kelsey, who held onto her by the belt loops of her denim cutoffs as if she'd float off if he let go, had stifled a laugh when she spoke to me. It felt like I'd walked in on an ongoing joke.

Hey, the Captain Morgan guy said to me. You were at Jenna's last night, right?

I didn't answer him, distracted by the threat I felt in the room; I didn't know what direction it came from, but something was aimed at me.

Look, said Kelsey, as she pushed her boyfriend off her and hopped down from the counter. I've got it right here. Twenty bucks a pill, special price just for you. She took a baggie out of the back pocket of her shorts and waved it at me.

Usually, I would take the time to tear into a girl like that who thought she could out alpha me, but I was shaken by the open discussion of what, for me, was so secret.

Still, I took the bag from Kelsey and sipped my warm beer while I looked at them: oblong white pills in a dusty plastic sandwich bag, unevenly shaped, like someone with poor knife skills had their way with them.

Those are Tylenols with the *T* scraped off, I said, tossing them on the counter as the dude bros killed themselves laughing. Here, I said, rooting around in my backpack and retrieving the Ziploc that held the small repository of pills I'd hid when the paramedics arrived at the house, scooping it up off the table like second nature before anyone saw.

I held them up in full view now. The people in the kitchen knew what they were, but they played it cool, Kelsey especially, and her boyfriend after she glared at him.

Want some? I asked. Special price, just for you.

She laughed, again like it was aimed at me, but I knew I had what she wanted. I licked my finger and lifted a pill from the bag with its wetness, then put it in my mouth and chewed.

Eyes went wide, but no one was laughing anymore. I handed off the bag to Captain Morgan, who looked me over like every part of my body had newfound significance. But the appreciation only lasted so long. He took the bag, turned to his friends, and it was like I vanished.

Who wants one? he asked. They all shrugged and feigned, but the want was apparent, I could read it on their skin. I sucked the bitter pill remains from my molars and resisted the urge to rush to the sink and retch, somehow succeeded in holding it in, and thankfully found the bathroom just off the kitchen as the pill took hold. Later, Someboy would tell me not to look in mirrors when you're high, mention this like it was common knowledge, but I didn't know that then, and the mirror held me in its sights for I don't know how long. Words and worlds ran wild in my eyes that I couldn't look away from. Outside the bathroom, they were yelling in the living room, cheering some new arrival. My body wanted to expel the pill and the flood of saliva its mashing up had produced but my will wouldn't allow it. It wanted all the poison in my veins. Wanted to prove something to the people I'd meet when I left the closed space of that bathroom.

And it did get in my veins, and I licked my lips with my chemical tongue, wiped at the makeup that had smudged under my eyes, and went back out.

They were gone, of course, along with both bags of pills. I asked myself how I felt about it and discovered I felt nothing. That cheered me. Another one of Steph's lessons was to never leave your purse—or, in my case, backpack—behind when you leave the room, so I had the rest of my stuff. I stuck my head in the freezer and drank deeply from a bottle of vodka I found in there, even though by then other party people had moved into the kitchen to fill the space left by Kelsey and those guys. That was also a trick I learned from Steph. What you can get away with if you do it right in front of their faces.

At that point, I had never taken more than one at a time, and even then I swallowed them, so it took some time for it to work into me. Never before taken two, one at the start of my walk and then the one I chewed and washed down with beer and vodka. I didn't know yet that if you take too much of anything, you can arrive back at what you were trying to evade in the first place. Full futile circle.

~~~

I'm still staring at Someboy's ceiling, and he's still sleeping, when my phone buzzes, and with it, my heart lifts. Maybe Ains or Tash want to go get breakfast, or they're wondering when I'll be home.

But no, it's another dick pic. I feel extra grossed out for having been so dumb as to think it'd be anyone else. This one's blurry for reasons I'd rather not imagine, a poorly lit shot taken in the driver's seat of a vehicle, jeans open just enough to reveal his junk and one tattooed tiger eye. Where r u? reads the accompanying text. The only person wondering where I am is Dick Pic Man.

I want to scream but can't even make a sound. This is an ugly room. Ugly man in an ugly room who I am waiting on no longer.

I slide out of bed, determined now to get out before he wakes up. Where to find my things, what could I have done with them. Bra, shirt, shorts, done.

Steve and Chris are both in the living room, groggy on the couch with coffee and cereal. I wave goodbye, head straight out the front door. I know the look I saw on their faces the night we met now. I still see that look sometimes. It meant, Oh boy, here we go again. It meant, You poor dumb girl, run. And maybe, I'm watching him do something he's done before and am increasingly uncomfortable with what it means about me that I never speak up against it.

That's the look.

I walk home trying to untangle my head. I never wanted to be more than new thing to Someboy. But now I am. Am I? I am and I'm not, somehow.

6.

When I get home from Someboy's, I hop down onto the balcony and waltz through the sliding door forgetting that it's Saturday and Tash will be home. She doesn't see me though—the kids are stationed in front of the TV, and I smell pancakes, coffee in the kitchen. Rick is probably sleeping, and Ains is in the shower by the sounds of it. I whisper good morning to Emily and Doug, who say it back without their eyes leaving their cartoon, and then I slip into Ains's room. Our room.

I flop down on the neatly made bed. Even though I've only just gotten out of Someboy's bed, it's a relief to be in Ains's. She washes the sheets every week and makes the bed properly each morning. I stretch out on top of the smoothly tucked-in covers and press one cheek to their coolness, happy for a few minutes to look at my phone, be alone.

Hey, says Tash, popping her head into the room. Wanna go to Costco? I just got paid.

When I don't budge immediately, she says, Come on, and slaps her thigh like I'm a stubborn pet, then walks off, expecting me to follow.

What about the kids? I ask, trailing her into the kitchen, unsure I have Costco in me today. It's an hour away, in the city. Tash already has her purse on her shoulder, keys in hand.

Ains will watch them, she says. And Rick's here too. Come on, I need someone reliable to pilot the cart while I eat samples. She wraps me in a sideways hug and squeezes. I thought it'd be nice to spend some time together just us, she adds.

I tense when she hugs me, her face close to mine, scared she'll smell something on my skin, see something in my eyes. Okay, fine, I'll come, I say, backing away quickly when she lets me go.

One-on-one time with Tash is even rarer than time alone, as is the chance to influence the grocery shop. Maybe it won't be so bad, I tell myself as I wait out on the balcony while Tash fills Ains in. I can't hear what they're saying, but I do hear Ains's tone upon learning the plan. We're not supposed to have to babysit on the weekends, that's the deal.

Tash's face is determinedly cheerful when she joins me outside, leaving whatever happened with Ains behind. It's a bright clear day as we drive out of Beauchamp with the radio on, Tash alternatively singing along under her breath and muttering to herself about other drivers. She lowers the volume and glances over at me.

So, she says. You don't have a mom—

Jesus, Tash! You don't have to rub it in.

Sorry, she says. What I mean is, you don't have a mom to talk to about things. Such as birth control. I saw you sneak in at 3 a.m. the other day.

I look over at her warily. What day?

Wrong answer, she says.

I fell asleep at a friend's house.

Listen, says Tash, if this is going to work, you need to be honest with me—

Before she can continue, I make a bold move. His name is Steve, I say. Like all my lies, it's unplanned, leaving my mouth before I can weigh its consequences on my tongue.

Oh, Tash says, trying desperately not to show how excited she is by my share. Tell me about Steve.

Well, I say, considering what I know about Steve. The best lies are built out of bits of the truth. He works at Valu Lots, I offer.

So, he's gainfully employed, Tash says. That's always a plus.

I need all the karma I can conjure right now, so I refrain from making the tell-that-to-Rick comment the moment begs for. He sure seems pretty recovered from his hand surgery at this point, always headed off to the gym or to jam with his buddies. And yet his convalescence continues, work-wise.

What else? Tash asks.

I don't know, I say, and shrug. He's from Durham. Big family. Sisters.

Have you met them?

Not yet, I say. But they seem really close.

Can I meet him? Tash asks, unable to contain her enthusiasm now. Why don't you invite him for dinner sometime? We could barbecue.

I hedge. Sure, I say. But, like, maybe next month. Don't wanna rush it.

Okay, she agrees. How old is he?

Umm ... nineteen, I say, though Steve is probably twenty-one.

To this, Tash gives a disapproving huh. Even my fake boyfriend is too old for me.

A song we both like comes on and I turn it up. Tash starts humming the first line before the big-voiced singer comes in, but after the first chorus, she shouts over the music, dancing in her seat, So are you having sex?

Tash pulled me for all the talks: sex talk, puberty talk, your-parents-may-have-failed-you-but-I-am-always-here-to-talk talk. Mostly, she just lumped me into whatever lecture she was giving Ains. Two birds, one parenting stone. All these talks made me burn not with embarrassment but something else: anger at not knowing everything already, hating having to be let in on things. Anger at them, grown-ups, always keeping something from me, even if it was only the knowledge of sex or bodies, though it was usually more than that.

I overheard Tash talking about me once when I was in sixth grade. She had a bunch of people over at their old place, where they lived when she was with Derrick. I was alone in the kitchen when I heard them through the screen door. Bria is a good kid deep down, said Tash.

Deep down, Derrick said. Like, way deep.

They laughed.

I worry, Tash said, that she's just like her dad.

But also: Tash smoothing back my wet hair from my forehead, her smell of baby lotion and menthol cigarettes before she quit, soothing me when I'd miss my mom when I was little and did things like that. Tash picking us up from school, always there on time, unlike my dad. Tash in her waitress clothes, tight and low, coming home with pockets of bills she let us help smooth out on the kitchen table for her to count. Leftovers from her staff meal in her purse, waking us up to kiss us goodnight and then cracking a beer with the babysitter before sending her home. Tash spending as much on me for Christmas as she did her own kids, even though the one thing Dad spoiled me with was toys.

I should have known this was a hijack. I wonder if Ains is in on it. In the small space of the truck, Tash is still talking, has moved on to birth control, injections, patches, pills. She runs down the pros and cons for them all. Tash's talks became a lot more like this once she went back to school. Stats and horror stories.

Bria? Tash is saying. You awake?

Uh-huh, I say. It's true my eyes are closed, but even in my sleep, I'm always listening.

Tash pauses. Well, I'm going to get you a big bulk box of condoms at Costco. Maybe we can split a box. How big is your guy? Rick is pretty—

Ahhh! I scream, hands over ears. I'm awake now.

Geez, I'm just joking, she says. But you should use condoms.

You're gross, I say. Then add, I have it under control.

And I do, and I didn't need anyone to help me figure it out. I've been getting my own tampons since I got my period, and I found a doctor and got the pill when I needed it too. Even went to the clinic in the city and got a bunch of it for free without anyone in Beauchamp needing to know. All of my money, practically, goes towards being a girl.

We're approaching the city now, its small skyline of tall buildings mirage-like against the otherwise uniform prairie horizon.

Plus, Tash says, all you've gotta do is miss a day or two and bam, baby. Or if he's a real asshole, he takes the condom off halfway through. Then bam, baby. Or, she says, you could be one of the unlucky four percent—

Okay, okay, I get it, I say. Bam, baby.

Bam, bam, bam, Tash says, hitting the steering wheel with one hand.

She lets it drop as we hit the city and she needs me to tell her when it's safe to change lanes. When she graduated and got her job, she bought a giant truck—some of the places she has to go for work are on country roads that are rough in winter—and she's a menace in it.

We're cruising through the suburbs now, the Costco sign visible on the horizon on account of the land being pancake flat.

Just don't get pregnant, she says. Not on my watch, not on anyone's. Okay?

Okay, I say. That much we can agree on.

At Costco I push the oversized cart as Tash walks ahead of me, talking all the while. I catch up and stand by patiently while she calculates price per unit and lectures me intermittently about how to budget. Remind me to get cat food, she says. It's so much cheaper here. And some of those all-natural fruit snacks we got for Em and Doug last time.

Kay, I say. Got it.

But I do not got it. Two seconds later, when she asks me what I was supposed to remember for her, I can't. Sorry, I say, and worry for a moment she's going to call me on my brain fog, examine my eyes, but no, she's on a shopping mission now, and I'm just along for the ride.

I always forget half of what I want to buy, even with a list, she says. Wait here, I'm going to run back to the dairy section for some yogurt.

Sure, I say, pushing the cart off to the side and leaning against it. The walk across the parking lot, so much more crowded than anywhere there is to go in Beauchamp, had made my head swim with anxiety. Too many people moving in too many different directions, all willy-nilly. Now that we're inside and she's off my case, it does feel a little good to be out with Tash, doing what she tells me to like a diligent robot niece. Or like she's my mom and I'm her surly teen angel daughter reluctantly helping with errands. I can probably even get by on one-word automated answers.

For the rest of the shop, that's what I do. Yes, we need laundry soap. No, I don't think we need forty gallons of trail mix. Yes, to cereal. No, to peanut butter. Yes, no. No, yes.

But always the ugliness creeps in. A tiny woman in yoga gear eyes me while she passes by with her equally slim and flexible children, as if she can see what I did last night all over me. I give her a fuck-you look and try to pretend again, but it's ruined. Nobody thinks I'm Tash's kid. They think I'm some trailer trash here to blow my welfare check.

Speaking of overspending, I do start to wonder where Tash is getting the inspiration to spend so freely when she comes back with not just bulk packs of yogurt tubes but also a block of cheddar the size of a two-by-four.

Even more so when we go to the mall afterwards and she buys me two new bras and a five-for-twenty-five underwear deal. I pick them out slowly, considering each pair. We go to a kids' store next, and she picks out T-shirts and pants for Doug and Emily, carefully sizing them up. For Ains, we get a new hoodie and leggings from her favorite store with the expensive sportswear those bitches on her team never take off. It's funny to see Ains with her teammates in her volleyball getup. Little booty shorts, sports bra, and a T-shirt. Strong and comfortable with herself. At ease in her body. When she steps off the court, it's like she distorts somehow, but on it she's crystal clear.

Tash gives me twenty bucks to buy some snacks for the drive home and leaves me in the food court while she runs to a few more stores. I get two big iced coffee concoctions, one chocolate and one caramel, and I'm standing in line to buy a bag of chips when I see this girl from school across the sea of tables.

I turn away quick, hoping she didn't see me, but as I do, she waves. I raise the iced coffees in acknowledgment. Figures. Tash isn't the only small-town girl who loves the mall. This place is always crawling with people from school. Me, I'd rather spend my time in the city looking at the old buildings downtown with faded signs painted on their sides, or people-watching on that street with all the Italian restaurants with sidewalk patios. Dad took me, Tash, and Ains out to one of those places once. They ordered an entire bottle of wine and drank it slow in the sunshine.

Hey, Bria.

The Beauchamp girl has crossed the food court and is standing in front of me. How did she do that? I really am out of it, underwater.

Hey, Jenna, I say, proud to have found her name in my brain. She's the rich kid whose grad party Ains and I went to at the end of the school year. Her dad works for some farm equipment company or something, and her parents let her and her brothers have a big blowout on their gigantic compound outside of town every June.

I don't really know Jenna, neither does Ains, but it's the kind of party everyone goes to, whether you know the people throwing it or not. The official unofficial end-of-school party. Was it safe to say that I had embarrassed myself? Talk of the ODs was still in the air, and to distract from my connection to them, I got spectacularly drunk and slid down the banister, hitting the round part at the end with one hip and summoning a bruise that two days later would be black and Someboy would trace with his finger.

Ains stayed with her friends outside, having claimed a circle of patio chairs a ways off from the house where they craned their heads back to look at the stars and sipped a shared bottle of something sweet and cinnamony. I felt like an intruder when I went over to them, talking too loud and saying too much shit. When I went back inside, I was sure everyone was staring. And whispering. About me? About my dad? Then the intense paranoia of a wasted person who thinks the room has turned against her.

What're you doing in town? Jenna asks me, back in the reality of the food court.

Just shopping. I shrug. You?

Same, she says. I can see now she's baked. Fried even. I relax a little.

It's my turn in line so I put my chips on the counter and hand the woman working the till my money, balancing the cardboard tray of drinks carefully so I don't spill in front of this bitch.

I can see Tash coming now, looking around the food court for me, her arms even more weighed down with bags. I've gotta go, see you later, Jenna, I say, not bothering to be nice anymore.

Hey, she says. I heard something about you.

I stop.

People are saying your dad's a snitch, she says.

Suddenly I have too many things to carry in my hands. I manage to accept my change from the cashier, but barely, and walk a few steps away before turning to Jenna. That's bullshit, I say and wonder if it would be better or worse for me if I also punched her. Worse: Tash has seen us and is headed this way.

But Jenna shrugs. We're having a social for my cousin's wedding next weekend. You should come. There's gonna be three kegs and a band.

Okay, I say, thrown by how swiftly she's switched topics—your dad's a snitch, wanna come to my party? Maybe, I add.

We part ways and I turn to Tash, who is dumping her bags on a nearby bench.

I got them in another color, Tash says, pulling out a pair of navy pants she'd previously bought in green. They'll be better for work that way. Show less dirt. What do you think? And I got you and Ains a six-pack of socks each. You should have everything you guys need for a while.

Sweet, I say, struggling not to show the fight or flight I'm feeling.

Tash takes the drink tray from me and wiggles hers out of it. Who was that? she asks, sucking on her straw.

Just some girl from school, I say, my tone impressively flat, given how shaken I feel inside. Snitch. Is that what people are saying? It was just a piece of meaningless gossip to Jenna; in fact it may have added to my social status in her eyes—that was certainly more attention than she had ever paid me before—but my heart was beating on high alert at what it might mean for dad, for me.

What's wrong? Tash asks, frowning. You don't like her?

I shrug, uncomfortable with how she's scanning me for information with her eyes.

Is it school? Don't worry about that. You've still got over a month of freedom before you go back. I just realized, Tash goes on, a tad manically, that frozen stuff is probably mush by now. Let's hustle.

We redistribute the bags evenly between us, and we're off, weaving to one side to let an elderly couple going the other way pass, then splitting up to hurry by some slow pokes.

I'm not going back there, I say, once we're beside each other again. I'm struggling a little to keep up with the pace she's setting,

73

legs flying beneath her as we motor through the mall towards our exit.

Where? Tash asks. Costco? I know it can be intense in there. Makes my blood pressure spike too sometimes.

But she knows I mean school, is trying to make light of it. Anger starts to mount in me.

Tash registers my mood, puts an awkward arm around me, bags and all. Chin up, kid. It's not so bad. We reach the doors, and she pauses. Fuck, where did we park?

Over there, I say, pointing with my chin towards the truck. We head in that direction, and Tash carries on.

You stay on with us through the fall and then we can see what happens with your dad. But you've got to go to school.

I'm about to step off the curb when I stop. Tash turns, then halts too. My skin is hot with what Jenna told me, my whole body pulses with whether or not to say it right here, right now. Ask if it's really true, if he snitched on the people he was working for and that's why he can't come home, has been so cagey about everything.

But now that I've got her attention all the way on me, I want to wriggle out from under it.

Chickening out, I take a page from Ains's playbook and demand, Who's going to take care of the kids when we're in school?

Tash sighs. That's not for you or Ainsley to worry about, she says, her voice clipped. Your job is to focus on school and being a teenager. The kids will be back in daycare full-time by this fall.

It's this way, I say, letting my voice go rude and unimpressed. Tash follows me between two cars to the row where the truck is parked. I move as quick as I can, in contrast to my earlier sluggishness, trying to lose her as much as I'm trying to lead her.

Summer has made it easier to forget that I'm an outcast for a litany of reasons, but when we get to the truck, I explode. I don't want to go back to school, I say. Just transfer me, anywhere but there.

Tash unlocks the doors and puts her bags on the backseat. I do the same. When we're settling into our seats she says, Look, I don't doubt you hate school. But you're two years out from graduating. That's nothing. You don't want to fuck that up and wind up like—

Lay off my dad for once, I snap.

I was going to say your mom, says Tash, but sure. That works too.

Screw you, I say, buckling my seat belt.

Hey, Tash says, buckling hers. Easy, I'm just kidding. She shows me her palms, like she comes in peace. I was going to say me, she says. Thirty-five with three kids and I just got myself through school. I did everything in the wrong order. Just started earning decent money now. I don't want that for you.

You're doing good, I offer, in spite of myself. She is doing good, aside from Rick.

Thanks, she says. It's not just me being an asshole parent, Bria. If you drop out while you're in my care, they'll take you away from us. And it'll fuck shit up for me at work.

She's taken the straw out of her cup and is trying to use it to scoop up the whipped cream and syrup sludge from the top of the drink.

I ignore how disgusting this is; in fact I try to ignore her completely as she backs haphazardly out of the parking spot and points the truck towards home. Except I can't ignore her, not really, because she needs me to give her directions from the map on my phone and answer when she asks if it's safe to change lanes.

Why don't you try to reconnect with Natalie? Tash asks.

I snort. She makes it sound so simple. Nat was my main friend when we were younger, but we haven't talked since high school started, basically. I didn't fully register the shift until it was a done deal. Nat had a new group of friends that her parents probably liked more, and I had . . . whatever social status it is that I have. Beauchamp's most popular pariah. I kept tabs on Nat for a while, but after Steph overdosed, I deleted all my social media accounts so I didn't have to think about people at school when they weren't in front of me.

You hear from your mom lately? Tash asks when I don't reply to her Natalie suggestion. We turn onto the wide and windy street that will take us through the city and out the other side.

I snort. That would be a no, I say. Mad she's made me say it. Mad in general now.

Hmm, says Tash. Well, she's a tough cookie, your mom. She might get it together one of these days.

Not holding my breath, I say, though what I want to say is please stop talking about my mother like she's a sports team that might turn their luck around someday. I look furiously out the window. Tash went to school with my mom. They were friends before Mom and Dad got together even. She doesn't talk about her though, not to me, except for these types of times. When it's just us and she wants to therapize me, break me down and put me back together. Today I am already broken down, and I won't allow it.

They should never have gotten together, your parents, Tash offers as the brief downtown gives away to the city's true nature. A place made mostly of green and gray. From what I've seen of other places in movies and TV, it's a shit city, but it's our mecca of convenience.

Why did they then? I ask eventually, long enough after her comment I can tell she has to search her mind to remember what she said, hopefully feeling bad about it now in retrospect.

I don't know, she says. Mutual self-destructive tendencies? Or maybe not. Sometimes people just attach themselves to each other. Sometimes, she says, it's very hard to tell if someone is good or bad for you.

I scoff. That's not true.

She looks over at me briefly, but long enough to let me know she thinks I'm full of shit.

Shut up, I say, though she hasn't actually said anything. We drive on for a moment, and when I open my mouth again, a question rises up from the deep cave where I keep them. Did Dad . . . get her addicted?

No, Tash says quickly, rushing to offer this. And then, it seems, not knowing how to back it up. Eventually she says, I don't think I can tell you who was the bad influence on whom. Your mom liked to party starting from when we were young, but your dad was the one always hanging around dirtbags, not the friends we all had in common, but other harder crowds. I don't think you can spend time around people like that without it rubbing off on you.

She stops talking and we both sit with that for a moment, me staring unseeingly out the window at the dwindling city.

Listen, kiddo, Tash says with a new intensity. We all did a lot of stupid shit. I got pregnant with Ainsley obviously, and that took me out of things. As it should. But plenty of girls we went to school with got pregnant, had the baby, and then went back to partying.

Tash trails off again, the way she always does when she accidentally says something damning of my mom. Mom being one of those girls, the post-baby partiers.

Then she says, You know, I think it's my fault, some of it.

Some of what? I snap.

She pauses. Then says, Some of the way things have turned out.

How? I ask, nay demand. Angry especially at the finality of "the way things have turned out."

I've been bailing your father out since I was fifteen, literally. I'm always there to save him from himself . . . and I don't know. Maybe I shouldn't have. Maybe I should have let him deal with the consequences sooner.

She's never admitted it to me directly, but Tash wasn't talking to Dad before he disappeared. She skipped Easter and Granny's birthday, dropping Ains and the kids off at family functions and then picking them up again later, claiming work obligations. At first, I thought she was just caught up in her new thing with Rick, but then Dad made some comment about Tash being a bitch lately. How she was back up on her high horse, all holier than thou. And when he took off, she didn't swoop in to save me like usual. I had Steph, and I guess we all felt that was enough.

I dig through a landslide of resentment and mean feelings until I find the words: Well, he's dealing with them now.

Yes, she says, he is.

The GPS lady on my phone speaks up to tell us to take the next off-ramp to the smaller highway that leads to Beauchamp. Usually this is where Tash would tell me to turn the directions off, but I leave them on and she doesn't say anything about it, both of us listening in silence as the lady tells us to keep going, urging us onward.

We both turn to look at All Stars as we pass. You can see it from the highway if you look at just the right time. The sign is pale in the daylight but still visible, its florescence drowned out by the throbbing green of the trees and a sky that drips blue. The patio around one side and the smoking area out front, coffee-can ashtrays lining the path like landscaped flowerbeds. In the daylight, it doesn't look like the same place I spend so many nights. It doesn't even look like something I know.

When did you find out Dad was in jail, exactly? I ask.

The truck swerves along with her body when she looks at me. Jesus, she says, straightening out. Why do you ask?

Maybe the fact I want to know the answer?

Bria, she says, hearing the venom in my voice and trying to find the antidote. Listen, it's not like I wanted to keep it from you. But I didn't know anything specific about his charges so I thought it would be better—

She seems to barely stop herself from saying something. Then restarts. We decided you'd been through enough already lately . . . with Steph and everything.

Who's we?

Well, I discussed it with your dad, and Rick agreed—

What does Rick have to do with anything?

Tash's face sterns. I notice now how nice she looks today, her hair pulled back and her face well-rested or freshly moisturized or something.

Rick is my main support system at the moment. I need it too, you know. And for now, he's a member of this household.

Though she looks like she wants to pull over and leave me at the side of the road, she sighs, seems to make the effort to soften. I think of the burden I am, how I get so much of her attention and I'm not even hers.

What I meant was, Tash says, your dad and I thought that you didn't need to know he was in legal trouble until we knew

79

how much legal trouble. The plan was to tell you once things were settled. That's just taken a lot longer than I imagined.

It's official: everything she says infuriates me now.

You know, Tash goes on, maybe we should call the therapist your case worker recommended. I didn't want to push it on you too soon, but since you're going to be in my care for a while—

I sputter. Care. What a fucking joke. As if I'm in anyone's care right now. You barely pay attention to your real children, let alone me.

Wouldn't you know it, we don't really talk after that.

~~~

The night after Jenna's party, the night I crashed that other party, the one with the people in the kitchen who stole my bag of pills, I eventually made my way over to All Stars, of course.

I must have made quite the entrance because Dave intercepted me between the door and the bar.

Bria, you can't be in here like this.

Like what? I asked, smiling in a way I imagined to be flirtatious. I remember a loose-headed feeling, like I had no connection to my body, and a frantic glee. I don't remember anything about who was there or what I was wearing, but Dave's reaction was outsized enough to make an impression on my vodka-and-beer-soaked brain. He wrapped me in the sepia-toned flannel work jacket he wore all four seasons, covering me up. And when I slunk close to him and adjusted the dish towel he had tossed over one shoulder, he said, Bria, stop it, grabbing my hand and moving my body back away from his.

The tone of his voice chastened me immediately. Dave never snapped at me like that. I couldn't do more than voice a few feeble objections and let myself be marched to his car, where I waited while he went back in to get someone to cover for him. Didn't even consider making a break for it, unsupervised as I was, too far gone by then to do anything but focus on trying to halt the way the world had recently started spinning.

But it would not halt, nor pause, nor reverse.

And then Dave was back and we were driving, making slow sick turns that spun me out even more until it finally became too much.

Pull over, I said, and as he did, I opened the door. I remember wanting to undo my seat belt and step out for some privacy, but also knowing that kind of coordination was out of the question. I was incapable of doing anything but trying to lean far enough out of the car to aim the contents of my stomach at the ground.

That's probably for the best, Dave said a minute later. You done?

I nodded, rolled down my window for some wind, and let that hold me together as we drove down the road.

Let's get you home, Dave said.

Oh no, I protested, let's not.

Bria, come on.

I'll get in trouble. I'm wasted.

He sighed stupendously, the human embodiment of being between a rock and a hard place. Won't you get in more trouble if you don't go home at all?

Please, Dave, I said, summoning all my faculties. Just let me crash at yours. I told Tash I was sleeping over at the party, I add, lying. Please?

He exhaled. Fuck, Bria, he said, but he put the car in reverse, turned around, and drove towards his house.

Dave set me up on the pullout couch in the living room with a glass of water and a bottle of Tylenol, which made me smile, thinking back fondly now on how I'd called that Kelsey girl out earlier for trying to sell me fake pills. While I was settling in, Dave called Tash, despite my best objections. Though he retreated to the kitchen to call, I could hear his voice, bright and reassuring when she picked up and then going quiet, out of range.

All right, he said, coming back into the living room. Tash says get some rest and she'll talk to you tomorrow. I'll drop you off there in the morning.

Okay, I said.

Goodnight, Bria, Dave said, turning out the lights and leaving the room.

Something went wrong in me immediately in the dark, but I fought against it. Said no again and again to the thoughts that tried to undo me. Still, they surfaced in a slaughter. I tried to think instead of good and simple things, like Emily's delicate fingernails and how she lets me trim them for her full of trust, translucent crescents I gather in a Kleenex and drop into the trash. Tried to remember Doug falling asleep against me on the couch, how it clears all my plans, having that kid decide to take a nap on me. Thought of the freeness of a day at the beach. How the sun blanks out the whole world when you lie down on the sand. Tried to feel the way it feels at work with Ains, us filling in all of each other's gaps. But not this. This she did not know. And then it was back to doomsday predictions and reaching for the proverbial paper bag to breathe into, anything to limit the panic that filled me.

Bad thoughts tsunamied through and washed away everything permanent I had to hold onto. In came my mom and dad and how I didn't know where either of them was, not really, or if they were okay, and then came Steph's body on the couch and the drugs in my own body, doing the same things to me they did to her.

Dave! I said, loud outside his bedroom door.

What? he responded immediately, voice a little panicked.

I think I'm dying.

There was a thump, and then the door opened. What's going on? He wore sweats and a T-shirt; his curly hair was rumpled on one side and a deep imprint from his pillow cut across one cheek like a scar. Had more time passed while I freaked out than I thought? I backed away, into the wall.

I think I'm dying, I said again. Not knowing how else to put it, how to elaborate in any way.

Dave put out a hand towards my elbow and then withdrew, as if afraid I'd be hot to the touch. What, he asked, do you mean? What makes you feel like you're dying?

What were my dying symptoms? I didn't know. Didn't know how to articulate anything other than that one thing: I was dying and dying. A devil had whispered my fate in my ear and now I couldn't breathe right—that in and of itself made it hard to explain what was happening in my body. A rising, roiling wave of something sharp and alarming. A total collapse of the systems that upheld my belief in the world maybe. Or no, it was more existential even than that. And it was straight, physical terror at what was working on my body, burrowing in, making connections I wanted nothing to do with. Or did I? After all, you can't run from what runs in your veins.

I admit, from an outside perspective, I probably didn't appear to be dying. Not fast, anyway. But I was drowning in something slow, and I didn't know how to put it into particulars, couldn't think of any words for it at all.

I kept it in as Dave stood before me, frozen, unsure what to do. I tried to think of something to say that could reasonably follow "I think I'm dying." Failing that, I commenced calming him down. Making it seem like nothing but stupid teenaged Bria being a whore for attention again. Even then, it pulled at me, dictating my actions. My want for the drug working for and against itself. Not me but it.

Dave was skeptical. Did you take something? Other than alcohol, I mean? he asked, rattled.

No, I said. No, just booze.

You'll be okay, he said, relaxing somewhat. You just had too much to drink. Come on, it'll look better in the morning. He led me to the kitchen and sat me down at the table with a glass of water, then went out and came back with the bottle of Tylenol and a wet washcloth. Here, he said, pressing the cloth to my forehead. Did you take one of these? he asked, shaking the bottle. When I said no, he opened it for me and gently nudged a pill out of the bottle and into my hand. I put it in my mouth and swallowed, committed to pretending nothing was wrong now. I nodded when he asked if I was ready to go back to bed, nodded again when he said one last time, You're just too drunk. Tomorrow, he said. Everything will be okay.

Tomorrow then. When it came, it was like he said. Or at least whatever had gripped me had lessened, which was technically better, I guess.

In the morning, Dave sat with me in the kitchen while I ate some cereal. He drank coffee and talked about my dad. Guessing, I gathered, that was what I was upset about. Was it? I wondered, sitting at the table feeling not so much hungover as maybe still high, still drunk, still whatever from last night.

Dave told me things I did and didn't know. Like how my dad used to run cross-country in high school and would train all year round; you'd see him at the side of the highway with a high-vis vest on before school on dark winter mornings, breath exiting his body like puffs of smoke. Dave tells me how he visited my parents right after I was born and how bright and excited Dad was to show me off, constantly carrying me around without his shirt on so that we could bond. How he never seemed tired when I was a baby, he seemed energized, thrilled to have me to take care of. Tells me how, when my grandpa died, eighteen-year-old Dad went for a walk after the funeral and never came back. Everyone was looking for him, and they found him the next day all the way out at this fishing shack my grandpa had, like thirty miles outside town. He'd walked the whole way there; said he just wanted some time alone.

Dave wiped his hand over his face as if he'd been sweating. He wasn't, but he did look nervous as he said, And he took me to the clinic in the city every day for months to get my methadone when I got clean.

This information didn't fit in my brain. Dave, addicted to opiates. Dad, helping him get off them. I put down my spoon and stared into the pool of milk at the bottom of the bowl, trying to make sense of it, without really knowing what was wrong.

Dave was too focused on his own discomfort to notice mine. At the time, he said, I had lost my license, but your dad made sure I got what I needed, even watched me take my methadone at first to make sure I wasn't messing around and abusing it.

My brain was trying to process this, flitting from thought to thought, holding up what Dave had said against my memories. I felt like a computer struggling to download a file too big for it. When? I asked.

Four years in September, he answered readily.

So, I'd have been about twelve. I try to remember what was going on then. It was right after Dad started making money and bought the house, back when he first started being out of town all the time for work. I knew Dave had quit drinking at some point, remember there being a shift when the days of him and Dad sitting out back late at night drinking beers had ended. I think it was around when Dave's mom, Glenda, died and he inherited the bar. It was never explained to me the way it was explained to me that my mom was a heroin addict. Just Dave doesn't drink anymore. No big deal.

But how can you work at a bar every night if you're sober? I asked him abruptly.

He shrugged. Alcohol was never really my issue.

That's stupid, I said with a vehemence that surprised both of us.

You already knew I don't drink anymore, Dave said, clearly bewildered by the turn this conversation had taken. He took a breath and tried to soothe me. What's so different now that you know I'm sober from everything? he asked. Wouldn't it be worse, working at a bar if I'd had a problem with alcohol?

Yeah, I said, my cheeks feeling fiery, not really sure what point I was arguing or why. My heart was thudding for some reason, and I felt miles more embarrassed by this than I had waking him up in the middle of the night or puking out the side of his car. Being so obviously upset and not knowing why I was. Upset, that is. That felt like a real failure, a humiliation.

I grasped for a point, something to justify the argument we were now clearly having, or I was having. Dave was calm, if a little embattled-looking, but my eyes were hot with tears and I got even angrier because of them. Why don't you drink then? If you don't have a problem with it? I demanded.

He laughed ever so briefly, but my face cut that short. Because, Bria, he said, I can't trust myself.

You can trust yourself enough to work at a bar, but not to drink? I snapped and stood up. The hypocrisy, the lack of clear logic completely befuddled me, and I felt both insane and like the only sane person I had ever met at the same time.

Dave called after me as I shut myself in the bathroom. With the door closed, my thoughts went right to Dad, driving Dave to the city, helping him get clean. Dave's own words.

I stayed in there for a few minutes, brushing my fingers through my hair and retying my ponytail, pinching a little color into my cheeks so I didn't resemble a teenaged corpse when I got home.

Let me just check I have all my stuff, I called to Dave when I emerged, going into the living room, where earlier I had done my best to put the pullout couch back together.

I'm good to go, I told Dave, throwing him for another loop with a return to normalcy.

I put on a chipper demeanor for the drive, hassling him about how sad the women's bathroom is at All Stars and trying to convince him to get us drive-thru breakfast even though we already ate.

Tash appeared on the balcony when we pulled into Paradise with a look on her face that indicated Dave had fully filled her in on how messy I'd been the night before.

Good morning, sunshine, she said as I dropped down onto the balcony beside her and tried to slip inside. But she caught my arm and pulled me into a hug. This was early days after Steph's OD, and at Tash's everyone was treating me with caution. Go on in, she said, releasing me. We can talk later.

I lay down on the bed and Ains sat beside me, put one careful hand on my head, and touched my hair for a second. She didn't say anything. Outside, Tash and Dave talked about me.

They were probably all the way over by his car, but we could hear them perfectly.

I don't know what to do, Tash was saying. She won't listen. I can't control her. Dave murmured something reassuring and then Ains went over and slammed the window shut.

In the days afterwards, I could see how Dave thought it was all about Dad, what was wrong with me in the morning, what I'd tried to tell him in the night. Maybe it was. When I'd go by All Stars, Dave started in without me even asking, saying he hadn't heard anything from Dad—but don't worry, he'd tell me if and when he did.

And rather than his talk with Tash resulting in some kind of crackdown on my middle-of-the-night excursions, both she and Dave seemed to ease up on me. As if they were scared of coming down too hard and crushing me in my fragile state. I felt I'd pulled something off. Fooled them all and felt sick with it.

7.

When we get back to Paradise Gardens from the city, Tash and I unload the truck without speaking except for Tash asking if I got the backseat bags and for me to answer in the affirmative, both of us clipped and polite.

Emily and Doug go briefly gaga over their presents before it sinks in that it's all practical things like socks and clothes. But still, with the kids around to lighten the mood, it's easier to pretend both Ains and Tash aren't mad at me. Or I'm not mad at them. Whatever the score.

Rick has made a rack of spicy ribs for dinner, his one contribution to the household being that a couple times a week he spends all day cooking a bulk amount of something the kids won't eat, and then when every dish in the house has been dirtied, he swans around like he deserves a medal. He and Tash eat out on the balcony, licking their fingers in between sips from frosty glasses of white wine while Ains puts away the groceries. They're going to some concert in Durham, I glean, listening from the couch in the living room where I fiddle with my phone, opening one app after another mindlessly. I retreated here after trying to help Ains put the groceries away, but I could tell my presence in the small space of the kitchen was irritating her. I guess Tash asked Ains to babysit tonight too? She must be livid—the deal was if we looked after the kids while Tash was at work, we could have every weekend to ourselves. But Ains doesn't get anything to herself.

A wave of proprietary affection floods me, and I'm relieved as it becomes clear: what Tash has done to Ains is way worse than anything I did.

Also, why doesn't Rick ever help out with the kids? Why didn't I think to ask that when we were fighting in the car today?

A sense of purpose would be good for you, Tash said when she told us she'd pulled them out of daycare for the summer. It's good to be busy, she said when we claimed to have said purpose in abundance. And then finally: I'll pay you a nominal fee.

Kind of like Dad, Tash has always liked cash. Liked having literal bags of it around. Whereas Dad keeps his in Ziplocs he hides in walls, Tash hid wads in an ornate beaded purse she kept in the closet. Growing up Ains and I knew where it was, but we never touched it. Tash knew how much she was hoarding in there down to the dime, saving it up until she deemed it time to spend. Then she would count out a stack of bills and take us to the mall, not unlike today.

Poor people syndrome, Someboy said when I told him how money moves in and out of our family. I'm the same way: Tash hands us both a few twenties a week, and I turn them into . . . what? Not savings like Ains, who puts it all in the bank and has a notebook that she uses to calculate projections of how long it'll take her to reach her financial goals.

After Rick and Tash go to their show and the kids are asleep, I follow Ains to bed with a desperate, throbbing need for her to talk to me. But she falls asleep quickly, or else she's a genius at pretending to breathe slow and unhurried like an unconscious person. I can just make out her face, slack in the dark.

I try for hours, really I do. Before I'm rolling out of bed like a silent ninja, scooping up the clothes I wore today from their pile on the floor, putting them back on, and climbing out the window.

~~~

When I walk into All Stars, I find Someboy right there at his usual table, talking in some girl's ear. She's older and pretty but nothing like me, so there's that. Still, it stings.

It was only last night that Dave dropped by Burger Shack to check on me, and when I walk up to the bar, he looks briefly like we're going to continue that conversation where we left off, but then he just asks, Are you okay? His eyes flick to Someboy's table.

I'm fine, I say. Can I get a Manhattan, please?

He laughs, as if I'm joking.

There's a mirror behind the bar so I can see Someboy clocking me. Not much of a reaction, but I track it as it goes through his spine, making him sit not taller exactly but more alert. To me. To my presence. Steve and Chris are at the table too. The girl is saying something, telling a story, and his roommates are leaning in to listen, but Someboy looks at me. Puts an arm around her waist and pulls her hips closer to him on the bench.

Okay, so he wants to get a punch in. I take my time, registering the blow, registering her.

Dave puts a glass of milk down in front of me and starts pouring Ron his hourly pint—they've worked out a schedule.

What's this? I ask about the milk.

To help you grow up big and strong, says Dave.

The new girl is snuggled into him quite comfortably now. Maybe they have history. He's old enough to have a lot of it. It's okay though, I understand. I'm just like him; I also want there to be a lineup of people who want me, waiting. To remind me when I need it that I'm worthy. I want to be a thought in many heads. I want to be the shape they call up when they close their eyes and reach down for themselves. It never works the way you want it to. Once you've got someone. I don't want the actual him. I want the him that existed before I knew him. Before we speak, that him. And I don't just want one of him; I want many. At least three at any given time. Guys who text me until I have to turn my phone off to make it stop. Who beg and plead for me. But who only ask for so much.

In the mirror, I watch the girl go to the bathroom. Memorize her back.

Seriously, Bria, says Dave. You okay? You seem . . .

Down? I ask.

Yeah, he says, uncomfortable, like I'm the one who made it awkward. That pisses me off about Dave. I express one thought or emotion, and he acts like I'm being a dramatic female.

I'm fine, I say. I'm excellent. I straighten, pull my shoulders down, and feel the length of my spine grow taller or whatever those yoga ladies Ains watches on YouTube talk about. I swing the stool around and stand up.

Bells, whistles, explosions of color and light, and all that jazz. I move so magic Someboy isn't the only one who watches me walk across the room. Hey, Steve, I say. How's it going?

What's up, Bria, he says and slides over to the chair closer to Chris so that I can sit.

Thanks, I say, accepting the seat at the table. Steve is a funny guy in the sense that he always looks happy to see me, even now, when it's clear I'm not invited to this party.

Who's she? The girl is back from the bathroom and she has questions.

I feel myself drifting downstream suddenly, away from this moment that demands my attention. I try to remember everything I've taken today, this day that never ends.

No one gives the girl an answer. Poor thing. She's prettier than me, smarter than me, cooler than me, and I'm still gonna get him.

I'm his girlfriend, I say, nodding at Someboy like I'm sorry about it, but only a little.

She rears back, enraged, appalled.

Listen, he says. It's complicated.

I laugh, and for his part, so does he. We enjoy a brief moment of eye contact, and this ignites the bitch even more.

Listen, he says again, glancing at her and then back to me. But I've turned, I'm leaving, gone.

He catches up just outside the door. What'd you tell her, I say, reaching into his jacket pocket and taking out his smokes. I light one and give the pack back to him.

Relax, he says. But he looks at me like I've surprised him, in a good way.

Let's get out of here, I say, and we walk off together into the sunset of my mind.

At least, that's how I'll remember it tomorrow.

8.

A couple of days later, Tash comes into Ains's room, startling me—I didn't even know she was home yet—and thrusts her phone at me. Here, she says. For you. Your dad.

I put the phone to my ear and listen to the familiar fuzz. Voices thin and sharp like tin, a big and windy room.

Hey, kid, he says, when I finally say hi. Tash says things are good?

Resentment dries up all my words and I have to search around for some. I've been better, actually, I say. And then wonder, Have I?

He laughs. Me too, he says. Good news though: my lawyer is working me out a good deal. So, you just hang tight, okay?

Dad, I say, what's going to happen to the house? I wasn't worried about it until this moment, when the worry lands in my lap like a premonition: what if we never live there again? Like, in a long-term, permanent way?

He pauses. You'll probably have to stay at Tash's for a little while longer.

I hear the air next to the phone move, like he's held the receiver away from him.

But then he's back, saying, This is important, Bria. You stay away from the house right now. And if anyone asks about me, don't say anything. Okay?

There's a full-length mirror on Ains's closet door, and I see myself in it, bag-eyed and hunched over on the bed. I sit up straighter. I wouldn't know what to tell them if they did, I say, though his tone tells me I'm in dangerous territory.

What? he asks.

If someone did ask me about you, I reply, I wouldn't know what to tell them. Would I?

I can hear him stuff down the frustration in his voice. I can't really talk about this right now, Bria, he says.

Hey, I say. You called me. Then I think, Did he? Or did Tash force him into it?

You know what I mean, he says.

No, I don't actually, I say, pissed now, or else I always was.

Listen, kiddo, I can't talk about this on the phone. I wish I could. I'll be home soon, I promise, and everything will start getting back to normal.

It is satisfying to hear him reassure me, even if I had to force him into it. Okay, I say, and he says it too, and we both say goodbye.

~~~

When I was a kid, it seemed to me that my dad just drove around all day and that was his job. He had a series of cars, never anything for longer than a year, sometimes slick new sedans or SUVs he leased from the dealership in Alma or, more often, patchwork pieces of shit he bought from Leech, one of the Rainbow boys, the family that owns the scrapyard and the dump.

Beauchamp is a blip of nothing in between several slightly more significant nothings. It's part of a trifecta of towns all about an hour southeast of the city, the scuzzy little sister of Alma and Durham. We share a hockey team and a casino, but you'd think the citizens were from different planets, the way some people act.

We're defined by our strip mall, one of two high schools in the area, a hockey rink, and a string of big boxes by the highway that have choked out the small businesses downtown, but what we're really known for is our drugs. Lowlifes from all over, not just from Alma and Durham but farther-flung places, all come here to buy their coke, weed, meth, and pills.

Dad got me when he and Mom split up. I was four and we went everywhere together for a while. When I was older, I'd wait in the car, playing games on his phone—he always had more than one—or listening to the radio, looking out the window at the houses and apartments and different places we'd go. Sometimes he'd bring me in, and I'd chat up and charm whoever he was there to see. Sometimes he dropped me off at Tash's for a day or two, sometimes a week, and I got my fill of people before going back to our house.

So, I knew some things by the time Steph came around.

But mostly I didn't know. How much, how deep. I knew there were drugs in my dad's life. He drank and he'd do shit at parties, sure, but he wasn't an addict. That was always my mom. Steph was looser though. She wanted to talk about her addiction; it was like a bad boyfriend she couldn't quit that all her friends were tired of hearing about. I was a fresh ear and pretty much her only person in Beauchamp, because by then he was splitting for a few days at a time for work. He'd leave us alone for five days, then come back and be mad we were getting along, that we were close. They'd disappear into the bedroom or out of the house for a day or two, and when they reappeared, he'd have relaxed, the balance returned.

What do you see in him? I asked Steph once when I was mad at him.

Oh, you know, she said, trying to lighten me up. Good looks. Charm. A big pile of drugs.

She laughed, a bark laugh that always made me wince internally because she never laughed that way at things I thought were actually funny.

I'm an addict, what do you expect? I heard her snap once on the phone with her mom. I think she'd missed a family thing.

Maybe *addict* is the kind of word I should wince at, like I winced at Steph's laugh. But I don't. I don't feel anything when I hear it. Maybe it's like how Someboy says the word *love* gets emptied of meaning if you say it all the time.

Do you know what intrusive thoughts are? Steph asked me randomly later that night, after I'd heard her fighting with her mom. I shook my head.

It's a symptom of OCD. My sister has it, the middle one. She started washing her hands obsessively when she was six and I was four. Like, all the time. My mom would wake up in the middle of the night and find her on a footstool in the bathroom, scrubbing her little paws down to the bone. Later she decided that me and my other sister, the older one, were making her sick. She refused to sleep in our room together anymore. I had to move in with our grandparents for a while. My parents were always with her at the doctor. In our teens, the germ stuff seemed to lessen, and other things ramped up. Imagine you can't stop thinking of all the worst, most horrifying shit imaginable. Your brain just continuously pukes up bad images on repeat. Like, incest or maggots falling out of—

Ew, I said. That sounds awful.

Yep, she said, suddenly cheerful or something resembling it. And now, I am the fuckup. Imagine that. I'm the one who's making my family sick.

~~~

If you take out the ceiling fan in the bathroom, in the space above it there's a duffle bag. Dad's spot.

Not long after Steph moved in, I woke up on the couch in the middle of the night. The bathroom door was open, light on, and I could see her standing on the edge of the bathtub, rooting around up there. She came down with a bulging baggie of pills and I watched her lick the tip of her finger, lift out one pill, and crush it on the bathroom counter with one of the smooth lake rocks I had lined up on the shelf for decoration. I like rocks, holding onto their cool weight. Steph arranged her deconstructed pill into a line and bowed down to it. At first it looked painful, going up her nose, then very much the opposite.

A little while later, when I was complaining of cramps one day, Steph offered me half a pill.

No! Dad snapped. Hard and mean like he can get in an instant. Don't give her that, he said.

Steph got me ibuprofen and there was talk of a heating pad, but when she went into the bathroom to look for one, Dad followed her in and ripped her head off.

These are the stories people tell about my dad. How in spring he'd get naked and jump in the lake while the ice was winning out over water. How he attended ninth grade for three days before faking a seizure in the hallway to get excused, never to return again. Granny found out when the school called and asked how Paul was doing with his epilepsy. How he did a computer programming course at the community college in the city, was at the top of the class, and then stopped going two weeks before he would have gotten his certificate. How he took me absolutely everywhere before I started school, strapping me to his chest or throwing me up on his shoulders and taking me to the bar or the shinny games he played with his boys.

But I know there are other stories too, that I don't get to know.

Sorry about that, Steph said later, after Dad went out.

I shrugged. I feel better now anyway.

It's funny, she said, brow furrowed. I think every kid thinks their parents are hiding something from them. That Mom and Dad can secretly afford to buy the new Barbie you want but just refuse. Or how kids believe that after their parents put them to bed, they break out streamers and balloons and have a late-night party with cake and cartoons. That something wonderful or terrible is being kept just out of sight.

I don't know, she said, really on one now. Maybe the secret is really just the gruesome realities of life, like when you first learn about blow jobs or what death is. Both of those things made me think, Ew, what is this life?

She lit a cigarette, blew the smoke up at the ceiling fan, and kept talking. I used to think my eyes were going to roll back in my head and stay that way in my sleep. My dad would do that awful trick where he'd flip his eyelids inside out to scare us. It was like he had little fleshy almonds over the whites of his eyes, little bits of meat. You know, I've never liked pink, as a color. I don't see it as girly and cute. The insides of us are pink. Pink is the color of the raw parts of things.

99

I remember being confused—I often felt like I couldn't keep up with her sideways train of thought in a way that made me feel stupid and lame—but then she circled back around.

I guess that's grim. Oh well. What I was trying to say is that all kids think there's something their parents are keeping from them, but what's fascinating is your dad actually is.

What?

Well, you know the basics, right? He works for drug dealers. She shrugged. Some very bad dudes.

As I sat with that, sifting through it, my heart pounded so hard in my chest I worried she would hear. My dad is scary. I knew this. But he didn't usually scare me. He did the day he warned Steph not to give me drugs though, or those drugs in particular. It was hypocritical—there were drugs everywhere, and he was the one who brought them into the house, into our lives. Or would they have been there anyway? I wanted to press him about it, scream at him about it, but I never did. It was too close to a subject we'd both sworn off. My mom died before I was born, I tell people sometimes at parties, and wait for them to tell me that can't be true. It totally can be though, and it almost is.

~~~

By Thursday, I can't take Ains being mad at me any longer, so I crawl into her room on my hands and knees to beg for her forgiveness. Emily and Doug come crawling in after me. Ains is lying on her stomach on the bed with her headphones on. Her makeup looks good and I tell her so and she rolls her eyes, but I see the edge of a smile tug the corner of her mouth.

Ains thinks all kinds of things are wrong with her. She doesn't ever say it out loud, but I read her journal once, so I know. I didn't mean to exactly, but when you share literally everything with someone, these things happen. The pages I read were an awful dump of words about how she hates herself, her body, how she's stupid and ugly and weak. All the things she's not. I have to pretend I didn't read it, or she would kill me, but moments like these I see how those thoughts own her.

Look, Doug, I say. Your big sister is so pretty and smart and hardworking. She takes such good care of everyone. Isn't she so special?

We sit there admiring her, and I compliment her excessively, and Doug and Emily agree with me, loving this game after the tension of the last few days. Doug jumps on my back and Emily clambers on after. I rise to my knees and neigh silly and horse-like, then dislodge them giggling onto the floor. Call for a tickle attack on Ains, but when I look back up at her, she's looking away, eyes flooded and shiny with tears.

What's wrong? I sit up and take her headphones gently from her ears. She shakes her head, and some of the tears slide out even though I can tell she's trying to contain them. We all climb up to join her on the bed. But she still won't talk or tell me anything, so we just cuddle her and pat her head until every last one of us falls asleep and we don't wake up until Tash gets home and starts calling out for her babies.

~~~

Wanna go to the park today? I ask in the morning. We're awake in bed, listening to Tash give the kids breakfast in the kitchen. The park in question is about a fifteen-minute walk away, and we usually only take the kids there if the pool at Paradise is too crowded or something, but I have something in mind.

Sure, says Ains, sleepy and surprised. I get up and leave her to relax a while longer, going out to receive Tash's instructions for the day. She's in chaos mode this morning, having turned the living room into a sorting station for the supplies she's gathering for people displaced by the forest fires a couple of hours north of here, filling reusable shopping bags with snacks and toiletries to drop off at the motels nearby where victims of the fires are staying.

Sunscreen refills are in the bathroom cupboard, she tells me, and there's a clean load of laundry that needs to be folded and put away.

I say okay over and over, even when it's to something deeply, offensively obvious. But I'm being too chill and helpful, and it attracts attention.

Are you feeling okay? Tash asks, looking me over.

I'm fine, I say and turn to the kids. Who wants to go to the park today? And then Tash can't say anything further, because Emily and Doug are over the moon at the prospect.

When Tash is out the door for work, we pack up the stroller and point it towards the park. Despite the fires being a couple of hours from here, smoke has muddied the sky, making everything smell like a barbecue. There are fires up near Ains's dad's reservation; she talked to him last night and they're on alert, ready to leave at a moment's notice on buses coated with special paint to help withstand the flames.

At a moment's notice. The phrase pings and pongs around my empty head as we head to the park. The walk over there is hot and shadeless, the ditches hum with mosquitos, and everything is begging for a breeze. I wore my hair down and wish I hadn't. I can feel it getting wet with sweat at my temples, the back of my neck.

We bribe Emily into riding in the stroller with Doug so we can get there faster than her legs will carry her. She's hyper-stoked by the outing and the fact Ains and I are getting along again, singing a song about ice cream in time with the rhythm of the stick Doug is dragging on the ground out one side of the stroller. It skips a beat every time we hit a crack in the sidewalk. Hypnotizes me, filling the air with noise so we don't have to.

Everything is fine, everything is fine, I chant in my head in time to Emily's song. I've got Someboy back. He even texted me good morning and sent me a song to listen to while I got ready for the day. Dad is sorting his shit out, or so he says. I should feel better than I have in forever.

At the park we stop at a bench by the playground, and I lift the kids out of the stroller. Emily makes shy eye contact with a little girl on the slides, and I gently push her forward, into the sandbox, then up to the slides, until finally they're playing together. Ains helps Doug thread his feet through the holes in a little kid swing and then steps back to push him.

Hey, I say, a few minutes later, when Doug has had his fill of the swings and they join me on the bench. Mind if I dip out for a few minutes to run an errand? I ask.

What kind of errand? Ains eyes me, on guard right away. Great.

I had thought about lying, saying I was going to get some snacks at the store or something, but nothing is getting past Ains today, I can tell. I take a breath and in a reasonable, straightforward tone, say, I just wanted to go grab a few things from the house, since we're in the neighborhood.

You're not supposed to go there, she says, automatic and authoritative, like she's shooting down a suggestion made by one of the kids.

I know, I say. But I'm not going to hang around. I just want to get some things.

What do you need? Maybe Mom and Rick can go grab it for you tonight.

I don't want them snooping around my room, I say. It's really no big deal. It'll just take two minutes.

What do you need to get?

Clothes, mostly, I say. I'm tired of wearing the same shit all the time.

She hesitates, shakes her head. Mom said you're not supposed to go there. Why don't you just borrow some of my clothes?

I already have. I laugh, gesturing at the shirt I'm wearing right now, which is hers. I try a different approach. I wanted to get something else too. Something of my mom's, I say.

It's soothing, how easily the lie comes. All of them.

Ains's face is like, Oh. Sad. And I know I've hit the sympathy jackpot.

I don't want to, but we bring the kids, Ains insisting the only way she'll let me go is if she comes with me.

As we turn onto the block Dad's house is on, Emily embarks on a question-asking tear.

Uncle Paul's house? she asks, as we cross the street towards it.

That's right, kiddo.

Is Uncle Paul home? asks Emily.

No, I say. He's away. For work.

Oh, says Emily, computing this.

That's why Bria is staying with us, remember? Ains says to Emily as she hot-wheels the stroller up over the curb with expertise.

Auntie Marie? Emily asks.

No, says Ains quickly. She doesn't live here. She lives far away.

I glance at Ains, and she mouths, Sorry. We don't really talk about my mom, ever. Emily has never even met her, so I don't know where this Auntie Marie thing is coming from. Maybe Tash is telling her stories, but I never hear them.

Em, remember we had a water fight here last summer? Ains says, changing the subject to one of Emily's favorites: she loves nothing more than a water fight. She sets off chattering about water balloons as we pull around to the back door.

Hey, says Ains, who's mowing the lawn?

Indeed, the grass is short and trim. Dave, I answer, even though I have no idea who's been mowing the lawn. It had never occurred to me. I search through my purse for the keys.

Dad surprised me with this house when I was eleven. Back then I'd go for sleepovers at Ains's that would turn into me staying there for days, a week at a time, never sure if it was our idea or one of the grown-ups'. He came to pick me up after one of those stints and instead of driving the usual way back to the apartment we came here, to this house.

All the houses on this block are the same, built for railway workers, little one-and-a-half-story homes with identical picture windows and the same chain-link fence surrounding every yard. The rest of Beauchamp is more varied, old brick farmhouses that the town grew up around, trailers with piecemeal additions made of scraps and ingenuity, and the big fat new builds the rich people like.

It may be just like the other houses on the block from the outside, but inside it was so renovated and new that I thought we must be rich and untouchable now. The fake wood floors were bright and clean compared to the beige carpet in our last place, and though it was small, there were two little upstairs rooms, one on either side of the staircase, with sloping attic ceilings and windows you could climb out of to sit on the roof and spit sunflower seeds at the neighbors. Two rooms, just for me.

I help Emily and Doug out of the stroller, then unlock the door.

It smells stuffy and sweet, like bad fruit. I should probably clean out the fridge, I think for the first time since I left here. The blinds are drawn and it's a relief after all the brightness of outside.

What did you want to get again? Ains asks, clearly ready to leave already.

I don't look in the living room, with the wraparound sectional couch we loved to watch movies on, and the giant TV Dad brought home after he'd been gone for an especially long time.

The kids throw themselves at the couch and start jumping around.

Hey, guys, stop! Get away from there, Ains says.

Why? asks Emily, freezing in place, eyes round. It's rare for Ains to raise her voice.

My eyes meet Ains's, and I read her mind because it's the same as mine. A lady almost died on that couch is what she's thinking.

Just be careful, she says. The furniture is askew from where the paramedics moved it to work on Steph, and Ains goes over and shoves the cushions back into place. There, she says, pulling the coffee table out so they don't crack their heads on it. Better now.

I go upstairs.

My room is a mess, but that's not from the paramedics, just me. Clothes on the dresser, bed, floor. Stacks of magazines on the floor, pictures torn from them arranged on the slanted walls. I liked to put up pictures of glamorous pillow-mouthed models and tried to channel their energy when I did my makeup. I liked to dress up in party clothes and take pictures I didn't post, just saved for me to pore over later, proof I was beautiful in a frozen, tangible way.

I get down to business. Grab some random tank tops and a hoodie I actually do miss and stuff them in my backpack.

Hey, Ains calls from the bottom of the stairs.

Anywhere you talk in this house, you will be heard. I used to have entire conversations with Dad from my bed when he was downstairs in his. Turn that the fuck down, I'd shout if his snoring got too loud. Or he'd wake me up by yelling my name, drawing it out forever until I got up for school. He'd still be in bed, ready to go back to sleep when I left.

Hey, Ains calls again. Bria?

What? I reply, coming back downstairs.

Hurry up. Let's get out of here.

Okay, I say, I just need to grab some stuff from the bathroom. To the kids, who're watching us, always watching, I say, And then let's get ice cream.

They erupt, of course. Ains looks pained.

I go to the bathroom and shut myself in. Come out a couple minutes later and make a show of all the bottles of shampoo and conditioner I've packed in a plastic grocery bag, the packs of five-blade lady razors and little green tubes of lotion for every part of the body. Eyes, hands, feet, body. Steph liked to stock up.

Ains and the kids are ready to go at the back door. Let's get out of here, she says.

I help her down the back porch steps with the stroller, and we wheel around to the front of the house. Just a sec, I say. I should check the mail.

I find three slim envelopes inside the mailbox and glance at them briefly before slipping them into my backpack. Just a couple bills, I tell Ains.

Is someone picking up the mail too? Ains asks.

I shrug. I guess. Like the question of the lawn, it had never occurred to me. Now I wonder if that's all the light was. Someone's been by to take care of the house. Dave or Tash maybe. I follow alongside the stroller, wondering what this new brand of betrayal I'm feeling is based on. Why I feel disappointed that could be the answer.

A couple of blocks later, Ains stops pushing the stroller and stands still.

You okay? I ask. Her eyes are closed, and she's breathing funny, shallow breaths.

Yeah, she says, I'm fine. But she's swaying on her feet. I ready myself to catch her if she falls.

No, you're not, I say. You're gonna faint.

No, she says, but I can tell she's woozy from her half-closed eyes and the way she's not moving forward when that's where we've got to go.

It's the heat, I offer, knowing Emily is listening, even though it's not the heat.

Ains bends over and puts her head between her knees. I squat down beside her. Mark said to do this when I feel light-headed, she says.

Is it happening a lot? I ask, irritated at Mark knowing something about her I don't know.

I just have low blood pressure, Ains says, looking up and a little less pale.

Let's get you a hot dog or something, I say in a lighter tone. Ains wouldn't eat a hot dog if her life depended on it, but we're just a few blocks from Valu Lots and they sell them in the parking lot in the summer.

Gross, she says, standing up again to her full height again.

When Ains is upset, Ains doesn't eat. Ains is always upset.

~~~

Last year, when she was spending all that time with Cole, Ains asked me what sex was about.

You mean what's it like? I had only done it myself a few times.

No, she said. What's it, like, about?

Cole was one of those kids that sneaks up on you and suddenly becomes hot. For years he'd been a target at school from both the boys and the girls, because he was sensitive, because he was small, probably because he was mixed race too. He had a big soft mom who loved him and his older brother, Alex, way too much. Or too much for us to tolerate. Their dad worked in the oil fields and was away a lot, coming home a stranger with presents to break the ice. Cole would show up to school on a Monday after his dad had been home with sneakers that pulsated with newness, or a jersey for a soccer team we had never heard of, so we resented him for that too. They lived in the corner house across from the lumber yard, a little white box with *Caragana* bushes fencing the yard. One of the houses Dad would stop at was down the block, and sometimes I'd see Cole and his family while I waited outside. Their mom was the elementary school nurse, and although I remember her as a nice lady, this only furthered the boys' unpopularity. Funny how things can work for or against your favor. Like how she let them express themselves. For Cole, this meant gelling his hair into long heavy-metal spikes for all of fifth grade. But by eighth grade, the spikes grew out and flopped attractively over one eye, and he got good at volleyball and all the guys on the team were forced to accept him. I didn't realize he'd also gained the girls' approval until I saw his name on a bathroom stall. *Cole is hot* with a heart around it in black Sharpie. And just like that, he was chosen.

For a while, he and Ains were almost a thing. Now she gets mad whenever anyone says his name, so I don't.

I think about that though. What sex is about. Is it about closeness and feeling good? Sometimes. Sometimes not. It feels like an exchange of something I can't express. Some kind of currency. Maybe the next time she asks, I'll be able to tell her.

~~~

Rick is out when we get home, and for that I thank him. Best thing he could have done for us in this moment. I get Ains a glass of ice water and a banana and leave her on the couch in front of the fan. Doug is already sleeping, his sweaty hair and scrunched-up face making him look like a tiny balding old man.

Popsicle? asks Emily. The ice cream mission was abandoned when Ains started feeling bad.

Good idea, I say. We hold hands on the way to the fridge, reaching out at the same time in a way that warms me a little. I take out three Popsicles in white wrappers and open the tops to see their colors. Emily picks purple.

You want orange or pink? I ask Ains.

Whichever, she says. I give her orange and help Emily up onto the couch, so she doesn't get her already-sticky hands all over it. Mouths busy with Popsicles, we go quiet, watching the cats fight over patches of sun. My backpack is on the floor next to the living room table, what's inside of it pulsing loudly, urgently, but only for me, and I must ignore it.

There's a buzz in the back pocket of my shorts. I reach for my phone, thinking it'll be Someboy telling me to come over tonight, but when the message opens, it's yet another dick pic. I press the button to darken the screen immediately. Emily is right beside me. Let's watch something, I say, to distract her, myself.

Yeah! says Emily, all enthusiasm.

Ains tucks her naked Popsicle stick inside the banana peel and curls up at the other end of the couch in a ball. I flip through channels, settling on the kids station Emily likes. Ains's eyes close by the first commercial break. Emily snuggles into the crook of her legs. Wait until everyone is peaceful and safe, then get up slowly from the couch. Grab my backpack, lock myself in the bathroom.

Inside my bag, wrapped in a hoodie, is a large Ziploc bag of pills, wrapped up in even more plastic until it forms a cellophane cylinder. Run the tap as I unwind and unwind it, until finally the bag tumbles to the floor. Bend to pick it up. Try to guess how many pills are inside, like guessing how many jelly beans are in the jar at the school carnival.

I've been taking pills since that night. That one.

I'm so careful. I only take a tiny bit. And wait. And wait. Then a tiny bit more.

~~~~

Later that night, when Emily and Doug are asleep and Tash and Rick are talking out on the balcony, Ains and I go to bed early. It's been building up to rain all day and now it's about to hit. The wind keeps sending the blinds smacking into the wall over and over, and you can feel the cool air mixing in with the thick hot stuff we've been walking around in for days. We need some rain, it's all anyone's been talking about, and now it's finally come. It's still sticky and hot in our room, but between the fan hitting me every thirty seconds or so and the breeze coming in the window, I know even though it's uncomfortable now I'll wake up reaching for a blanket in the middle of the night.

Thunder cracks and I listen for the kids, but Tash is home and so is Ains and they wouldn't be crying for me, anyway, if they did wake up. I'm never around this time of night.

Do you ever want to talk about it? Ains asks.

I'd thought she was asleep. Race through thoughts, keeping quiet, quiet.

A moment passes and she whispers, Bria? You awake?

Instinctively, I do my best impression of a sleeping person. One minute later, wish I hadn't. Why can I talk so much when it doesn't matter? Never when it counts?

Later, when Ains is out cold, I slip out of bed and go down the hall to the bathroom.

The bills I saved are still in my backpack. I take out Dad's credit card statement. Wasn't ready to look before, but now I do, quick before I lose my nerve. Scan the list of charges. Dad has an account for Mom at a pharmacy in the city where she's lived for the last couple of years. Every month he lets her charge a couple hundred bucks to it. Not too much and not too little. Just enough to keep her alive, based on his calculations.

There they are: biweekly charges from the pharmacy Mom's tethered to, in among the automatic payments for phones, hydro, mortgage. I haven't seen her since I was eight, when she borrow-stole some stuff from Dad for the final time and took off. I still got calls from her until I was ten or eleven, but by then I'd stopped believing anything she said, and that didn't leave us much to talk about. Started hating when her calls came through collect or from some unknown number. A burner she'd managed to buy for herself, or more likely the phone of a friend she was sponging off at the time. She's better far away. I don't even have the good memories Tash and Dad have about her. I have the hole she left in my life and that's about it.

I slip one more pill between my lips and make a silent vow to be better tomorrow, to put my foot on the brake, and swallow.

9.

On Sunday the pool is closed. Rick offers us a ride to the lake, and it's hot enough in the apartment and on the patch of grass outside that we take it.

Tash is sleeping off a coworker's bachelorette from last night, but the rest of us pile into the truck with Rick, Ains wedged in the back with the kids and me up front. Even as we're buckling seat belts and driving out of town, east towards the lake, I'm still expecting Ains to backtrack, say never mind, take us home. When she said yes, I zipped around packing everything we might need for the day while she gave the kids breakfast and Rick did whatever he does on his phone all the time, trying to get us out the door before she could have second thoughts. Why so committed to the idea of an excursion today? I don't know. The cicadas were buzzing obnoxiously in the trees beyond the Paradise Gardens parking lot, and we never do anything fun on the weekend. Weekends are me slinking in or out. Avoiding this or that. Why not have a nice day together for once.

I feel lighter as we leave Beauchamp with the radio on, kids chattering in the backseat. Hell, I'm even feeling half-kind towards Rick by the time we stop in Alma for some chips and drinks.

What do you guys want? I ask Emily and Doug, who've joined me in front of the fridges. Ains is in the snack aisle, having a staring contest with some trail mix, and Rick is leaning against the counter up front, telling the cashier about his carpel tunnel.

Water! Emily says, smacking the glass in front of some bottles of water.

I brought water from home, I say. You can both pick a juice.

Emily gets in close to examine her options. That one, she says, pointing at a mango-apple blend. Doug wants what his sister wants. I add their juices to my basket, along with a bag of chips and the trail mix Ains is agonizing over. At the counter I reach for my wallet, but Rick pulls our stuff towards him and nods at his cashier friend to ring it through.

Anything else? she asks. Rick's already got gum, some beef jerky, and a couple king cans of Labatt.

You girls want anything else? Rick asks.

I look to Ains, who shakes her head. We're good, I say.

Throw in a six-pack of those fruit punch coolers too, Rick says, tossing a few more bills on the counter. He looks over at me. That's what you like to drink, right?

My eyes flick to Ains's again, but she's staring down at the kids, holding onto Emily with one hand and Doug with the other.

Sure, I shrug. The cashier puts the coolers on the counter in front of me. I pick them up and we move towards the doors as Rick waits for his change. He got his unemployment check yesterday, Ains mutters.

I see, I say. That makes sense, hence the celebratory mood. I wonder if he gives Tash anything for staying with us, eating all the good sandwich meat she buys for lunches and hogging the window A/C unit in her bedroom.

Before we get back on the road, Ains takes the kids to the gas station bathrooms. I get in the truck with Rick, which has become a sauna in the few minutes since we parked. My thighs are plastered to the seat and I peel them off periodically, waving my elbows to get a little air under my arms as we wait for the A/C to kick in. Rick is in his standard jeans and boot combo, which he's stayed committed to throughout the summer, but he did toss a rolled-up towel and swim trunks in the back of the truck. I'm already wearing my bathing suit underneath my shorts and T-shirt and am starting to sweat through everything when Rick rolls the windows down, letting in the outside air for some relief.

Thanks, I say.

He seems distracted, flipping through radio stations and then searching out his smokes, then back to the radio. You want one, he asks, nodding at his pack, which he tossed on the dashboard when he was done with it.

Sure, I say and then regret it when he beats me to his lighter. Holds out the flame for me to lean into, cigarette between my lips. I hate when people do that but lean in anyway.

What, he says when it's lit, no thank you?

Thanks, I say, flooded with the feeling that maybe this wasn't such a good idea. Maybe my wanting to get away made me overly enthusiastic, too soft towards Rick, whose invitations for rides or freebies I always refuse. I shift my knees away from him and blow smoke out the window.

A brown mutt lies in the dirt near the entrance to the gas station's small parking lot, long pink tongue lolling, panting steadily in the heat. Wordlessly, I step out of the truck.

Hey, boy, I say, squatting down and holding out a hand to the dog. He springs up and runs over, best friends at the first offer of attention. I can tell he's not a stray but a badass parking lot dog from his name tag that reads Brutus and from the way he acts like this high-traffic zone is his living room. It makes me nervous. Dogs and tires. Trusting humans to be mindful of the safety of others. Trusting humans, period.

Come over here where it's safer, okay? I say, trying to lead him closer to the store entrance. I sit down on a low cement parking block and give him some pets, my cigarette making me sick in the heat. I smoke it anyway. After a minute, a white truck even bigger than ours pulls in and the dog runs up to greet it, tail wagging, zero regard for the height of the wheels or if the driver sees him.

I stand up. Hey, buddy, come here, I call to the dog as an older guy gets out of the truck and walks towards the entrance.

Country dogs, he says as he passes, like it's the answer to a question I was asking.

I think he has a death wish, I say.

When Ains gets back with the kids and we start moving again, I feel better. Being stuck with Rick isn't ideal, but it'll be worth it for a proper swim. The lake is deep and cold and so much crisper than any pool. We'll have a real good day, I tell myself. We need one.

But Rick seems different when we're back on the road—restless and radiating a foul energy. He takes the turn off the highway onto the gravel road that leads to the lake too fast, making the kids shriek with laughter as the back end of the truck fishtails.

Slow down, I snap.

Rick turns to the kids behind him and goes, Weeeee!

Cut it out, I yell. Ains is having a silent conniption in the backseat.

What? They like it, says Rick.

That doesn't matter, I say. Now I see he's been off all day. Way too cheerful at first and then this. They're too young to know you're a dumbass, I add.

Rick's phone buzzes and he glances at it, then tucks it in between his legs, muttering, Fuck. He's quiet after that and drives properly.

We park in a spot near the head of the path to the beach, right by the big map that shows the boat launch about a mile further up the road and lists some facts about the meteorite that made the lake a million years ago. I'm only just out of the truck when Ains grips my arm.

Cole's here, she says.

What? Where? I ask. The lot is half-full, but there's literally no one around at the moment except us.

That's his car, she says, pointing at a generic-looking silver hatchback. Well, his mom's car, she says, babbling now. No one else in town has that car.

Easy, I say, trying to soothe her, while also hiding my amusement at how much she's freaking out.

Bria, don't, she warns, looking murderous.

Hey, it's no big deal, I say. Lighten up. Who cares about him?

See you guys in a bit, Rick says, from somewhere behind us.

We turn around. Our bags and the cooler are unloaded on the ground. Rick is in the truck again, pulling out in a long slow arc, one arm hanging out the open window to give us peace fingers.

Where the hell are you going? I ask, stepping quickly out of the way.

I'll be back soon, he calls. I've got errands in the area. Then he straightens the truck out and toots the horn as he drives off.

That fucking guy, I say to Ains. Errands. Incredible.

Emily is still holding Doug's hand like we asked her to, waiting to see what we'll do. Ains looks like one of those slow-mo videos of a building imploding in a controlled and expert manner.

That's okay, I tell everyone, including myself. Who needs him anyway? I address the kids, summoning some cheer. All right! We have to carry all this stuff by ourselves. Let's see if we can do it in one trip.

It's a five-minute walk to get to the beach through bush too low and sandy for a stroller, not that we have one anyway. We pick up bags and shoulder flotation devices.

Shit, I say, looking around for my backpack.

What? Ains asks.

Nothing, I say, though it doesn't feel like nothing. I left my bag in the truck, I explain, but it's okay. I don't need it.

With that, Ains and I grab one end of the cooler each and off we go.

The beach is a stretch of about a hundred meters of sand in a little bay where the water is shallow for this lake. On the walk I tell Emily and Doug about how the lake is special because it's a space lake, touched by the universe.

We break through the bush and survey the sand for a good spot. Across the lake there are cliffs where teenagers drink and take leaps of faith into the deep water, but this is a family spot, where the steep drop of the water is offset every spring by a few big dump trucks' worth of white sand.

Today, though, an obnoxious red speedboat is parked beyond the buoys. A crowd of guys are whooping it up, music blaring, spread out between the boat, the water, and the shore about twenty feet away. That'll be where Cole is.

I turn in the other direction. Let's set up over here, I say, kicking off my flip-flops and scooping them up with my last free fingers. The sand is burning hot, but if you sink down just a bit below the surface it gets cool enough to stand. We walk until we reach a nice open expanse and drop everything. Emily helps me spread out a big blanket for us to lounge on while Ains tackles slathering Doug in sunscreen and getting him changed.

Should we go check out the water, Em? I ask, but her eyes are big and worried. She mimes needing to pee.

Already? Ains asks, uncharacteristically irritable (usually she saves that for me). The outhouses are back in the direction we came from.

I'll take her, I offer. You guys good?

Yeah, says Ains. Thanks. That fucking guy, she says, out of nowhere, and I know she means Rick.

Hey, at least he got us here, I say. And provided snacks, I add, nudging the cooler with my foot. That's more than he's ever done before.

True, she says, leaning back on the sand and looking like she might consider relaxing.

Doug starts to dig a hole in the sand as Emily and I head off down the beach, hurrying the last stretch when she starts tugging on my hand. You sure you want to go in by yourself? I ask.

She nods and I close the door behind her, holding it one iota open in case she needs me. I'm relieved she didn't want me to squeeze in there with her, not that it smells much better from where I'm standing.

As I try not to breathe in the outhouse fumes, sewer smothered in soapy faux-flower perfume, through a thin veil of bush, the boat flashes red. The radio is distant from here but present, like a buzzing in the ears you get used to.

I close my eyes. Just beyond the outhouse smell is forest, sun-warm pine needles, wet rock, and deep water. I relax a little, in my bones. I can get through one day without taking a pill every time something upsets me. Last night when I couldn't sleep, I promised to the sun and the moon and the cats watching from across the room and the sleeping cousins beside me that I will be better. I'll fix what's gone wrong with me.

Eyes open, I watch the blur of boys with less concern. I can only see their outlines from here, but it's definitely the guys Cole hangs with from the volleyball team. They all look the same when you squint: same height, same shoulder-to-arm ratio, same loping confidence.

Emily is moving in the stall and I open the door more, then wide as she pushes to get out.

Gross, she says.

Agreed, I say. Next time just pee in the lake, I add, and she laughs.

~~~

Good news and bad news, I say when we get back.

What? Ains asks, cheerfully enough. She's eating watermelon and reading a book.

Bad news is that's definitely Cole. And a bunch of other guys from the team.

Ugh, she says, lying back on the towel she's positioned under her head. Who?

I don't know, I shrug, distracted by her body—her legs look much the same as ever in her cutoffs, but where are her ribs underneath that white T-shirt? Are her elbows knobbier than before? I haven't been paying enough attention. I can really be a piece of shit sometimes.

I shake it out of my head and answer her lightly. Ryan and Curtis and Harrison, I think? I can't tell those idiots apart from afar.

It's hard enough up close, she admits. Despite the boy drama, she looks relaxed, lying there in the sun next to Doug, whose hole in the ground has grown pretty big in the time we've been gone. What's the good news? asks Ains.

I sink down onto the sand next to her, throw an arm around her, and squeeze her tight. I missed you, I say.

What, when you went to the bathroom?

I hold her tight, not letting go. You know what I mean! I hate fighting. No more please. Never again.

Let go of me! Ains shouts and I squeeze ever tighter. Emily and Doug are transfixed, amused but unsure whether or not to approach. We do literally everything together, Ains says. What more do you want?

More! I yell, and next thing Emily and Doug have joined the pileup and we're rolling around, scream-laughing like always.

I'm glad he's gone, Ains says after we've settled back down.

Me too, I say. I don't know for sure who she means this time, which him, but I lean into her arm and say, Who needs him?

We still have the coolers Rick bought us chilling, but I don't even want to reach for them. Ains drinks water, and the kids drink their juice. I munch on Doritos, and Ains eats four more chunks of melon. I count them, and so does she. We play Frisbee in the water forever, jumping and diving to make miraculous catches, which then evolves into a headstand competition in the shallows with Emily and Doug judging from shore who can stay down the longest, whose legs are straighter and steadier.

Ains keeps her T-shirt on in the water and it billows white and ghostly around her. She floats on her back between head-stands, moving her cupped hands back and forth to stay afloat. It's hard to tell if the T-shirt is making her more buoyant or sinking her.

We stay in the water so long that Ains's lips turn dusky and blueish. All right, I say. Everyone out.

Back on the blanket, I direct the kids to lie down and dry off in the sun. Maybe it'll trick them into a nap, I think. It almost tricks me too, lying out on the warm sand, feeling Emily's soft body curled into my back.

I saw Mr. Abrams at the end of the year, you know, Ains says out of nowhere, like everything she says about herself.

Oh yeah? I say carefully, the sun bright through my closed eyelids.

He said I can graduate at Christmas if I try. I mean, if I want to.

Whoa, I say, opening my eyes to find her curled up on the opposite side of the blanket, watching me. What would you do? I ask. What about university?

She shrugs the shoulder she isn't lying on. The wet T-shirt is pulled out taut towards her knees to further camouflage what's underneath; the outlines of her bathing suit faintly showing through as the sun quickly leeches out the wet. I can still go, she says. Apply for next fall and just work till then. Or whatever. I don't know.

But Ains is not an "or whatever" type of girl, and I sense she does know. What about volleyball? I ask. I'm tired of everything shifting all the time. I can't handle Ains changing too.

She rolls onto her back. I don't really care about volleyball anymore, she says. Or I don't know if I do.

Everything I want to say sounds dickish, even to me. All I can fixate on is that I'm already a year behind her in school; if she speeds up, she'll be even more ahead of me. I'm trying to find a response that won't turn us against each other again when someone walks up to us and drops a pair of boots heavily onto the sand. Rick.

There you are, he says loudly, projecting his voice as if for an audience.

I sit up, and so does Ains, both of us blinking at the sun and the sudden intrusion. Doug and Emily are conked out, hats pulled over their eyes. Rick grabs a beer out of the cooler and settles onto the sand next to our blanket. He's changed into swim trunks, a camo pair that inch up as he leans back on his elbows, legs stretched out in front, revealing the lower portion of a large tattoo on his thigh. It looks like a tiger, though only the mouth is visible, teeth bared in black and white, the typical shit attempt at verisimilitude that you see on gym bros like Rick. Except why do I feel like I've seen that exact shitty tiger before?

Where else would we be? I reply finally. My eyes stuck to the tiger.

There's an accident on Highway 1. Took me a while to get back, he says.

Cool story, I say, still feeling like there's a thought fighting through the fog of my brain. I stand up as it dawns, and my heart thuds to my knees, then to the ground, rolling across the sand so that it'll never be clean again.

Fucking Rick is the one sending me dick pics. I don't know how I didn't know it before.

Somehow no one's noticed my heart falling out of my chest. Ains is asking if Rick has heard from Tash.

No, says Rick. Why don't you text her?

There's no reception on the beach, she says.

I'm going to go get my phone, I say.

Okay, Ains says. You good?

Yep, I say. Keys please, I say to Rick, holding out my hand for them.

He takes a long drink of beer and then fishes them out of his shorts pocket. Taking his time digging around in there. Smiles with his tongue showing through his teeth. There you go, sweetheart.

The word *sweetheart* flips some self-destructive switch in me, sparks a flame I need to douse. I pluck one of our vodka drinks from the cooler and walk off across the hot sand before anyone can mention it.

〰️

The truck is unlocked. Idiot Rick strikes again. I hobble across the gravel of the parking lot barefoot, having neglected to storm off wearing shoes, and climb in the front seat where my backpack is lying on the floor. I chugged the entire bottle on the walk through the woods. Should have saved a sip because, before I do anything else, I shake a pill into my hand. I brought a few in the usual old ibuprofen bottle I keep in my bag. I know I said I'd be good today. I know I shouldn't have them on me like that, but I also know I need them right now. It's nonnegotiable.

The air in the truck burns the back of my throat going down, but I don't move for the windows. Sweat pools in every nook and cranny beneath my bathing suit, runs down my temples and behind the lenses of my sunglasses, where it burns my eyes.

When I'm ready, I take out my phone and scroll through the pictures Rick's been sending me since I moved in; many of them I now recognize were taken right here in this truck, which he's constantly borrowing from Tash even though he has his own car. Says he's going to check in on the restaurant and coming back five hours later. I avert my eyes from the images and try to only see my words, my responses. Everything I've ever said in response sickens me.

Who is this?

Fuck off, creep.

Get a life.

I should have blocked him. I go to do it now, but when my thumb hovers over the button to delete his messages, I stop. I can't delete them—what if I ever need proof? The idea of telling Tash . . . I don't know if I can. I scroll back to the first one. Right after I moved in with them, before he was staying at Tash's even. That creepy fucking fuck.

After a few minutes fuming, a wetness registers on my foot. Bright red smeared all over my pale instep. For one confused second, I think it's anything but blood—strawberry jam, ketchup, I don't know—but then the pain reaches me, and my eyes find the diagonal gash the blood flows from. Must have stepped on a rock or something when I stomped through the woods and across the parking lot. I wince, fingering the edge of the cut, but the pain holds at a distance.

I'm searching the glove compartment for a bandage or some paper towel when I find the knife. Dad probably gave it to Tash to keep in the truck. His number one housekeeping rule is always keep a weapon in every room. Not guns necessarily, but a crow-bar beside the bed, a hammer in the living room, a baseball bat by the back door. He buys me knives like other dads buy their daughters . . . whatever normal people buy.

I sit sweating in the truck, thinking mostly about Dad and what he would do if he knew about Rick, or about anything I've been up to lately, when momentum comes out of nowhere, seizes me, and I hop out of the truck into the much cooler air.

The breeze moves the poplar leaves, a flutter of green gold coins, and it cools the sweat on my forehead, underneath my arms. Maybe it was too hot in there. If small children and dogs can die when left too long inside a vehicle on a hot day, what about strung-out teenagers? What's the math on that?

For a moment my head swims, but then my sense of purpose returns. I bend down and push the knife into the hot rubber of the truck's front tire. It parts smoothly, sinking in. Much better. I plunge the blade deep, then pull it down, lengthening the cut. The tire lets out air like a sigh of relief. I go to the other three, do the same.

Only after I'm done do I look up and see Cole standing there at the foot of the path, stopped short. I close the blade, tuck the knife quickly into my bathing suit top, and straighten.

Hey, Cole, I say, walking towards him. Did he see me? I can't tell.

Bria, he says. I didn't know you were here.

How would you? I ask, tidying my sweaty hair into a knot.

Are you okay? he asks, looking a little stung.

Though I don't think it's what he meant, I brandish my foot at him. Was just looking for a Band-Aid or something.

Cole makes a yikes sound. I've got a first aid kit in the car, he says. You should clean that up.

I look at the bloody bottom of my foot for a moment, trying to see a way around it, but he's not wrong. It looks nasty. All right, I say.

Cole helps me over to a picnic table and goes to get supplies from his car. The sun pulses while I wait. I pull my sunglasses down over my eyes as the buzz of cicadas oscillates around us, growing fainter and then into a crescendo again. I feel claustrophobic, all of a sudden.

Cole comes back with a roll of gauze, bandages the size of my head, and alcohol wipes.

Jeez, I say, what a Boy Scout.

It's my mom's car. She's a nurse, he says, though I know that.

I've hurt his feelings but don't care. She got anything good in there? I ask.

Cole ignores that, tearing open one of the wipes. This might hurt, he says and then dabs gingerly at my cut.

It's fine, I say. And when he keeps acting afraid to touch me, I say, Oh, give it here.

Sorry, he says, blushing as I take the wipe from him and begin to clean off the blood myself.

What are you doing in the parking lot, anyway? I ask, gasping a little at the sting. Are you leaving already?

He shades his eyes with one hand and looks at me. Motions behind him towards the beach, his friends. Just needed a break, he says.

Oh, I say. Me too.

You're here with Ainsley? he asks.

Yeah, I say. Stupid fucking Cole. His shoulders are so broad, I bet he'll fill out in the next couple years and be a real big guy, but for now he's still gawky and awkward. I can see it though: he'll get a scholarship for one of the sports he plays and move away.

Get really, truly hot after high school and meet people who never knew him before his growth spurt, before he shaved off his gelled spiked hair and embraced normalcy. Be an asshole for a few years, to girls specifically, drunk on his newfound position of power, and also he's so totally weak. I see that now. He'll be easily influenced by the frat-boy culture he's sure to encounter. I wonder if he'll date rape someone someday, I think, and then ask, Why don't you ever talk to Ains anymore?

He stares, then offers me a bandage warily. You said to stay away from you, he says.

I take the bandage and tear it open. I didn't say to shun Ains though, did I? I press the large rectangular bandage over my cut. You guys were friends, I say. Like, what the fuck.

Bria, I didn't mean for anything to happen that night, he says, looking away from me. I really liked her, you know.

I stand up. Right, I say. So, why'd you go for me then?

He fumbles, like I knew he would. I don't know, he says. You're just . . . He trails off.

But he doesn't have to say it. Easy. That's me. Great answer, I say, pointing off into the forest. You can go now.

Bria—

Seriously, I say. Just go.

And it's not as mean as I'd like to have said it, but it's mean enough that he goes.

~~~

What's up? Ains asks when I get back to the blanket. She and the kids have moved a few feet away from Rick, who's laid out on a towel, hat covering his eyes, one hand circling the beer can nestled in the sand beside him. Since I've been gone, they've expanded Doug's hole and connected it to the lake by way of a complex irrigation system, which Emily tells me about breathlessly before dumping a pail of water in to demonstrate. The water splashes into the sand, but there's not enough to flow down to the lake—it just soaks in and disappears. Doug bounces in excitement anyway, and Emily runs back to the lake to refill the bucket and try again.

I cut my foot, I tell Ains.

Oh no! she exclaims, seeing the bandage.

It's fine, I say. It was just hard to walk on without a shoe. I ran into Cole, and he got the first aid kit from his car, cleaned it up for me.

Oh, she says.

I think I'm gonna go for a swim to the point, I say.

What about your foot? Ains asks, her face hasn't recovered from my mention of Cole.

It's fine, I say again. Doesn't really hurt.

Which is true. After Cole left, I took another pill.

I'll change the bandage after, I tell her, feeling much better now, unbothered almost, even by Rick over there.

Okay, she says. Watch out for boats.

I can watch the kids when I'm done, if you want to go for a swim, I say.

She waves me away. It's fine, she says.

It's not fine. But I don't let that stop me. We both love swimming to the point, usually do it together, resting on the warm rocks when we get there before swimming back. The knife is still in my top, between my breasts, the spandex of my suit holding it close while I walk to the water. No hesitation, like a warrior woman, I submerge myself.

The cold catches my breath for a second, but I kick forward under the surface for as long as I can keep myself from rising.

When I do, I put my head back down and swim out into the deep water.

Soon I'm far enough out that the voices are faint and unthreatening. I flip over onto my back and float.

Imagine all the water disappeared and we ended up on bottom of the lake, Dad said to me once when we came here for a swim. It was so deep, he explained, because the lake formed when a meteor smashed into the Laurentian Plateau, blasting a crater in the rock. If all the water vanished, we'd be in a valley filled with strange rock formations and crevasses.

On his command I'd pictured it, imagining the fall, or imagining no fall but just appearing at the bottom of the empty lake, transported by a genie or a witch's spell. If it was meant to spook me, it didn't, or I trained it not to. Instead, it made the fact of the water feel more miraculous, holding me there.

Now I feel the slightest pull of the current trying to hurry me along, empty me into the river the lake feeds into. For the moment I let it, going limp like a baby leaf, carried along the surface of the water.

But then the weight of the knife reminds me, the metal a different temperature on my chest.

I roll back onto my stomach and stroke forward towards the middle of the lake, pausing to check my trajectory across the bay.

When I'm far enough, I reach into my top and pull out the knife. It's small but sharp, not a dull Swiss Army knife like the ones boys keep on their keychains to open beer with or maybe to slice an apple for show. I have a rape whistle on my keychain. Boys get knives and girls get rape whistles. Except Dad gave me both, and he showed me how to close the blade by pushing aside the metal bar at the center of the handle and easing the blade back down, holding the sharp part away from your body. These weapons never made me feel better or safer. If anything, they planted the seed of fear in my mind and now it's blossomed in strange directions.

I tread water and open the blade with cold fingers. Feel afraid, finally, at how its edge was recently so close to my heart. Let it drop. Watch it disappear into the dark. Feel a rock of satisfaction sink to the bottom of myself and settle there, out of sight.

The second pill hits me as I'm walking out of the water, breathing hard from swimming straight back to shore without taking a break first. I get heavy, need to sleep. Lay down on a towel, the sand beneath me warm and yielding.

~~~

Emily shakes me, her small hands on my shoulder, my arm. Time to wake up, she says.

Oh, I say, sitting up. Ains and Rick have everything packed already, are standing to one side, waiting for me.

He has plans apparently, Ains mutters as I drag my body up and into action. You were out cold, she says.

I remember both things at once: Rick's dick pics and how I cut open the rubber of the tires to even the scales. He did something to me, and I did something back at him.

This sinks in slowly as we walk across the beach, into the woods. I move my legs and the rest of me follows behind, my mind too messed up to wonder what'll happen next.

Rick sees from all the way across the parking lot. The truck sagging towards the ground.

For fuck's sake, he says, dropping the bags he's carrying.

What? I ask. This will require all my crisis actor skills.

The tires are fucking flat, he says, walking over and kicking at a tire when he's close enough. All of them, he says. Fuck.

Ains and I look at each other. While I'm grateful for sunglasses to hide my eyes, I don't even have to pretend; I just look as miserable as I actually am.

Rick bends down to examine the front driver's side tire and puts his finger in the slit in the rubber. Someone fucking slashed them. He stands up, swearing steadily.

Hey, says Ains. You're scaring them. She means Emily and Doug.

But Rick's eyes go right to me. You know anything about this? he asks.

What would I know? I ask. The way I say it is perfect, the exact same snark I always have with him. For one weightless moment, it's worth it, all of this destruction, just to have wiped the smug look off his face.

Did you cut someone off on the highway? Ains asks.

Yeah, I say. Where'd you run those errands, anyway?

He looks back to the truck and, still swearing, gets in and starts rummaging through the glove compartment.

We can call Mom and get a tow truck, Ains says. It'll be okay.

Emily lets out a sharp cry that I think, for a second, is in response to the idea of having to wait for a tow to show up. But she's clutching her arm, face screwed up in pain.

Oh no! says Ains, spotting a bumblebee on the ground at Emily's feet. Did you get stung?

Shit, I say. A red welt has appeared on her arm.

It's okay, kiddo, says Ains, examining the spot. You're not allergic. Plus, it's good luck.

Is it? I say, as Emily breathes in a deep and trembling breath, like a wave gathering momentum, then lets out a drawn-out wail. We gather around and I scoop up Doug, who's close to tears himself in sympathy.

Remember? Ains asks, speaking into Emily's hair. There aren't very many bumblebees anymore, so getting stung by one is lucky.

Oh yeah, I say. That's right, Em.

I'm going to the top of the hill to call, says Rick. Reception is shit down here.

For Christ's sake, says Ains as he walks off down the road towards the boat launch.

Here, I say, finding an ice pack in the cooler. Ains presses it gently onto Emily's forearm.

Everything okay? someone asks from behind us.

It's Cole again. Does he just lurk in the bushes waiting for us to require first aid?

We're fine, says Ains, though both kids are crying.

You guys need a ride back to town? Cole asks, looking at me now.

Well, I say, trying to take stock of the situation, do you have enough room for all of us?

Bria, Ains warns.

Sure, he says. I came out by myself. Met the guys here.

I look at Ains. Come on, I say. Let's get out of here.

She looks pissed but softens when she glances at the wilting kids. All right, she says.

We grab the car seats from the truck and Ains throws herself at Cole's backseat, so I climb in the front. The car smells new and Cole is a good driver, better than Rick, deliberate in all his movements, taking turns at a slow and soothing pace. Emily's cries quiet and soon her chin is resting on her chest, sleepy head rolling onto Ains's shoulder.

You know there was a famous UFO sighting out here? Cole asks, after a few minutes.

Oh yeah? I reply. I can tell Ains is listening.

Yep, he says, nodding towards the north side of the lake where the cliffs are high. This guy from the city was hiking the cliffs in the '70s looking for rocks—

Sounds like a weirdo, I offer.

What's it called when you study rocks? Cole asks. Not geography . . .

Geology? offers Ains from the backseat.

Right, he says. The guy was an amateur geologist from the city out for a hike. So, he's walking around, eyes on the ground, looking for rocks—

Again, I have questions, I say.

You're always bringing rocks home! Ains says, incredulous.

If I see a cool rock on the beach, sure, I might bring it home. I don't, like, go rock hunting.

But do you charge your crystals in the moonlight? Cole asks.

I ignore this genuinely good jab.

It's a unique landscape, Ains says. We're lucky to live here.

I turn around in my seat to look at her. She's watching the world stream by outside the window. Trees, sky, and yes, rocks.

What? she says, meeting my eye. It is. We're right at the edge of the Laurentian Plateau, where it mixes with the prairie. I think it's cool. Two different types of terrain overlapping.

Her talk of the plateau reminds me of Dad, and I look out the window and see what she means: how somewhere between the lake and Beauchamp it gets flatter, the trees thin out, and the sky looms larger overheard. It distracts me for a minute from Cole's story, which is continuing.

—he looked up and there was a strange silver object hovering in the air about twenty feet off the ground. Like a classic UFO shape.

So, are you some kind of alien buff? I ask.

I listened to a podcast about it, Cole says. The guy got near the UFO and ended up with a strange burn on his arm. Experts from all over came to examine the site, he continues. Apparently, there was a big circle cleared of all vegetation, high levels of weird metals and stuff in the soil.

Cole keeps talking, telling us about the theories debunking the sighting, about how there's an exhibit at the planetarium in the city about it. I glance into the back again: Emily and Doug are both snoozing and Ains is staring out the window, listening to Cole's stories about UFOs. I close my eyes too and sleep.

~~~~

Any illusion of peace is shattered when we pull up to Paradise Gardens. We've barely opened the doors to Cole's car before Tash starts.

Ainsley, Bria, get your butts over here right now. She's on the balcony with the phone to her ear but drops it, climbing onto the lawn clumsily.

Emily bursts into tears upon hearing her mom's voice. Come on, kid, I think, cut us a break. She was fine the whole way home, but now the pain of her sting comes flooding back full force and she holds out her arm for Tash to make better.

I just got off the phone with Rick, she says, reaching out for Emily.

Relax, Mom, Ains says. I can see how wound tight she is with Cole here watching this unfold.

Look, Dougie, we're home, I say, helping him out of his seat. He looks sleepy but unharmed. I hoist him onto my hip and aim him in Tash's direction for protection. Thanks for the ride, Cole, I say. You should probably go now.

136

Hold on, snaps Tash. No one's going anywhere yet. Explain, please.

Like I texted you from the car, Ains says. Emily got stung by a bee and Cole offered us a ride home, she says, then shrugs and adds, Basically.

Well, according to Rick someone slashed the tires on the truck and then you guys took off without telling him.

That's not what happened, Mom, says Ains.

Well, I say, it kind of is, but—

Ainsley Dawn Chambers, get inside right now. You too, Bria. I see you there.

Uh, I'm not exactly hiding? I say, and then regret it. I haven't seen her mad like this in forever.

Well, I see you eyeing the exits, Tash says. Go.

Ains and I grab our bags and the car seats, which Cole has already efficiently unloaded for us. I salute him. See ya, buddy, I say, about as freaking platonically as it gets, so he's not confused.

Thanks for driving them home, Cole, says Tash. Say hi to your mom for me.

See ya, Cole says to Ains.

See ya, she says back weakly.

Once we're inside, Tash starts in on us again. You know the rules, she says. We have to know where you are, always. Rick was very concerned when you guys disappeared.

Ains is full infrared in the face. Rick took off on *us*, Mom. He was gone the whole day!

You do realize that Ted Bundy liked to hunt girls at the lake?

That was in the '70s. And nowhere near here.

So what? Men like him are everywhere, prowling public places in the summer looking for undersupervised kids. I see it all the time at work. You have no idea.

Please, says Ains, really getting into it now. Whose fault is it if we're undersupervised?

I back away slowly so as not to attract their attention and start unpacking our wet towels and beach toys. Ains is dredging up all her resentments about babysitting this summer, dusting them off and bringing them out to play, while Tash sticks to her horror-story tack, how our high-risk behavior will be the death of us, of her.

I don't get it, personally. Tash tells us all the time how our cognitive functions are still developing and need another ten years before we graduate from our baby moron starter brains to our well-balanced badass adult women brains. She uses a grab bag of metaphors to describe how we're teenaged embryos, butterflies cocooning, phoenixes rising from the dust of our dumb prairie town. So then I don't understand why she seems so surprised by our bad decision-making when she's the one who told us that's all we're currently capable of.

I take in her lecture anyway: the tales of girls gone wild, gone missing or addicted or what-have-you that she deals with all the time at work. All the pedophiles and murderers and heartless drug dealers and tragedy after tragedy, dancing around what she's actually thinking, which is my mom. You don't want to end up like your mom, now do you, is the subtext of all her stories.

Everyone tells stories like this. Teachers, parents. Told to scare us into behaving. But bad shit happens whether you behave or not. You only have to turn on the news, look around you, to know that.

I remember Ains and I obsessing over a girl who'd been kidnapped in a town about four hours away when we were like nine and ten. We didn't want to be her exactly, but we definitely wanted to be close to her, to stare into the face of the man who'd done evil to her, to be the people who found her left there in a field to become dirt. We wanted to be lifted up out of our world by a horror so big it made everything before and everything after seem enviously calm. And steady. And still. We read the news stories to each other after school and at sleepovers, emphasis on everything, especially the worst parts. We kept our eyes peeled for white vans and other bad-man signs. We told ourselves we would kick him in the balls if he tried it with us, whoever he was, whatever *it* was. We'd take our fingernails to his eyes, and our feet would connect swiftly with his crotch. We wanted to see the worst things happen to make what we had seem good. No matter what it took.

~~~~

The fight with Tash makes me and Ains even more on each other's side. That night we lay in bed with the window open wide and an actual breeze coming through so that the sheets are cool against our slow-roasted skin. Because, of course, we applied sunscreen liberally to Emily and Doug all day, but not to ourselves.

What do you think they're fighting about? I ask. Rick and Tash started arguing as soon as Ains and Tash stopped. I don't really care though, because lying here, studying the dim ceiling in a lazy way, my hair pulled into a reassuring ponytail, I feel a little okay for once. I even took a shower to rinse off the lake in case there's unpublicized swimmer's itch like last year. I had to stay home from school I was covered in so many bites. Ains and I got to eighty before losing count.

I don't know, she says. Maybe they'll break up.

I wish, I whisper.

Do you know what happened to the tires? she asks.

No, I say, and the lie feels round and whole in my mouth.

Probably someone Rick pissed off taking it out on Mom's truck, she says.

How was it seeing Cole? I ask, trying to say it lightly, so as not to betray too much interest in her answer.

Fine, she says, like she's trying to convince herself. I see him at school and around the gym all the time, she adds.

It was nice of him to give us a ride, I say. We'd have been waiting there with Rick forever for a tow.

I guess, she says, unconvinced.

He wouldn't have done that if it was just me.

Yes, he would have, she says.

I don't respond, and a few minutes later, I look over and her eyes are closed. I close mine too and run through lists in my mind. Lists to keep my mind from going where it wants to go. I list known quantities like all fifty states and the countries in Africa, but I also list things that are harder to quantify. Like the number of times I remember hearing from my mom on my birthday or how many guys I've fooled around with. I list brands of whiskey and menu items from Burger Shack, starting over when I lose track, always losing track.

I told Steph about my way of falling asleep. She asked if I had OCD and I said, No, I eat food off the floor all the time.

Anxiety then, she said, when I explained the why of it.

I guess, I shrugged.

You should get diagnosed, she said. They give you good drugs for that.

Eventually, I run out of things to list and admit to myself what I've been trying to ignore for ages: I have to pee. I ease myself out of bed as gingerly as possible to not wake Ains and hustle down the hall quiet as a ghost.

When I'm done in the bathroom, a light's on in the living room that wasn't before. I creep forward to see who it is, but when I get to the end of the hall, there's no one. Go into the kitchen, turning the tap on and letting it go cold before I fill a glass, drink it, fill it again.

I hear him one second before he touches me. Soon enough to flinch but not soon enough to move away from his hands on my waist, the bare skin between my shorts and tank top. Smells like dank cigarettes and motor oil. He speaks into my neck, says, I know what you're up to at night, out at All Stars, sleeping around—

The door to the kids' room opens and we both turn, Rick stepping away from me at the same time. It's Emily, blinking tiredly. But I'm afraid she saw.

10.

When Someboy finds out how old I am, he throws a fit. Throws me out. Asks me back in. Chases down my back when I refuse. Takes me home and silent. Rages at me. Falls to his knees and begs. Rubs up on me with his hard dick. Breaks down sobbing, like I've never in front of anyone, not even Ains. He says it's my fault we're in this mess. I led him here. Uses words like *lure* and *vixen* and *masterplan*. And maybe I am and maybe I did. What did I do again? Went out to meet a man who could provide me with some things. Mostly the chance to evaporate what's going on. And it was him, he was the one, to make it serious, to make demands. I was in and out and easy, I made sure I was, but he kept requiring more and more of me until he got it and didn't like it, and how is it my fault except for the fact it always is?

And I'm thrown torn. Ashamed and angry. Running fast inside my head away from everything.

When he cried, I hated him. And I knew I couldn't leave as he lifted his wet face to mine, open-mouthed and urgent, pushing up my shirt, hands scrambling for my bra and then all over uncovered skin. That once was mine. Now the wet meat of tongues mashing and him issuing a moan that sounds so much like distaste, then he's even more urgently at my pants, and I take over because he's going to ruin my zipper and we can't afford that. Naked now, he yanks me to the floor; nothing about it is about me. It's over before you know.

He takes a long time in the bathroom and I use it. Gather-gather-go. Through the living room and if there are roommates watching whatever on TV and pretending not to have heard, don't worry about it. Shame cherry on top. Just get out and go.

~~~~

Except no. That's not what I did, not what I do. I don't leave after. Don't pick myself up and go. I stay. Stay longer than I've ever stayed before.

~~~~

When Someboy finished high school, he took out all the credit cards and student loans he could and went gambling. He made fifteen thousand dollars and got high for a few months. Then money gone, habit formed, he had to do things he would've rather not done. Sleeping on couches and mattresses in basement city squats. Hanging off gross people for a place to crash and a chance at their supply. Crack houses and SROs when he had the cash. Always trying to make the money he needed for another night and also not to feel.

After the fight, I'm mostly naked in his arms. Been in bed for hours, first sex and then just talking. He tells me stories and traces letters on my skin. Like how when he was nineteen, he moved in with some older druggie guys, and one of them, Wade, was standoffish and conspiracy-theorist-y, but not crazy to their knowledge, per se, until one day he put liquid LSD in the milk they all used for their coffee. How it took until the second day for Someboy to realize he was tripping. Wondering after that if he was really seeing cockroaches in the kitchen or if Wade wasn't just at it again.

That's why I take my coffee black, Someboy says, drumming on my back.

And another one about him and his ex-girlfriend, the one who features most in his stories, and the time they acted as mules for some heroin headed to Montreal and stayed there for weeks afterwards on the profits, going to strip clubs and seedy bars, buying each other clothing and massages. She sounds like an older version of me in his stories, so who knows what she's actually like, because I'm not really like the things he says about me. Or I'm not only what he says. Every story he tells about himself seems calibrated to make him make sense, or to explain to me his damage, make him seem good or something. And then suddenly it's my turn. Tell me yours, and I'll tell you mine. He makes me talk about my family, about my mom and dad, about Steph. The pillow is wet beneath my face, but he doesn't mention it, and after a while I wipe my damp hair away and let my bare skin breathe. He reaches and smooths the hair back further off my face. Whispers me sweet. Talks quiet in the dark. And I let him and I let him.

~~~

When Someboy finds out how old I am, it bothers him enough that he does drugs in front of me. First time. I'd thought the coke and booze I'd seen was all of it, but that's not it at all. Color me surprised.

It's so late the sun is creeping through the blinds, casting long lashes of light across the floor, and I can hear through the open window the sound of neighbors getting into their cars, going to work. But we're still firmly lodged inside last night.

Drugs I've tried:

Weed when I was eleven. Hit off a joint from Jared, a kid a couple of years older who hung around the building we lived in, a bored dropout with a baseball bat who'd talk shit about all the stuff he smashed, but I never saw it, and who was always pulling stubs of joints out of his pocket and hauling on them. Liked it right away, the laughs it loosens and the bliss of shoveling chips into your face mindlessly, and the lovely-feeling fog.

Cigarettes for show, sneaking off for puffs of smokes Ains and I lifted from Tash's purse before she quit, or from older kids at the park. Mostly liked the way it looked in my hand and how it added emphasis to things, then later like the itch, it licks inside when I'm wide awake and wired.

Beer sips from Dad, starting when I was young. He'd go, Here, Bria, try this, and I'd sip and make a face, or when I was older, pretend I wasn't going to give it back. Either way making him laugh.

Whiskey when I was twelve, which made me pass out pretty quick, but again learned to like the powerful way it burns you down. Now I'll take it if I can get it but also need to keep an eye on how it can mix with weed or whatever and make me way too far gone. Nobody likes the puking girl, Steph warned sometimes when I was getting ready to go out.

Case in point: mixing whiskey and shrooms with these guys Kyle and Spencer from school, throwing up in the bathtub and spending so long cleaning it up, bits of puke swirling and spinning in patterns. Worrying about what everyone thought I was doing in there, when really they were all sitting on couches in Spencer's basement, staring at the home screen of their video game and clutching the Big Gulps we got because Kyle's sister said the sugar would help you metabolize the drugs faster and more efficiently.

Wine's not my thing, but Steph liked the pink stuff and showed me how to taste it right, holding the glass by the stem and swirling.

Mostly getting drunk and high in the fields behind school at summer bush parties, and then, only later after Dad left, did I go to bars.

So, I'm no sober ally, I'm no angel, but there are a few things I don't like. Don't like meth. Scares me. Makes me think of picked-apart faces and machete rampages. It's always on the news what meth heads are up to. Wielding weapons at the mall, breaking into homes in the brazen afternoon, then burning them down and getting trapped inside. And heroin I don't like either, for obvious Mom reasons and some other shit I'd seen.

But these pills upend me. Steph called them green monsters, poison, friends, down. Got excited when they were super strong. Told me about hot spots, about how with these pressed pills like the kind Dad sold, there could be too much of the drug con-centrated in one pill. That made it dangerous to smoke or snort them, she explained, as she was snorting one.

That's why I just swallow them whole. It's easy to pretend like I haven't. Take one and get on with the day and wonder later why my feelings are drifting away from me.

The challenge I've set for myself, the game I play, have been playing for weeks, is getting high enough that the world gets swimmy and so do I, but not so high that I can't function. At work, the till still balances at the end of the night. I can hand people drinks without missing my mark. Pay actual attention to the kids. Eyes on them, monitoring. I don't know why—it's not like I need the added challenge of fighting not to seem high, even as I am—but it sets up blockades in my brain where I need them. And when.

What happens is, Chris brings over a girl I know. Or I know her sister, and she knows me because of that.

It's late Saturday night, in the backyard, and we've been together since the night before. It's been a week since we went to the beach with Rick, and I've been avoiding home as much as possible. Sneaking out at night to come see Someboy and relying on Ains to cover for me when I'm not home on time in the morning. Assuming she will, not even trying to check in with her. There will be hell to pay with Ains later, but I made it to the long weekend, when Tash and Rick took the kids out of town. Someboy doesn't seem to mind me here; every time we see each other now, it's a twenty-four-hour stay, blur of a day. I lose thoughts of trying to fix the various messes I'm in and don't try to find them. I lose everything except for what's going on between me and my pills. I've never, not like this, and I get a little loose.

Megan, the girl Chris is chatting up, is the older sister of this girl Shannon who's in my grade. We were friends for a minute when we were like twelve or thirteen; I've been to their house and everything, though not in a million years. I never say hi to Megan when I see her around, and she in turn acts like I'm not there, but I'm feeling fine and generous, so after we've been hanging out for a few hours, I try to strike up a conversation.

Hey, Megan, how's Shannon doing?

She gives me a fresh once-over from across the circle. You know my sister?

I don't know if she really doesn't know who I am or if she's simply being a bitch, but I tell her as Someboy comes back out from inside and sits next to me. He's back and forth all night, sitting down beside me, but it's never long until he's up again. Changing the music or clearing bottles or lighting a cigarette or flicking all the butts off the picnic table and into the coffee can that's three-quarters full already.

Oh shit, Megan says. You're Bria Powers?

She says my name as if it's a punchline. I nod, knowing I've messed up. Beside me Someboy is watching this unfold with a look I can't read.

Well, you've sure grown up, she says.

I think, If I had a bullet for every time someone said that to me.

Someboy stares at her, his arm a threat around my shoulder. Shut the fuck up, Megan. You're just jealous because she's hot, and you got fat after your kid.

He gets up, goes inside. This time, he doesn't come back.

Megan sniffs like he's not worth her time. A beat passes and then the party carries on, the music just as loud, the people just as fucked up, except something has shifted horribly. But I smile. Say, Shit, Megan, I didn't know you had a baby. Boy or girl? And I help Chris with the joint he's rolling and involve myself in everything until it's undeniably over.

Still, I stall, try to get Steve to stay up by the fire, or watch a movie, or drink another beer, but I can see his reluctance. So I say goodnight and go inside.

Spread out on the bed is all of my shit, the entire contents of my backpack and wallet. Makeup case, clean underwear, shirt, and deodorant for tomorrow. Band-Aid, Pokémon sticker from

Emily, paper clips, and a couple of pens. Bank card, library card, buy ten burritos get one free punch card. My school IDs from the last three years: eighth, ninth, tenth grades.

Someboy is smoking in the corner. What's this? he asks, tapping the dresser beside him. On it is the bag of pills I took from home last time we were there. I bring them with me now, so that no one back at Tash's finds them. And not only that: he's found all the secrets I carry with me, my bottle of ibuprofen, the small one from the dollar store, that I keep in my purse. My just-in-case-pills, what I bring with me in case he's mean. Or nice. Or work was slow, or busy, or I couldn't sleep, or I have a blank slate of sleep that I wake up from and all I want to do is get back to it. He's seen me pop pills from that bottle many a time.

What does it look like? I reply finally.

The fight unfolds from there, and what's clear in the aftermath is that rather than my secrets tearing us apart, they fuse us together. We're different now: I am, and he is, and we are. Since Tash is out of town, it's easy to stay the weekend, acting the part and sometimes feeling it. Sometimes unfeeling it. We go out to All Stars, and Someboy orders shot after shot from Dave, who surely sees him bring them over to me. Pisses me off, for some reason, that he lets me be. Where's the big brother routine now, Dave? I want to ask, but Someboy gets weird when I talk to him too long.

On the Tuesday morning after the long weekend, we sleep too much, and I wake up panic-sad, having to get out fast—I need to be there to help Ains with the kids, I've been gone way too long already—but before I can go, he wakes up too and looks at me with all this love.

Bryan and Bria, he says. See, we're the same.

11.

What's wrong with her? Rick asks Ains when I walk across the living room later that day. I'm not wearing any makeup, and my body feels like an old suitcase I'm dragging around.

Nothing, Ains says. But we aren't speaking again since I disappeared for the weekend. So how would she know.

We go to Burger Shack together all the same. The wind must have changed in this direction because the smoke is back, changing the texture of the sky to soot. Or maybe the fires are getting closer. I don't know. I haven't been paying attention.

At Burger Shack, only work-related words are exchanged, but even those soften the air between us.

Two cheeseburger meals to go, I say.

Low on onion rings, she replies.

We switch automatically when it gets busy because Ains is better at moving the line along whereas I always talk to everyone too much. Darcy fills in the gaps wherever we leave them, letting me take over the grill and supporting me on the fryer, while also wrapping and bagging orders, filling drinks for Ains up front, and delivering every order to the correct customer—he also probably knows them by name. I've worked alongside Darcy when a tour bus stopped on the way to the casino and saw him add up a six-person order before the register could, reaching for a tray with one hand while he poured coffee with the other. Darcy also has an encyclopedic knowledge of local hockey stats, a strange thing to be devoted to, but it's made him universally beloved in our trifecta of towns. He shows up at every game with his face painted like a human mascot and has a fundraising social sponsored by Burger Shack for the junior team every spring. Like, people adore him. Ains and I constantly have to put up with customers who regard us suspiciously and ask, Where's Darcy? when we try to take their order.

By seven, it's slowed. Darcy clocks out and fixes himself a burger to eat before he goes. There are no orders up, and I could use some fresh air, so I ask Ains if I can take a break outside with him.

Sure, she says, as though I am profoundly disappointing her for the fifty-thousandth time.

We all take our breaks out back, away from the eyes of customers and the stream of traffic that goes by most times of day. Darcy and I kick a couple of milk crates away from the dumpster and sit down. What're you up to tonight? I ask.

There's a practice, he says in between bites.

Why do you go to those? I ask, feeling a surge of something in me, a pushiness. I've seen a lot of people treat Darcy like . . . I don't know. Some charming sideshow. You know that high-pitched tone some bitches take on when they're talking down to you? When people talk to Darcy like that, I bristle at best, but he doesn't seem to notice. I guess it's just me with the problem, again.

Darcy shrugs, as if it's obvious. I always do, he says. It's fun.

Usually, I can count on a simple leading question sending Darcy on a ten-minute ramble about the Nighthawks' defense strategy, but today, for once, he's uninterested. He swallows and motions inside with his head. What's going on with you guys? he asks.

What do you mean? I reply.

You and Ains, he says.

Oh. She's mad at me, I say and shrug.

He says nothing, considering this. Darcy is like the rest of the world in that I would expect him to automatically take Ains's side in any fight between me and her. Complete strangers could look at us on the street and conclude everything was my fault.

Well, you guys should talk, Darcy says. You both look miserable. And crams the rest of the burger carefully into his mouth.

I go in feeling sorry, feeling like pouring my heart out and getting everything out there, over with. I just can't handle being questioned or pressured or judged, so she needs to be over it too. Sure enough, Ains turns right to me.

Is that him? she asks, nodding at the window.

It's Bryan. He's parked in the lot of the insurance broker next door, leaning against his car and looking at us looking at him. Calling him Someboy doesn't work now, even in my head. He's too real.

I better go talk to him, I say.

She rolls her eyes. Do whatever you want. You always do.

Punch-drunk from her words and the last six months of life, I look from her to him and back. Walk away not so much feeling like I'm choosing him over her as I'm walking out of one burning house into another. And like moving through the air is preferable to staying still right now.

Sorry, he says when I approach with my eyes down, considering the ground. I just wanted to see you.

Can't look. Make myself. It's okay, I say, giving a weak shrug. It's not though. I'm not. I'm burrowing into myself, goosebumps breaking out on cold-sweat skin.

He drops his cigarette and stomps on it before coming towards me. Takes me by either elbow, lowers his forehead to the dampness of mine. Come over when you're done work?

Sure, I say, and breathe again as he steps a little away from me.

He seems overjoyed, energized. Great, he says. I'll see you later then.

But he doesn't go. Hey, he says, as if it's suddenly occurred to him. Did you bring anything with you to work?

What do you mean? I ask.

You know, he says low, like a sexy whispered thing. Some of your pills.

I look at him and imagine what his day has entailed so far. A shower, I can tell from his hair's lack of grease and the way he smelled when I breathed him in, but probably nothing else since I left him this morning. A shower, then he would have sat around the living room with Steve, talking shit. An errand maybe, some simple trip to pick up something for the house that he would have acted like was a monumental task. And then me. He came to find me.

Back inside, back to Ains, back to work.

What was that about? she asks.

I shake my head. It was nothing. Sorry. You should take your break now. Take an extra fifteen.

She's pissed, wants to say more, but gives me another one of her looks like she can't even handle trying, and goes.

Ains still isn't talking to me when I take my last break. I'll be out back if you need me, I say, before getting myself a root beer and going outside.

I didn't tell Bryan, but I did bring pills to work. Everywhere I go, they come with me.

It's not a good idea to get too high at work, but I don't really feel so high from one pill anymore. I feel better, feel more whole. What I'm trying to say is I wouldn't normally do this mid-shift, but I pop a pill into my mouth and let it melt on my tongue a bit before sipping my drink and swallowing down. The bitter chemical taste reassuring me while I wait for it to work. I sit down on a milk crate, stretch my legs out in front of me, and close my eyes to the sun. Warm and okay. That's what I am.

A rustling in the dumpster interrupts, alerts me, and then a loud noise rings out, metal and gong-like as something hits the wall of the container.

We keep the dumpster padlocked now because of the bears moving into town, but the lid is flipped open, the lock and chain coiled on the ground in front of it.

More noises come from inside the dumpster, something big rooting around.

I rise from my milk crate and freeze. Hear snuffling, muffled breathing. A hump of fur appears at the top of the dumpster, blue-black in the sun. It's a bear, scavenging for food.

Unfreezing, I move quickly to the door, eyes on the bear's rounded back, which is still visible as it pokes around. When I open the kitchen door, the bear hears me, looks over its shoulder.

Its eyes aren't afraid but evaluating, taking me in to see if I'm a threat, if he needs to be territorial over his jackpot of half-eaten burgers and the dregs of chili we scrape out of the bottom of the pot at the end of the night. Whatever test he gives me, I pass, and the bear drops back down into the dumpster to focus on his meal.

Darcy keeps a hockey stick with the mop and brooms next to the back door, for reasons unknown—so that in case an impromptu game of street hockey breaks out, he's ready? Or maybe it's to slap shot the occasional mouse we get in the kitchen back outside. I grab the stick and open the door again a crack in time to see the bear pulling itself up over the side of the dumpster and jumping down, looking a little human for one long-limbed moment. He's even bigger than I thought and rubs his snout on the ground before lumbering off towards the tree line beyond the service road that runs behind Burger Shack, without casting me a backwards glance.

As I watch him go, I feel weirdly abandoned, bereft. I wish the bear had looked at me longer with his brown animal eyes, that he'd bobbed his head and nodded at the trees off in the distance, inviting me to follow him, to join his bear family and live as they do. I wish he had pushed his way into the restaurant, sniffing the air for meat, swiping at me with his claws when I tried to get away and leaving slashes in my skin for the blood to come through. I wish he'd knocked over tables and made himself at home, ending my shift, ending Burger Shack once and for all. Instead, it's only the end of my fifteen-minute break, and I have to go back to work.

Ains is busy sweeping and self-righteously restocking everything before I can help. I don't tell her about the bear, hurrying through closing duties so we can get out of there early.

When we've locked up, I start off in the same direction as her, and she falters in her stride for half an instant but then decides not to comment, walking quickly towards home.

That's fine. She can be mad at me; I still want to be around her a bit longer before going back to Bryan. That's what I tell myself as we walk beside each other not talking, until finally I burst out.

I saw a bear earlier, I say, as we round the corner onto the block occupied by Paradise Gardens. Out back, I add.

Really? she asks, her eyes dart over to me, then away.

It was in the dumpster. During my break. I forgot to lock it, I guess.

No, she says, it must have been me.

I shake my head. I took the garbage out, remember?

No, she says, I did garbages today. Are you sure it was a bear?

A minute passes as I take this in. Then she says, almost kindly, as we start up the driveway to the courtyard, My dad told me something weird about bears once.

What? I ask. She doesn't talk about her dad much lately.

Bear fur feels sort of sharpish, she says. And when you skin a bear, it looks a bit human. Too human to eat almost, even when you're hungry.

~~~

I try not to see him in the days after that. Really. I get his texts and don't respond. I don't want to do anything about anything. But he finds me. Comes by work every night and walks me back to his place after my shift with arms around each other, cumbersomely close. Now that we know each other's secrets, he wants to be always together. Now he wants to know what I've done, when, with whom. I tell him some things, make up some others, hide some away. Tash seems relaxed after their weekend away, but I know I'm pushing it, staying overnight at Bryan's and getting back to Tash's later and later the next day. By Thursday, he's convinced me to stay at his place all day, go straight from there to work. I text Ains, ask her to make an excuse and hope her silence is acquiescence. Meanwhile Bryan and I lie in bed till late. Then shower. Coffee in the kitchen with Steve and Chris, who's home from work because he hurt his back last week. Gives the house a holiday feel because he's happy to be off.

Come here, Bryan says, calling me into the bedroom where he has a line ready for me.

I didn't do this until him. Was just swallowing them whole and then looking away, as if it hadn't happened. But he treats pills like they're all four food groups, chomping on them when we're out at the bar, crushing them into powdery lines in the living room, smoking them, like he did the first night, when he scared me. I don't do that, I tell him, but now I guess I do.

A week goes, the heat thick and unmoving, making time pass both slow and fast, without me noticing. The world seen through molasses. We have everything we need right here, he says one night, and he means each other, my bag of pills, and the mattress we're lying on. We walk into All Stars together holding hands and Dave eyeballs me all night, but I can avoid eyes as easily as I catch them. Bryan brings me glasses of water in bed and makes us toast and eggs in the morning. Meets me at work, waiting on the far side of the parking lot for me to say what I have to say to Ains to excuse myself, and she inevitably says, Just go.

~~~

Of course, he starts harping on me to move my stash. Where to? One guess.

He doesn't admit he's mad that I won't tell him where it is. I like watching him restrain himself for once, stuffing down the urge to mention it and in the meantime being sweeter than I've known him to be. One day he shows me how to use one of the ancient cameras gathering dust in his room, how to load film and focus the world through the viewfinder. Tells me about how his mom was awful at taking pictures of him and his brother when they were kids, always with her thumb in the frame, film canisters lingering in the fridge for years. It's the first I've really heard of his family, and of keeping film refrigerated for that matter. That's how I got into photography, he says, because my mom was so bad at it. He pulls a box out of the closet and shows me pictures of them, this mother and brother that suddenly exist. Only then, after giving me this, does he ask me for more pills. This is the kind of control I have now: the power to make him tiptoe around this corner of mine. Now it's not just his eyes on me, but his thoughts on me too. For a few days, it feels like something. Finally, some deference around here. I'll be pulling my hair back smooth and tight for work as he puts on his boots to drive me when he asks, casual-like, Can you leave me something for later? Or, Can you stock up before you come home?

Home, he says. The word rattles through me; I wish he wouldn't say it. The thrill of having something he wants this badly drops off and the unsubtle guilt trips he lobs my way start making me want to kill him. Or myself.

Just breathing in the dust could kill a kid, he points out.

Don't say that, I say, stung. Not because I don't know. I know.

It's true, he says, as if it's plain and simple.

As if truth could ever be simple.

For fucking instance, us. I don't know how to explain us, the dance we do now. I care and then I don't care. I'm afraid, angry, and okay again all within a minute. I decide he's the most pompous, obnoxious person in the world and then I'm desperate for his attention. He gets mad at me for chatting with Steve too long in the kitchen when I'm getting a snack or for telling a dumb party story from before him; ignores me to pay all the attention in the world to some lady we cross paths with in the Valu Lots parking lot, but then the next minute he's fawning over me anew. Tells me tales of what we'll do when we get the money. Because, oh yeah, he doesn't just want to store the stash at his place for safekeeping; he wants to sell them to this guy he knows outside town. Says no one from Beauchamp will know. Says we'll make ten grand easy. More maybe. Because I'm sketchy on the details of how much I have, which is partly me trying to keep something to myself, something only I have access to, and partly I just don't know. I try not to look that closely. I've been pretending this wasn't happening, and now it's his favorite thing to talk about.

His drug creation story goes like this: he was fifteen and the world took on a new blurred brilliance. He felt he'd found a system of being, a calling. You had to be smart to find drugs of the order he wanted at that age; you had to be ruthless and subtle. And once you had obtained the contraband in question, you had to be made of strong stuff to survive it. He was very, very good at getting fucked up. There was an art to how he got high. There was a tragic beauty there. Or that's how he tells it. Short on details, tall on delusions of grandeur.

His second favorite story is about how he was sober for a few years, the grind of that. And how, at the same time, he had the feeling he was building something. Something so big it wouldn't be completed in his lifetime, like a pyramid or a cathedral. Something beautiful and lasting and impossible for anyone else to really visualize until it was complete.

He tells me all of this, gets me unguarded, then there's another guilt trip, another ask. What he doesn't ask is how it is for me. Using.

For me, it's not like that. For me, it's something I don't want to think about. Can't stop thinking about. The pills fuzz out the edges of my feelings, hold up a lovely lens to everything. Sometimes the feeling swells: the distance they keep me at gets too great and I almost drop Doug or fall asleep over the deep fryer at work or stare at the walls too long thinking beautiful nothing. These days though, it's the opposite. It wears off, and I want to be blanketed in that weight again. So, I have to take another. And another.

Bria, he says, and I look over at him from where I'm lying on the bed. He's sitting at his desk with the fresh bag of pills I went by the house the other day to grab, since we already blew through the last one. I took two big bundles with me this time, gave them all to him, almost. Time to tell me where you're getting these, babe, he says.

I should hate them. The pills. Because whatever Dad did or didn't do, I know it was the pills that took him away, and it was the pills that killed Steph, until I brought her back. I wonder if it should have made me feel powerful, being the one to do something like that. Or in control. Because it really, really did not.

12.

Hey, says Ains as I slip behind the counter at Burger Shack, two minutes late for our shift.

Hey, I say back, tossing my bag in the staff area by the dish pit and washing my hands.

Your dad's back, dickhead, she says.

And thank god she doesn't say it mean. I wouldn't be able to take that. Because even delivered kindly enough, it breaks the tender grasp I had on normal and spins me out, sucker punches my heart.

What do you mean *back*? I ask, confused by the word. I woke up an hour ago at Bryan's and barely had time to shower, apply coffee, and walk over here.

Ains shrugs. He got out, I guess. I didn't get many details from Mom. She waits a beat, then says, She's been trying to get a hold of you all weekend.

My phone got smashed, I say, which is true, then add, stuttering, I didn't think I'd miss anything important.

She shrugs again. Well, ya did.

I had managed to convince Tash that I'd been invited to Natalie's cottage for the weekend, invoking the coming school year and acting happy for this chance to rekindle our friendship, and while Tash bought it initially, I have no idea how well my story has held up over the weekend. I meant to get a cheap burner or ask Bryan if I could use his phone to check in, but it kept slipping my mind. Maybe it was nice, being all the way out, unavailable, lost in that townhouse, that bedroom, that guy. Maybe being completely unreachable is what I'm after, after all.

I told Mom Natalie's cottage doesn't have cell reception, Ains says, penetrating my thought spiral.

You did? I hadn't even consulted Ains about the Natalie story. I didn't expect her to back me up.

Ains shrugs, says, Whatever. And then, You can work the back if you want.

It's true, I'm not fit for public consumption, and she can see that. I stare at her a minute before I go: she looks different, some subtle alteration in her face, but I can't figure out what it is, so I just say, Okay, thanks, and head to the kitchen.

I put on my apron and tie my hair back, feeling alien, like a robot or some other poor imitation of a person. I shouldn't be sorry Dad is back, shouldn't be panicked, but I am, and I ricochet back and forth between guilt and fear and maybe some gratitude because even in his shit he is familiar and comforting in so many ways, and I do want to see him. So, why then the feeling of falling apart?

Jesus, there are orders. I shove it out of my mind and become someone else. I become Robot Bria.

Robot Bria drops chicken strips in the fryer and shakes baskets of fries free of excess oil. Goes over everything with enough salt to satisfy. To make them want to quench their thirst with an extra-large drink, because Robot Bria's good for sales. She sweats it out in the tight kitchen space between the fryer and the grill, waiting for that moment when the patties release, and she can slide her spatula under and flip. Expedites everything, works without a break all through the evening rush until realizing she feels ill, overheated, underfed, and chooses the right moment to pop into the front and ask Ains for a drink with lots of ice when she has a minute. Robot Bria doesn't think about things. She reacts. She's good at that.

In the slow time after the rush, we put the cassette tape we love on in the kitchen, an '80s compilation, and when there are no customers, we spin right round baby right round. Robot Bria sneaks in a few smoke breaks when she's not needed and burns those puppies down like it ain't no thing. She eats cigarettes for breakfast, Robot Bria does.

It's a fun enough shift actually. Brought back in close to each other by the overwhelming shittiness of things. I only have to suffer some new catastrophe for Ains to like me again.

You coming? Ains asks at the end of the night, like it's even a question.

We walk home together, stepping off curbs and cutting corners at the same time and place.

The heat's been steady for days, the kind that sits on your skin like dishwater air, like the unwanted breath of a close talker, but tonight there's a breeze and thank fuck. It takes the edge off everything.

Back at Paradise Gardens, it seems like everyone's up. It's after ten but the day's dragging itself out. Light lingers on the playground where a group of kids race after each other, their parents watching from balcony deck chairs, too content to instigate bedtime yet. Mark, Jeff, and Cindy are sitting at the patio table outside Mark's apartment across from ours, drinking wine and watching the action with the same self-satisfied late summer air.

Outside our apartment, Tash is stretched out on a blanket on the grass chatting with Pam and Dan, our neighbors to the left, while Emily dozes next to her. Rick sits in the recessed space of the balcony, balanced on the back legs of a chair with his feet up on the railing, sunglasses on even though it's not exactly bright out. For a second, all I can think is that the slightest kick would take him down.

Tash breaks off her conversation with Pam as we approach. Her face sterns. I have the familiar unpleasant sensation that they've been talking about me. Bria, she says. You're back.

Emily blinks sleepily and everyone else ogles me, examining me for signs of ruination. It's only been, like, two days, I say. You guys act like I've been away abroad or something.

You heard about your dad? asks Tash.

Ains is standing aside, not paying attention even, eyes glued to her phone. Yeah, I say, and then ask, begrudgingly, So, where is he?

Tash shakes her head. I'm not sure.

I balk. Well, when did you last see him?

Yesterday, says Tash, looking to Rick for confirmation, which gets my hackles up even more. He said he had to go out of town for a few days, but that he was going to try to track you down first.

Well, I say. He didn't.

Why didn't you check in all weekend? I left you a million messages. We could have come get you early so you could have seen him.

Ains seems to take this as her cue to go inside. My eyes land on Rick, who's listening. Anger spikes, and I want to lash out in every direction.

My phone got smashed, I say to Rick. His eyes may be obscured by his glasses, but the rest of his face is as punchable as always.

Meanwhile Tash is looking at me as if this proves every point she's ever made.

What? I demand. Her face. I can't stand it either. That's a totally normal thing to have happen, I say. Phones get smashed every day.

She laughs.

They do, I insist.

Why don't you go inside and chill out, says Rick, turning back to Dan, like I'm wrecking their party.

For once I listen to him and go in. Tash comes after me, hauling Emily on her hip.

Bria, we're not done talking about this.

What're you doing up, Em? I ask.

I couldn't sleep! she says, a perfect imitation of Ains saying the same thing.

I laugh. Want me to put you back to bed? I ask, and to my immense relief she immediately lets go of Tash and throws her arms at me.

Tash has no choice but to hand her over. Later then, she warns.

Doug is asleep in his new big boy bed, with its half wall to keep him from rolling onto the floor. I put Emily down in her own bed, a proper single opposite him and touch a finger to my lips to signal we should be quiet. Sleep reduces Doug practically back to infancy, one arm thrown over his head and the other thumb in his mouth, his cheeks round and flushed. I kiss both of their foreheads, tuck an almost-asleep Emily in with exaggerated thoroughness, and then go to the bathroom.

In the mirror I look like shit: dark circles decorate my eyes, hair grown out and greasy from my shift. I haven't dyed it in forever, and I've got inches of roots. I examine myself for what they might have seen outside. Signs that I'm a user, that I'm used. But I look the same, I think. Thin enough. Pretty enough. Not that it matters, guys mostly seem to see my boobs. It's like nothing else exists, like they're the bestselling toy this Christmas season and I'm the only kid in class lucky enough to get them. Everyone's had my ass typecast since puberty.

It's stuffy in the small space of the bathroom and I'm sweating again on top of the day's dirt, but before I do anything, I take a pill. Then take off everything, turn the shower on medium cold, and step under, inching the cold water tap more and more to one side until it's icy. As cold as I can stand. Punishingly cold. Let it run over me until my scalp, my skin, everything is numb.

I dress fully before leaving the bathroom, putting my dirty work clothes back on so I don't have to walk across the hall in a towel. The kind of thing I did without thinking about before Rick revealed his true perv colors.

Ursula the cat shadows me down the hall, slipping between my legs to beat me into the room. She hides under the bed, which Ains is stretched out on, typing avidly on her phone.

I watch Ains in the mirror as I brush my wet hair back, cold steadily leaving my skin. Who're you texting? I ask, after she's ignored me a minute.

No one, she says. And then: I was looking at apartments in the city. Here, check out this one.

I sit down next to her, and she flips through pictures of a cute one-bedroom with hardwood floors, a tiny sun-filled kitchen, a bathroom with a clawfoot tub. A text notification appears at the top of the screen and she dismisses it quickly, but I catch the name Cole. And not just that: he's sent her a smiley-faced emoji with heart eyes.

Now I see. The aftermath of the lake fiasco for Ains is she's talking to Cole again. And he has heart eyes for her.

I collect myself enough to offer a coherent thought. It's nice, I say. How much?

I could afford it if I worked full-time, she says. Her face is alive with her fantasy, the thrill of imagining rooms all her own, or maybe hers and Cole's.

Oh, I say. We always used to make elaborate plans about moving to the city together and getting an apartment. She was going to go to school, and I was going to work at a bar and make lots of money, then travel. I'd get home from work so late it was early and crawl into her bed to tell her about my night, and she'd scoot over and make room for me, same as always.

So, you're leaving then? I ask her. When you finish school at Christmas?

I'm just looking, she says, noncommittal. Doing research.

Even as she shows me more apartments, she feels far away, like there's more she's not telling me, plans she's making, dreams she's dreaming. I start to sweat again, not really listening to her at all.

I don't think I can stay here, I say. The words fly out, full of alien emotion I don't know the origin of.

You have to, Ains answers automatically. She's back to texting, half smiling at something on her screen. You have to finish school and see what happens with your dad, she adds.

No, I say, I mean tonight. It's like a door was left open in my mind, and my feelings have escaped out it like a dog hell-bent on freedom. Now I'm chasing them around the yard trying to catch them, but I can't. It's true as soon as I've said it aloud: I can't be here.

Oh, says Ains. Are you going back to his place? She gets that look she gets when she talks about Bryan. Pissed off and irritated. And more than that, judgmental.

Feeling like I'm toeing the edge of a cliff, I repeat, I don't think I can stay here, Ains. Then add, Because of Rick.

She looks even more irritated at the mention of Rick, rolls her eyes, and groans. I know, I hate him too. I was hoping she'd get rid of him after their fight about the truck, but the weekend away only seems to have made them stronger.

I say the words like stepping out onto ice you aren't sure will hold you. Rick's been . . . sending me pictures.

She stares at me, a bit slack-jawed, hands still gripping her phone, mid-text with Cole.

Like, dick pics, I add, less carefully. I didn't know it was him, and then I figured it out at the beach and since then I just . . . I can't be here. I say it in a rush, needing it out.

What? she says finally, uncomprehending.

I hadn't factored in how high I am before embarking upon this conversation, hadn't factored in anything at all, and now I falter to explain, falter underneath her gaze. I can practically see the terrible wheels turning in her mind. It started after I moved in, I try. Maybe a timeline will help.

That's disgusting, she says, really sounding the word out.

I know, I agree readily, but then I don't know what more there is to say. Luckily, Ains has found her words.

We have to tell Mom, she says.

I know, I say, but—

I don't understand, she interrupts, shaking her head. How did he get your number? What did you say to him?

I don't know! From Tash's phone or something?

Keep your voice down, she says, even though I am. The window's open, she adds. They'll hear you.

She means Tash and Rick out on the balcony. I can hear Pam yammering from here.

I didn't say anything to him, I tell her, voice as controlled as I can make it. I asked who it was and told him to fuck off. I thought it was someone I met online or something.

What, you get so many dick pics they just blended into the crowd?

I don't know! I say, louder again. I didn't think it was fucking Rick, that's for sure.

And how do you know it was him? Did he, like . . . come on to you? Have you guys done stuff?

No, we didn't *do stuff*, I say.

Jesus, Bria, I know you have a thing for older men, but can't you just—

She stops short of whatever she was going to say.

Say it. I can't stop, need to make her hurt me more. It's not something she's doing to me; it's something we're building together now.

Can't you just let anyone have anything? Ains demands, at last.

What's that supposed to mean?

She looks even prettier, cheeks bright and angry, but it's too late to tell her, because then she says, I know what happened with you and Cole last year. He told me.

Time staggers to a halt. Shaking, I turn away, take off my shirt, change my bra, and pull on a clean tank top. Drop my shorts and underwear, my closed back telling her I know what I am. She doesn't need to remind me. Once dressed, I scoop some clothes out of the drawer she gave me in her dresser and stuff them in my backpack. Finally say, It was nothing.

Ains doesn't answer at first either, staring into the abyss of her phone, scrolling blindly. I know, she says. He told me.

Are you guys, like, together now? I ask, realizing that's what's different about her today: she hasn't forgiven me; she's in love.

Yeah, she says, then adds, I mean, I guess.

Since when?

Since the beach.

Why didn't you tell me?

She's not looking at her phone anymore, but she's not looking at me exactly either—she's looking at my hands. Or at my backpack, which I'm holding in my hands. It's unzipped and open, stuffed with clothes. But also poking out from among the things I carry with me is a bag of pills.

It's just a small sandwich bag, almost drained of the original amount. I left way more with Bryan.

Where are you going? she demands, but I'm quick. Before she can say anything more, before I can even really know for sure if she saw them, I've grabbed my shoes and am out the main door of the apartment, careful Tash and company don't see me leaving.

~~~

Dad's not at the house, but he's been here: the couches are disheveled again, and there's a water glass by the sink that wasn't there before, I don't think. It's more that I feel him here, a different buzz in the air, something that alerts me, leads me to the bathroom where, above the fan, in the hole in the ceiling, all the pills are gone. All of them, every last plastic-wrapped bundle. Every pill.

I go upstairs. It doesn't look like he's been in my room—all my shit's untouched. Feel a phantom urge to check my phone, same way I have every ten minutes or so since I broke it.

An idea occurs to me, and after spending a few minutes rooting through drawers in the kitchen, I find an old phone of Dad's. Plug it in upstairs and curl up on the bed, waiting to see if it works.

I didn't mean to smash my phone, but I got so mad, I needed to do something. It was Friday night at Bryan's and he invited some guys over, buddies of his and Chris's in particular. Dudes who acted like I wasn't there except for when they talked low to each other, side-eye on me, leading me to assume the topic of discussion was my body, some other girl's body, or drugs. Otherwise, it was a circle of loud talkers telling stories about people I didn't know and their various feats of manly strength.

Only Steve paid any attention to a single thing I said, and eventually I went inside feeling angry and unwieldy. When I get like that, I don't know what I'm going to do, say, or destroy. Steph could tell when she had a migraine coming on: she'd get a sort of tingling sensation in her limbs, feel lightheaded, see auras. I felt that way, like something bad was coming over me.

The kitchen—which I'd tidied earlier, putting all the dishes away, wiping down counters, sweeping the floors—was a sprawling party disaster zone again already. I felt a searching need for motion, opening the fridge to stare at some bottles of pop and wilted vegetables, then shutting it again. Went to the living room and ran my eyes over all the surfaces, the table cluttered with keys, remotes, empty beer cans. His room, bed made because I made it, piles of clothes on the bathroom floor, the toothpaste-spattered mirror, and me in it.

I wanted to scream but couldn't, and to leave but couldn't, and to tear my skin off and step out of it. But obviously couldn't.

I needed to take something, but my little pill bottle wasn't any-where in my backpack or the bedside table. I'd just given Bryan two bundles of pills for "safekeeping" and didn't know where he'd put them. Something caught my eye in the garbage can under the sink. The blue and yellow bottle, so small, that I keep in my bag as if it's for cramps or headaches I get from the heat. Empty, because he'd taken them all.

That's when I smashed it: throwing the phone as hard as I could at the tile shower wall was all it took. The screen shattered completely, glass crystals I swept down the drain with my hands, not even really hoping I'd gotten them all.

I felt better. I went back to the party.

Now I lie on my bed, my real bed for once, waiting for the burner phone to charge, with my shoes still on, uncomfortable but without any sort of inclination to do anything about it. I wait, exhausted and blank.

When it's been long enough, I power it on and find there's no code to open it. Amazing.

No contacts saved either. I try to think of a number I know off by heart. Dad. Ains. Tash. I can't call any of them to mind. I'm too tired to talk or type anyway, so I get under the covers and close my eyes.

A thump comes from below, at the back of the house. I hold my breath, terrified it's Ains or Tash come to find me. Or who knows, anyone could be out there. Maybe it wasn't Dad who cleared the ceiling of pills after all.

The bed is pushed up against the wall where the window looks out into the backyard, but the blinds are closed, and I don't want to risk moving them if there is someone out there.

I stay still for the longest time, listening. Then slowly sit up, stand. After an agonizingly slow descent downstairs, I check the doors and windows, closets and corners. But there's nothing, no one. Go back to bed and peek out the blinds to the backyard one last time, just in case.

My tiredness is gone now, and I'm wired instead. Reach for my backpack and shake out a pill. Tomorrow I'll make a plan.

Close my eyes and try again to sleep. But my mind is running. Remembering. How every bad thing leads to the next, like a virus spreading.

Like the time last April when Dad got beat up. It happened right out back, in the carport next to the garage. I'd spent the night before at Tash's because he had to work, and we picked up my favorite Thai takeout on the way home. As I got out of the car and walked towards the house, a pickup truck pulled up in the back lane with two men inside.

One of them said something to Dad out the open window—I didn't catch what—and Dad answered back with a vehement fuck you.

The doors of the truck flew open and they were on him with their fists, hitting and hitting him, as I stood at the back door holding the Thai food, grease from the spring rolls spreading across the paper bag.

It seemed he was on the ground immediately, and he shouted at me to get inside, but I didn't have keys on me. The neighbor's house was right there, their door across from ours. We weren't friendly with them though, and their windows were blank and unwatchful like nobody was home, or if they were, they didn't care. I froze, wondering if I should pound their door anyway, or yell to call 911. Was this the kind of thing you called 911 for?

I don't know how long they punched and kicked him for, but when they were done, they got back in their truck and drove away. Dad got up, assuring me he was fine before he was fully on his feet. His face was already swelling, one eye turning purple as it closed, blood and saliva dripping from his battered lip. He ushered me inside, drawing the blinds and pressing a dish towel to his face. Swearing a little under his breath, mostly he went soft, telling me not to worry, it was fine, to watch TV and eat my dinner. He got on the phone. I put some food on my plate and ate until my belly was uncomfortably full, then went upstairs to get ready to go out.

He was still making phone calls when I came back down. Where are you going? he asked, hand over the speaker of his phone.

I told you, I said. There's a bush party tonight.

It was Easter weekend. All the best bush parties happen between Good Friday and Easter Sunday in Beauchamp, sometimes raging three days long, better even than the ones in the summer when the weather was actually nice.

When he protested, I whined, preparing to throw down a full teenaged tantrum, but he cut me off before I could get it off the ground. Fine, he said. I'll drive you.

The bush party spot was beyond the high school football field, through some trees and in a clearing that backed onto a row of new-build houses. Someone at the party usually lived in one of the houses that bordered the field and would run extension cords out for music; their mom might let girls use the second bathroom. But all that was really needed was the empty space of the field and the dark, which enclosed us in our own world, different from the school world or the world of our homes.

One of the people Dad had called while I sat in front of the TV and shoveled Thai food down my gullet was Tash. She rushed over even though Doug was a little baby then, arriving after Dad got back from dropping me off and making him ice his eye and lip immediately. When she found out I'd gone out, she came to find me.

An adult moving through a party full of teenagers is an interesting phenomenon. Some didn't notice Tash at all, as she walked through the crowd looking for me, but when they did clock her as a grown-up type, their posture would change, joints and beers would be tucked behind bodies, music dimmed. I was around the fire knowing none of this, nicely drunk and at the center of some stupid conversation that stilled as Tash intruded.

Bria, she said, loud enough to get my attention.

Hey, I said back, in surprise.

Come on, I need to talk to you.

At least one of the boys made an "Ooooo Bria's in trouble" sound, but mostly the circle looked embarrassed for me briefly and then turned away as I followed Tash towards the edge of the party.

Are you okay? she demanded, eyes searching me for damage. She told me she'd been to the house, tended to Dad, but wanted to make sure I was okay. Do you want to talk about it? she asked. Come back to our place. I can draw you a bath, and you and Ains can sleep in the living room. Watch a movie, take your mind off things?

I had genuinely been having fun before Tash arrived, at least I thought I had been, but she'd ruined it. Now I was thinking about Dad's battered face again, the way they hit him so many times, one hit after another so he couldn't get up or defend himself. The way his eye had already begun to resemble the closed eye of a baby bird when he'd dropped me off at the party. The way, when the first man stopped hitting him and went back to their truck, I had been so sure he was going to get a gun and shoot Dad dead.

No, I said. I want to stay. I'm fine.

Seriously, she said.

I made myself hard. I'm fine, I said again. I'll see you tomorrow, okay?

I walked her back to her car, and before she shut the door, she said, I wish you would let me take care of you, Bria.

I repeated goodnight as firmly as I could, and then went off to reclaim my spot by the fire.

The next day, we all went to Tash's for Easter brunch. Dad picked up Granny from the care home in Durham, and she said nothing about how swollen his face was behind his sunglasses. I wonder what it's done to me, seeing the way these women took care of him. Tash rushing over to tend to his wounds. Granny ignoring what was right in front of her. And where did that leave me? Standing by and watching him get beaten to a pulp? Putting it away and going out into the night? Yeah, that's where.

~~~~

Or wait, maybe not. Maybe it leaves me next to the fire after getting rid of Tash and turning to see Cole beside me.

You okay? he asked.

I hadn't realized I was shivering. I forced myself to stop, stand straighter. What are you doing here? I asked.

Lots of people are here? he replied, not offended, even though he was within his rights to be. I was always annoying, annoyed, at him and Ains's other friends, bothered by their closeness, their interest in TV shows I didn't care about and sports I didn't play. This was around the time I realized Cole had changed, going from a short sensitive boy who only hung out with girls to a tall broad dude who fit in. His easygoing nature, which had made him weak, a target, before had been tweaked, and now he was appealing to girls and guys both. I couldn't help but hate people like that. Who somehow changed the way they were seen.

What happened to you? I asked, yelling to be heard over the party.

What do you mean?

All this, I said, indicating his entire being, then changing my mind and the subject. Can you get me a beer? I asked. I'd rather not deal with Harrison over there right now.

The two kegs were set up on the other side of the fire on some picnic tables that had been dragged into the field eons ago. No one knew whose beer it was really; kegs were the domain of the older, connected kids, and everyone simply drank until it was gone, but that night a group of guys had gathered around the kegs proprietarily, performing stunts that would surely land someone in the ER before morning. Currently Harrison was trying to bench-press the keg, while also drinking from the tap.

Yeah, sure, Cole said. He moved deftly through the crowd of jocks and came back a minute later with two full red cups for us. Wanna go for a walk? he asked me.

All right, I said, swallowing the top inch of beer so that it wouldn't spill.

We walked to the edge of the party and kept going through the field that ran behind the new development area of town neither one of us was from.

Was that Ainsley's mom I saw you with earlier?

I opened my mouth to deny it, then stopped. Yeah, I said. He knew Tash; there was no point in pretending. But what happened next surprised me.

Is everything okay? he asked.

He sounded so fucking nice. The way he asked. So, I told him what had happened with Dad. All of it, almost.

We had reached the edge of the field by the time I finished talking and turned back. The houses to one side of us were far enough away that they were reduced to the shadows of roofs and fences, nondescript patches of light, and when I stopped talking, Cole started, making up stories for me about the people who lived in them. I began to notice things about him. Like the square of his chin and his full lips, which for some reason I was wondering what it would be like to kiss, and the way he slowed down to stand in front of me a little too close, which made it seem like he was wondering too.

He licked his lips in quick preparation as my mouth made its way to his, and they were soft when I met them. He pulled me into him, and sometimes the shape of it is all you need. Love or whatever. Just having someone act it out with you is enough.

We made out for ages in his car, the front seat, emergency break boring a hole in my thigh, his hands on my hair, shoulders, waist.

He drove me home in his mom's car. The sweetness left me as he turned the key and the engine stopped. Don't, I said.

Don't what? He smiled.

Don't talk about it, and don't tell Ains. Just stay away from me, okay?

13.

I sleep forever, or until noon at least, waking up roasted by the sun that's snuck through the slats in the blinds. My eyes hurt and I want sleep to close back in around me, but my first thought is the fight with Ains, and then I'm all too awake. Way back at the beginning of the summer, we booked the next two nights off work for my birthday, which is tomorrow. I don't imagine those plans are happening, and while I don't have anywhere to go, I feel decidedly unsafe here today, like at any moment someone is going to barge in the door and make me take accountability for my actions. You don't have to go home, but you can't stay here, I tell myself, getting out of bed.

First things first, I hunt for pills. Whether it was Dad or someone else who took the stash, the bathroom ceiling spot is really and truly empty. I need to know for sure how many I have to work with.

The answer is nine, and whatever is left of what I gave Bryan. I do some googling. The internet tells me it's called a taper.

When you've been taking them like I've been taking them, you can't just stop.

~~~

Darcy is behind the counter when I walk into work in the late afternoon, a line of customers stretched to the door. Greg, one of the daytime staff, is in the kitchen working the grill but it's clear Darcy is swamped. I stopped in to get a drink and a break from the sun on my walk over to Bryan's—he is not expecting me; I was supposed to be with Ains today—but I dump my stuff in the back and grab an apron.

I can bag orders, I say to Darcy, coming back out to the front of the restaurant.

Thanks, he says, sideways, as he finishes filling up a cup at the soda fountain. The grease trap overflowed again. It's been a nightmare shift.

Worst smell I've ever smelled, I say, remembering last time.

Not me, he says with authority.

Oh yeah?

He nods. Locker rooms. Much worse.

I admire your positive attitude, Darce, I say, and try to summon some positivity of my own as I pitch in to help them with the rush. But it's not always easy to stuff down your emotions. I haven't taken anything today, not even half a pill. I can feel it already, the want of it, working beneath my skin.

After a frantic fifteen minutes or so, we clear the line of customers. You can take off now, thanks a million, Bria, says Darcy.

No, it's okay, I say, glancing in the back, where Greg still has a mountain of orders to get out. I can stay for a bit longer.

Don't you and Ainsley have big plans today? Darcy asks.

Uh, yeah, but not till later.

Darcy mops the sweat from his brow with a napkin. All right, if you say so, he says, and before he heads in the back adds, You're a lifesaver, Bria.

But once he's gone, I start struggling. Robot Bria is nowhere to be found today—my face is red with the effort of not crying, and every time I turn around to fill a cup or swirl an ice cream cone, I let a few tears drop and try to subtly wipe them away before turning back. I think it's working; nobody seems to notice, or else they just don't care that the teenager selling them their Fat Boy combos is silently weeping.

Out of sheer desperation, I slip into the back and, careful no one sees, plunge my hand into the depths of my bag until I feel the shape I'm looking for. Pop one pill into my mouth and try not to feel too guilty about it. Like the internet said, you can't just stop.

After a few minutes, I calm down. Manage to maintain it even as I'm dealing with this awful upwardly mobile white trash couple who want to express their individuality through their Burger Shack order. No, we don't have that fake meat burger she's heard about online. No, we don't do salads. I answer automatically, trying to wipe my face of any emotion as their questions keep coming. Can he have the off-menu Fat Boy his buddy told him about? And don't put too much ice in her Coke. Actually, can she have a separate cup with ice that she can add as she pleases? Usually, I would try to exact some sort of revenge on customers this awful, but I just give them what they want and brace myself to be nice to the next fucker in line.

That's when I look up and see Dad behind a family of four. My dad. He holds up a hand in greeting, but I still have to keep looking back to check that it's really him. I take deep breaths to keep from shaking as I hand people change and pack burgers into a to-go bag.

Hi, I say when I've finally served everyone but him. I walk around the counter, and we hug.

Smells like him. Jean jacket cigarette smell. But also clean laundry, because he is a man who loves a dryer sheet. Looks like him too. Less tanned than he'd usually be at this time of summer, and maybe a little thin, the lines beside his mouth deeper.

He grabs my shoulders and holds me away from him to take me in. I avoid his eyes. Wonder if I look different, in what ways. Squirm out of his grasp and try to get a hold of things.

Surprised you made it through the summer, he says. He sounds bright, forced.

What? I ask, freaked out by every little thing.

The job, I'm surprised you lasted.

Asshole like him, I think. Say, I didn't really have much of a fucking choice, did I?

Hey, I've been sending Tash money.

Well, I'm not Tash.

He snorts, still finding me amusing. Sometimes I hate it when I see him feeling proud for what he had to do with creating me. And then sometimes I don't mind it. I don't understand that. How sometimes it feels like love and sometimes it feels like suffocation.

Can you take a break? I need to talk to you. He says it all casual-like, and it makes me blink dumbly, too overwhelmed to be angry.

Hey, Darcy? I go all the way into the kitchen instead of calling to him through the pass, like I usually would. Are you guys good now? My dad's here.

Darcy's cheeks are burning red from the exertion of the rush; the air conditioning doesn't even begin to touch the heat back in the kitchen. Of course, he says. Thanks again for your help.

I told Dad to meet me around back, but he's not there when I go out through the kitchen. I'm walking towards the service road so that I can see around the back of the building next door in case he's over there, when I hear a ringing metal sound behind me. The thought that grabs me in the milliseconds it takes to turn around is that the bear in the dumpster is back and due to my foolhardy nature it's about to take me down with one paw swipe.

But it's Dad, having kicked the dumpster by accident as he rounded the corner. He looks rattled by the sound too.

Good to see you, kiddo, he says and again pulls me into a hug.

I allow it.

Happy birthday tomorrow, he says.

Thanks, I begrudge.

We'll do something special to celebrate soon, okay? He lets go of his hold on me and presses a wad of folded bills into my hand. I tuck it into my back pocket without counting it.

Thanks, I say, searching for a start. So, when did you get out?

He hesitates. Doesn't want to say.

Asshole, I say.

Hey, he says. Take it easy. It's . . . uh, complicated.

Complicated how?

He again looks around, scanning the open field behind the row of businesses, the trees beyond the service road. What's the line from that song he loves to quote? It's not being paranoid if they're really out to get you?

Finally, he says, I can't tell you very much right now, Bria. I've gotta go away for a few days and take care of some things, and then I'll come back and get you.

Get me? I say.

I can see him working through his frustration with me— he thought this would be a joyful reunion somehow, that I'd welcome him with chill vibes and open arms. You know how much I've missed you, right? he says.

I am silent. I do not know. But this, him saying it, is supposed to soothe me. I stand very still and wait to see what happens, what I do.

I'm sorry about Steph. That must have been scary. You did good though.

Neither of us says anything.

I eventually ask, So where have you been?

He sighs. The new people I was working for, things didn't go so well. I promise I'll tell you everything soon. It's almost over.

Why'd you even come back then?

To see you, kid, he says lightly. I missed you.

I hate how looking at him is like looking at me too. All the parts of me I owe to him, can blame on him. Both of us erupt in freckles every summer, have eyes that are sort of hazel in the sun. Both of us stubborn like metal that won't bend. Except aren't I always bending for him? Why'd you really come back? I ask.

He shakes his head, touches my arm. To check on you and Tash, make sure everything is okay here, at the house.

The house. I want so badly to throw the pills in his face, tell him I know that's why he really came back, but then he would know I've been into them too, not just Steph. He'd know I've been taking them and can't stop taking them now.

I'll talk to you in a couple of days, he says. I love you, Bria, okay?

Okay, I agree.

He leaves after that. I go back into the restaurant, through the kitchen and out into the front in time to see him get into a car driven by someone else and pull away.

I wish I'd been nicer and meaner to him while I had the chance. I need a thousand cigarettes and a million hours alone, but all I do is fix myself a ginger ale and sip it, taking stock of things. Dad's back, but not really.

I wish that I'd asked him about Steph. If he's talked to her, if she's okay. I wish I'd asked him to take me with him. Wish I'd acted any other way than like I didn't need him, like I wanted to be alone. Because now I am, and how.

~~~

Darcy tries to insist on me leaving. Get out of here, he says, go enjoy your birthday plans.

I'll take off in a second, I say. I have my backpack on, ready to go, but I can't make myself leave. I'm stuck, sticking around and chatting to Darcy while he sweeps the dining room. I keep thinking about terrible things, such as school and how my birthday always signals the countdown to going back. And Dad's face when I asked him where he's been. And who was driving the car he left in? Another thought: the eight pills remaining in my bag.

Finally, I say bye to Darcy and leave Burger Shack. The smell of the fires, which usually mutes when you've been outside for a while, smacks me in the face anew. Something about the sun, sinking like a giant red orb into the highway horizon as I wait at the intersection for my chance to cross. Reminds me of what? Smells like campfire or charcoal barbecue. Skews my memories, sending me at once to childhood cookouts and last summer's bush parties until a generalized nostalgia chasm opens up and threatens to swallow me.

Easy, I tell myself, testing my eyes on the setting sun. The smoke so thick you can finally look directly at it without going blind.

The light changes, and as I walk to the other side, I remember the wad of cash in my pocket and some semblance of a plan emerges.

I've had my hair every color pretty much but right now I need it new. Go to the Drug Mart across the street, walk back and forth in the hair aisle scanning boxes until they blur.

Can I help you?

I look over at her to see what I need to do. Salespeople always think I'm stealing, and I ready myself for an altercation, but she looks genuinely helpful. She's young but not as young as me, and her hair is a purply red magenta, cut in an angular bob with bangs that reminds me of wigs they sell at the mall. Rows of disembodied lady heads in shades of blue, purple, and green lined up in the window right when you walk in.

I need to do something about this, I say and grab a handful of my ponytailed hair.

Looks like it's been through a lot. She comes close, peers at my head, the white blonde ends we burned my scalp bleaching, anchored by my brown roots.

I tell her everything.

~~~

The salesgirl's name is Jackie, and she went to high school in Durham with Steve's older siblings, we figure out after talking for a while. She's about to finish hair school and lives with her grandma out here while she's saving up to move to the city this fall. Her boyfriend is in a band and lives there already; she pulls out her phone and shows me pictures of them together at festivals, her wearing band T-shirts tied up in knots and tons of gothy makeup. I ask her one question about mascara, and she offers to do my makeup for free; I just have to commit to buying one product she uses on me. Dad's wad of money is uncounted in my back pocket. Why not spend it on some birthday presents for myself?

Alana and I used to smoke joints in her family's minivan at lunch. Do they still have that thing? asks Jackie. When one of the wood panels fell off, they replaced it with, like, an actual piece of wood.

Alana is Steve's sister; Jackie seems to think I know her. No, I say. I think they got rid of it.

It seated, like, twelve. Their family is so fucking big, man. I'm an only child so I was always jealous.

Me too, I say.

We'd hotbox the van at lunch, steal cookies from 7-Eleven, and then take naps in the drama room for the rest of the day. Those were the days. I wonder how she's doing.

Alana? I say. I don't know. I can ask Steve next time I see him.

This is a mattifying primer, she tells me, spreading some cold white goo over my cheeks.

Oh cool, I say. To help set my foundation?

Exactly, she says. She seems to relish in looking at my face. It's nice to be so closely considered, and I pay attention to everything she says about the products she's using on me, like it's my best bet for survival. You know, she adds, you have ridiculously tiny pores.

I do?

Yep, she says with absolute authority. The tiniest. All you need is some light coverage to even out your skin tone. This stuff is incredible, she says, turning to the display next to the tall leather stool I'm perched on and selecting a tube in my skin tone. It'll cover the red around your nostrils but still let those freckles show through.

I didn't even know my nostrils were red. I peer into the mirror behind Jackie and see that she's correct. Usually lighting this florescent would kill me, but tonight it feels just right. Phony and bright.

Jackie squeezes some of the foundation onto a clean sponge and dabs it all across my face in tiny kisses, evening me out. She gets up close and I can see her own makeup in detail, long spiky lashes, bronzed cheekbones, and black wings that lift her eyes up at their corners. I can also smell her breath—black tea and something minty, maybe gum—and I close my eyes as she moves over my skin with the sponge. Next is blush and bronzer, applied with a series of puffy brushes she uses to buff my cheeks to a shine, then my eyebrows need to be defined, before she settles in to shade my lids a subtle taupe sunset.

I have this way of unfocusing my vision, so that I can't see some things that are right in front of me. I can do it with my ears too, pulling a blanket of fuzz over my hearing at will.

I do it now with the mirror and my face, trying only to see where Jackie's changing me and not who I was before, beneath. And I talk, about nothing, anything, free-associating stories while she works on me.

Oh my god, I say when she's done. I don't look at my face as a whole, but each part individually. Lips glossy and pink-beige, cheeks carved out of burnished gold, eyes like brown holes in my head. I look away.

I'll take this, I say, pointing to the bronzer she used on me. And this and this, I add a few other items to the pile, which includes the hair dye she helped me pick out before.

How long do I leave this on for? I ask Jackie about the dye as she starts to ring me up.

Depends, she says, stopping to look at me again. I feel better as soon as her attention is on me, undivided. That's, like, six months of roots? she asks, guessing correctly. It might be better to strip it first, she says. And ... if it were me ...

What? I ask. What would you do?

She doesn't move for a second, glancing around the store like she's making sure there isn't something else she could be doing. Then she considers me again anew. I'd cut it—bring it up to here, she says, indicating my collarbone. No, maybe shorter, just above the shoulder. I do hair in my grandma's basement, you know. I could do it for you.

Really?

Sure, she says, eyes on the computer screen.

Can you do it tonight? I ask, taking out my wad as the total appears. I hand her four twenties and count at least ten more.

She pauses.

It's my birthday tomorrow, I say. Please?

It's your birthday?

I nod, bouncing up and down. Please? I can pay extra or whatever.

She looks at me for a minute. Okay. I get off in twenty minutes. We can do it right after that.

~~~

Whose house is this? I ask as we walk up to a bungalow with butterfly decals attached to the front of the house, pretty flowers in the beds below.

My grandma's, says Jackie, leading me around to the back and unlocking the door.

Oh yeah, I say, remembering she said that already. Where is she? I ask as we step into the kitchen. I slip off my shoes.

Come meet her, says Jackie. Hey, Grandma, she yells ahead, going through the living room and down the hall. She doesn't hear so good these days, Jackie says over her shoulder to me, opening the bedroom door.

Her grandma is asleep upright in bed, with the TV on the

weather channel, volume blaring. Jackie takes the remote from her hand, turns off the TV, and puts it on the bedside table, kissing the top of her grandma's head before turning off the lights and shutting the door.

We go quietly back down the hall to the kitchen. Jackie grabs two wine glasses and leads me to the basement.

So, she says. Wanna do drugs?

Shit yeah, I say.

Drugs to Jackie is weed and wine she pours from a box in the basement fridge. It's big and open concept down here—one half is set up as a family room, with a sectional couch, recliner, and TV, while the other side is Jackie's bedroom. There's a kitchenette and a big bathroom with a laundry sink Jackie has rigged up to wash hair in.

I'm so jealous, I say, completing a circle of the room.

It's all right, says Jackie. She's on the bed, rolling a joint using a stack of magazines for a surface. I hate how damp it is, but at least I can do hair here.

Jackie keeps talking as I continue to poke around. My whole family hates me, she says. Only my grandma and my aunt talk to me. Makes it awkward at family gatherings now that I live here, she says and laughs.

I'm in the bathroom, looking at her bottles of perfume. And also rooting around my backpack for my stash. The plan was to cut up the pills and take them slowly over the course of the day and then less and less as the days go on, but instead I pop a whole one in my mouth and wash it down with wine, for maintenance purposes. Bryan has more anyway, if I need them.

Step back out into the main room as Jackie lights her joint. When she's ready, she sits me down in a chair in front of the mirror and positions herself behind me. Okay. How do you want to look?

I think, Older. Dangerous-er. But I just say, Different.

Jackie runs me through some options and makes sure I'm on board, but I would do anything she tells me. The pill seems strong, and I feel blurred, giddy. I try to do everything I can to make Jackie fall in love with me. Not in a romantic way. I just want her to also want this night to never end. I don't know if it's working, but she refills the wine I don't remember drinking and starts to paint my head with dye.

~~~

Later, when my hair is cut and colored and we're both wasted, we trade stories of terrible things. I tell her about my mom; she tells me about hers, etc. A few stories in, she mentions a friend who ODed last year, and when it's my turn again, I tell her about Steph. About how slowly the information moved from my eyes to my brain. What I saw when I got home from one of those first nights with Bryan. Steph on the couch. Not sleeping. Something else. It was like every rule about time erased. Like someone moving across the room to give me bad news, except it was only my eyes and her on the couch.

The way my voice shaped her name was like no word I'd ever said before, the sound of it rattling me more than anything.

Steph? I rushed to her. Shook her still-warm shoulders. Then harder. Begged her eyes to open, her lips to move, her lungs to breathe for me. Then freaking out, knocking things off the living room table looking for it. Naloxone.

Her purse was on the floor. I dumped everything out and could see right away it wasn't there, that red canvas pouch with the first aid symbol on it. Should I do CPR? I didn't know. Probably more important to find the kit. That's what she said to do if it happened. That was the thing: it was happening and I wasn't doing anything right.

Where was my phone? Or hers? Realized mine was in my pocket. Shake dialed 911.

It didn't ring for so long that I took the phone away from my ear to check I did it right, turning it to speaker as they finally picked up. What was my emergency?

My friend is overdosing, please hurry. Then I remembered the kit they gave us at school. And I ran.

It was there, tucked into the drawer of my bedside table next to nail polish and lip chap. I grabbed it and ran back to the living room, then slowed again.

The voice on the phone was asking if I was still there.

I'm here, I said. I found it, the naloxone. Now what?

Hold on. Do you know what kind of drugs your friend took?

Pills. I unzipped the package.

What kind of pills? asked 911.

Fentanyl.

That must have been the magic word because then they told me exactly what to do. What kind of kit is it? Nasal spray? No? Then it's important to sterilize. Get all the air out. Fill it up with every last drop, then plunge it in.

I wasted one second wondering where, then stabbed her in the meat of her arm. Rubbed the spot. Steph! Shook her again. No response. Told the woman on the phone she wasn't waking up.

What's your name, dear?

Bria.

Bria, sometimes it takes more than one dose to reverse a fentanyl overdose.

What? I touched her face, cool and slack. Eyes a little rolled back.

Do you know if she has another naloxone kit somewhere in the house? Maybe in her purse?

Someone somewhere was wailing. Or no, it was sirens descending. Opened the door for them. Said which room for them and what drug and how long for them. Rattled off stumbled answers. How old she was and what she took again and again.

Steph, they yelled at her. Stephanie! Like the movies, they repeated her name to bring her back to life. Come on, sweetie. Open your eyes. Then back to questions. Who am I to her?

She's my stepmother, I said. Even that a fairy tale.

Called my dad. And called him. Called Ains and Tash instead. They came.

～～～

For a while, Steph wanted to keep a record of her dreams. A dream journal basically, except she kept such strange hours, she was never near the journal when she fell asleep, and when she'd wake up, she wouldn't remember to write them down. So, she set an alarm to go off every hour. And when it went off, she'd check to see if she'd been dreaming, and if she had, she'd record a voice note on her phone, copying it into a notebook later.

I brought the journal with me when Tash drove me to the hospital to see her the next day, because I didn't know what to bring someone like her after something like that.

She'd told me she had sisters, but I hadn't imagined them like this. Beautiful and cool and so sad over her. They were quietly talking, leaning into each other, one of them all animated and worked up and the other exasperated, tired. Both with eyes red from crying. Then the angry one said something and the tired one laughed too loud, clapping a hand over her mouth to tamp it down.

Her parents were there too, a sweet, worn-out-looking couple who had their heads together looking at something on a cell phone.

I imagined them all driving out from the city to the hospital in Durham where the ambulance took Steph, camping out here in the waiting room to see her, taking turns going to nap at a motel. No matter what she'd put them through up to this point, they still came. They hadn't given up on her. You could see that clearly by how her parents' eyes flew up every time someone walked in the room.

Not me though. They didn't see me, at least not as someone who mattered in their emergency. I recognized them from the pictures she'd shown me to go with her stories. It's different though, seeing people in the flesh, in motion. All these people who belonged to her and who were more important than me. We were a scuzzy holiday for her. A stop on the addiction train, almost the last one, but now who knows. She could keep going for years, because I saved her.

I thought about the kind of conversation I could have with her family, trying to explain who I was to her, and I saw how little claim I had. Practically none.

I walked back to the elevators, hit the button to close the doors until they did, and met Tash on her way in.

Sorry, she said, I had to park, like, five blocks away. The hourly rate in the parking garage is highway robbery.

I kept walking past her, outside, put my sunglasses on. It was so bright, it hurt.

Did you find her? Tash caught my arm, slowed me.

I nodded. Let's go, okay?

She looked me over, evaluating me and the situation like she would one of her charges. Clients. Whatever they call them. Okay, she said. Let's go.

As penance, I endured being momentarily squeezed into a hug and then followed her back to the truck.

I didn't read all of Steph's dream journal, but I did scan the pages in search of my name. It only came up once, in a description of a dream about being late for work, and even though it was a mundane dream like that, it still soothed me, knowing I had made enough of an impression to show up in her unconscious.

At some point in the days after Steph's overdose, Tash went to the house and packed up her things and got them to her family. I didn't mention the dream journal. Like the times I read Ains's notebook, it was something I knew would only be mine if I stole it.

~~~

Where is she now? Jackie asks, after I've told her everything.

Steph?

Jackie nods.

I shrug. Her parents got her into treatment somewhere.

Well, that's good, right?

Right, I say. We're both sprawled out on the floor in the bathroom, having landed on it as the most comfortable option at some point during my hair transformation process.

You know, says Jackie, cheersing me with an empty cup. It's shit like this—here she gestured at the space between her and me—that makes me feel better, you know?

I do know, I say and press my cheek to the cold white tile of the bathroom floor. Can I hear that song again? I ask, about the one she's just played for me.

It's so good, she says.

So good, I agree. Are you hungry? I ask.

No, she says. Wait, now I am.

We should order pizza, I say but we don't. We just keep telling stories until it gets too sideways to talk.

14.

For my birthday, Ains and I were going to buy a sheet cake from Valu Lots and make them write "Bittersweet Sixteen" on it. We were going to eat it with forks, no plates, all of us, the kids included, because I've always wanted to do that. Mark was going to let us up onto the roof of Paradise Gardens so we could look for shooting stars, though he didn't know it yet. But a birthday can be very persuasive.

Since my daytime plans with Ains aren't happening, after I leave Jackie's grandma's house, I walk towards Bryan's, even though he isn't expecting me until tonight.

It's a long walk. I keep checking my phone. No messages. Right. Why would there be, Bria? You dummy. No one knows how to reach you.

I barely knew where I was when I woke up curled into the corner of the sectional, the fabric beneath my cheek wet with drool. Jackie was snoring in her bed as I uncoiled my body slowly, remembering what we did, how late we stayed up, some of what we said. Brushed my hair back from my face and remembered that too: I have bangs now. And another thing: my birthday.

A candy-colored movie played on the TV—Jackie can't sleep without a romantic comedy in the background—and the sound covered for me as I crept around the basement gathering up my things, seized by the sudden urge to leave before anyone could wake to find me.

The blinds are drawn and the windows dark when I walk up to Bryan's, but when I try the door, it's open.

Inside, Steve has his feet up on the coffee table, drinking a soda in front of the fan. Hey, cool hair! he says.

Thanks, I say, touching my fingers to it for the thousandth time already today. Jackie convinced me to go shorter, to a bit below my chin. I realized on my walk over here who my haircut makes me look like: her. She gave me the same haircut she has. I'm one of the disembodied lady heads at the mall now. I can't tell if I mind yet; my shoulders and neck at least feel naked and free.

Birthday present to myself, I tell Steve.

It's your birthday?

He jumps up to give me a hug, and his can of soda touches the back of my neck briefly. I shiver. It was a long and stinking hot walk over here.

Here, says Steve, presenting me with a joint he had tucked behind his ear. Happy birthday.

Thanks, man, I say, accepting it with ceremony. Where is everyone?

Don't know, he says. I just got off working a night shift. Was going to smoke that and take a nap.

I get myself some water from the fridge, and Steve puts the TV on and we sit in the dark living room and chat. It's afternoon already, but I'm glad Bryan isn't here, even though part of me is wondering if he has anything planned for my birthday. We didn't make any plans, but he knows it's today, knows I'd be over later.

Eventually the wine from last night starts making me feel like shit, and I retreat to Bryan's room. Though I should snoop around to see if I can find the bags of pills I left with him, I take one of my remaining few instead and fall deeply asleep for a few hours.

When I wake up, Steve is humming in the kitchen, doing the dishes. I grab a dish towel and join him; he puts on some tunes to accompany us and soon the kitchen is clean. We tidy the living room too, and by the time Bryan and Chris come in the back door an hour or so later, we're stoned and giggly.

Steve's been telling me about how his first job was picking rocks out of the field for the farm down the road from them, returning with a bucket full at the end of the day for the farmer to dump out and count. Ten cents a rock. About how he fell asleep in the field once and almost got run over by a tractor.

Steve! I say. That's so quaint! You little farm boy.

It sucked, he says. I was so sunburned. I had these weird tan lines for, like, a year after.

Chris comes into the living room with a beer, Bryan behind him. He doesn't look at me at first, greeting Steve and then examining the living room table as if for evidence of what we've been up to. Unless he's hiding it in the kitchen, I see no signs of birthday paraphernalia of any kind and immediately feel stupid. I hadn't realized I was expecting some kind of celebration and quickly stuff down the disappointment.

What did you do to your hair? Bryan asks when he does acknowledge me. He bends to kiss me on the cheek before I can stand. When I do, he kisses me again, on the mouth, and then backs away a few feet to examine me.

My friend Jackie cut it, I say.

Who's Jackie? asks Bryan.

My friend, I repeat. She's a hairdresser. She knows your sister, Steve.

Oh yeah? he says. Which one?

Alana, I answer.

It's cute, says Bryan. Happy birthday, he adds in a strange, obligatory way. Like a birthday is something uncool I opted into. Let's go out for a smoke, he says, not to me but to the room. We all move to follow him.

What were you guys talking about? Bryan asks me as we pass through the kitchen. He says it low, but Steve hears, I guess, because he slides the answer smoothly into the awkward space Bryan makes with the question.

I was telling Bria how my first job was picking rocks out of a field, Steve says.

Outside, we settle into chairs around the patio table. Bryan takes time arranging the contents of his pockets on the table— wallet, cell phone, keys—before he lights a cigarette.

Steve continues his previous topic of conversation, as if tension isn't being kicked around in the air like a hacky sack between us. All my siblings became lifeguards and had the coolest summer gigs, he says.

Why not you? I ask, trying to match his tone. Not lifeguard material?

Not quite, he says. I think the parents figured four lifeguard offspring was enough, and they could just let me, you know, be me. I was always jealous though. Alana worked at Wet n' Wild at the top of the slides.

She was a go girl? I ask. No way.

What's a go girl? Chris asks.

I let Steve explain the importance of the go girls while my mind drifts. I remember thinking they were the coolest: they sat on lifeguard chairs at the mouth of the slides in their red Wet n' Wild tank tops looking bored and unimpressed, florescent bikini strings around their necks, and yelled go every fifteen seconds so that the slides didn't get clogged up with kids. I snap myself back to reality, find Bryan watching me.

She did it every summer when she was in university, until they closed, Steve is saying.

I didn't have summer jobs as a kid, says Bryan. I had jobs all year round and an extra one in the summer.

Did you walk uphill both ways to get to them? asks Chris.

Steve laughs. I only picked rocks until I was ten, then I switched to cans. Me and my best friend, Shay, would bike into town and hit all the party spots, keep going until we had enough for a loosie and a hot dog, maybe a gram of weed.

Like a very precocious hobo, I say.

You know the best spot? My place. My parents would always have these big family parties, and once all the grown-ups were drunk enough, we'd start collecting cans. All the aunties thought we were being good boys helping clean up. Little did they know. It was a beautiful time.

I've always sensed from Steve's stories that he comes from one of those weirdly happy families. You know that rare freak family unit that doesn't just put on perfection for Facebook, they really are that functional and photogenic? Steve's the kind of guy who's universally beloved, with popular older siblings who paved the way for him from birth, their cute kid brother to the end, even if he is a tiny bit of a fuckup. He's their fuckup and they love him for it. Plus, with a supportive family like that, you know Steve will turn out fine. His folks live in a big house outside Durham that he visits every Sunday for dinner and to let his mom do his laundry even though there are machines in the basement here. There are three sisters and a brother all older than him, a few nieces and nephews that adore him, pictures all over Facebook of Uncle Steve.

I'm starting to feel sad now in all sorts of directions, but I try not to show it. These days Wet n' Wild would be a good spot for collecting cans, I say. Everyone parties out there now.

The slides closed down when I was around nine, and by the time I started partying, the whole water park was transformed into a graffitied skeleton of the place I remember as a kid. Weeds growing in the cracked concrete of the giant hot tub, bumper cars long abandoned, but the slides still stand, begging to be fucked with.

No way, says Steve, I didn't know that.

Bria's got her finger on the pulse. What else are the kids up to these days? asks Chris.

Oh, you know, satanic rituals. Group sex. Same old shit really, we just broadcast it on the internet now.

I see, says Chris.

Why don't you take us there? Bryan says to me suddenly.

Where? Wet n' Wild? You guys know where it is. It's not like you need a tour guide, I try, teasing.

Come on, he says, it'll be fun.

I don't know, I say. If you want to, I guess.

Eyebrows up, he looks at his roommates. You guys wanna come?

Chris defers to Steve, who shrugs his bony shoulders and puts down the lighter he's fiddling with. Yeah, he says, sure.

No one moves though, and before long Steve's talking about the flat earth movement, explaining how one of the guys at work made him watch a YouTube video about it on break last night. We sit there smoking and shooting the shit for long enough that I think Bryan's forgotten about the water slides, but when we all finish our beers, he grabs his keys from the table and says, So who's driving?

I try to think of a distraction, but the boys are all forward momentum, and to say I don't want to go would piss him off for sure. It'll be fun, Bryan says, pulling me into him.

Let's do it, I say, slipping around him to get my backpack.

We spend a few stoned minutes gathering supplies, everyone remembering and then forgetting what we need to bring along. I make sure I have my wallet and phone but even that is hard to remember through my fog. I want to ask Bryan where all the pills I left here are, but he's the one who decides when we smoke, when we drink, when we get high.

Steve brings a six-pack and then goes back into the fridge for a couple more cans and Chris rolls not one, not two, but three joints, lighting one and tucking the others away for later.

Bryan comes out of the bedroom, and again I don't know how to read the strange combination of cold and hot he's putting into the room.

We'll take your truck, hey? Bryan says to Chris, who has a giant Silverado.

Sure, says Chris, surprised but happy, the way he is anytime someone mentions his truck. He doesn't have a girlfriend, seems to be devoted to the truck instead.

I'm pleased because that means hierarchy dictates I can settle into the spotless leather backseat next to Steve, instead of riding shotgun in Bryan's cramped and cluttered car. I roll down my window as Chris backs out of the driveway.

You'll wanna take the 15 to the 20, says Bryan.

Why? asks Steve. The 15 goes straight there.

I want to stop and see Leech on the way, he says.

If either of the guys knew this was part of the plan, they don't indicate it. Leech and his family own the dump and scrap-yard, plus various side projects that ensure everyone around here knows them, whether it's from taking their kids to go watch the bears at the dump, selling Grandpa's collection of hub caps to pay rent, or picking up a quarter from Leech's trailer.

I try to focus on the good clean air hitting my face, waking me up, which is something I sense I need to be. Awake.

Steve won't stop moving next to me, rocking in his seat and tapping his knees. He's like a puppy, restless and gangly. Chris turns the radio to the hard rock station, and we drive into the night outside town to the sound of a heavy, pulsing beat that seems to signal some sort of doom. He slows as he takes the turn off the main highway and pulls onto the two crumbling lanes of the 20, the old highway as people call it around here.

A nicer song comes on and I'm grateful. What's this? I ask.

Bryan laughs.

Nirvana, Steve answers.

Kurt Cobain, says Bryan, humming along, in love with his own voice, which isn't half-bad. You would have liked him, he says. He shot himself in the head.

I know who Kurt Cobain is. I just don't know his entire discography, I say, reaching for the last word and, thank fuck, finding it. Talk a big talk to hide the rising feeling that I really should have distracted him, gotten us out of this somehow.

What generation are you, Bria? Chris is asking me, as if I come from some other planet. And maybe I do?

I don't know, I say.

Why? asks Steve.

Nah, we're Y, says Chris. How old did you turn today anyway, Bria?

Slow down, says Bryan. The turn off's up here.

Leech's trailer is away from the main house, off behind the scrapyard. Bryan says something low to Chris, who responds in the affirmative. Eventually lights appear ahead, and we slow to a stop, parking next to a row of broken-down cars. Outside the trailer, those multicolored lanterns are strung up around a crude fire pit and a few plastic lawn chairs, but no one is outside. Chris turns off the truck, and he and Bryan get out.

We'll be right back, says Bryan, and they leave without further ado.

What, we're not invited? jokes Steve.

Apparently not, I say. Should we steal Chris's truck? He left the keys.

Steve laughs.

I arrange my face into faux seriousness. I mean it, Steve. Run away with me. Let's leave this all behind.

Something weird happens then: I don't mean it, but as soon as I say it, I do. In one long moment, it all plays out in my mind. How we'd run into each other somewhere, maybe at his work or mine, and I'd do the thing where I pop a hip while I put my number in his phone, somehow holding the phone in front of my chest suggestively at the same time. How he'd see me different, start inviting me to family stuff on weekends, and I'd make friends with his sisters and his buddies' girlfriends. His mom would be cold and indifferent but slowly warm to me, and his dad would like me right away. We'd stay in and watch movies, get a dog, and be loved up on the couch forevermore. Until something happened to fuck it up, like he'd say something presumptuous about my past, insinuate I'm some kind of victim whore, and I'd do something big and bratty in retaliation to prove him right and wrong at the same time, and we'd end up rotten, just like everything that starts out sweet.

I think all of this in a moment, and in the next Steve laughs obliviously. He unbuckles his seat belt and leans into the front seat. They could have at least left the windows rolled down for us, he says and then exclaims, Aha! He holds up a pack of smokes triumphantly. Chris left his weed, he says, fishing out a joint and opening the door. You coming?

I glance at the trailer. It's true they'll probably be awhile. We shouldn't, Chris rolled those special for the slides, I say, only partly kidding.

Come on, says Steve. Don't you think they're in there getting high right now?

True, I say, sliding across the seat and getting out on his side. Careful though. I feel like Leech probably has the place booby-trapped.

I shut the door softly and follow Steve away from the trailer, back towards the road. The motion sensor lights are on, revealing the area immediately around the trailer, but as we walk under the trees that mark the edge of the yard and the start of the bush, the lights go out. We're swallowed by the dark.

Steve lights the joint and takes a few hits to get it going, then passes it to me and cranes his head back to take in the stars. Under some unspoken agreement, we smoke in silence, but it's never really quiet in the country. There's the rhythmic cricket creak, the endless oscillating drone of mosquitos as they buzz around your ears before settling on a good spot to binge. There's the distant wail of semitrucks speeding by on the highway, mournful and fleeting as they come and go. And then there's the voices, too muffled to pick out words, coming from inside the trailer. I listen to the shapes they make instead, square and impenetrable, like a brick house, then easygoing, then imploring. Talking without saying anything, but then getting to it, short punches of words, back and forth. Everything quiet becomes loud when you're outside in the middle of nowhere at a drug dealer's trailer. Steve passes the joint back, and I take three long hauls before handing it off.

Wanna take bets on how long they'll be? I ask, when I'm good and stoned.

He laughs. Who cares. It's kind of nice out here.

It kind of is, I say.

The voices are louder now, moving closer to the doors. Steve and I walk back to the truck and slip into either side of the backseat as the trailer door opens and light empties out. Then the motion sensors are triggered, illuminating the yard even more. Chris comes out first, Bryan hanging back to exchange a few more words before he goes. I can only make out: Thanks, man, see you soon.

The truck bounces with their renewed weight. Before anyone says anything, Chris has the keys in the ignition, and with a turn the truck fills with sound. He reverses quickly and heads back down the gravel road faster than we came.

What'd you guys get? I ask. Even though I know not to.

I'll tell you later, says Bryan, after making me wait a minute. He and Chris continue some conversation that started in the trailer. The music is too loud to follow from the backseat, but I think it's something about a boat.

I give up listening and watch my reflection flicker in the window as the landscape flies by on the other side. The road is bumpy, and Chris is driving so fast the back end of the truck fishtails on the loose gravel. It feels like if I pay attention to everything, then we'll all be okay, but I have to really focus on every detail around us or this will spin out of control.

Chris slows at the stop sign, which is good. He even signals as he turns onto the new highway, and around here that's considered pretty optional.

The slides rise up out of the flatness of the prairie, lording their height over the surrounding fields and parking lots like a coil of faded turquoise entrails. Why is everything aquatic painted that same bright blue? Give me a soothing navy swimming pool any day. Or a fucked-up fuchsia. Anything other than this fake tropical bullshit. There are two high slides and two lower ones, all of them winding and circling around each other in a tangle before emptying into either side of the main pool at the bottom. It's always reminded me of seeing the guts spill out of a deer's belly once after Dad went hunting.

We turn off the highway and off-road it a bit outside the bounds of the parking lot, not that it's clearly demarcated these days anyway. Chris pulls in close to some bushes, hiding us from sight of the main road, and turns off the truck.

Wet n' Wild, says Bryan, hopping out. It's the youngest I've ever seen him look, having gotten his way right up to this moment.

One by one, the truck doors slam, and we take a moment to face down the hulking form of the slides in front of us. I lead the boys back around to the main doors, though they seem ready to walk the perimeter and look for a good place to climb the fence. Not necessary. The same old iron revolving doors that you've always needed to pass through to get inside the park are still standing, and kids cut through the chains that they used to keep the doors from turning. I go first, stepping into one triangular chamber of the doors and pushing the metal bars with their flaky black paint until they start to turn reluctantly.

When the doors spit me out, everything is overgrown but familiar. Like walking through the halls of your childhood. Different but the same. Ruined but the same. The guys come through the doors and immediately fan out, loping through the grass in the direction of the slides while I hang back. Bryan sees me behind them and slows. You good? he asks, as we fall into step beside each other.

Yeah, I say, noticing again the distance between us. Hands hanging at our sides when usually his would be on my waist, in my hair, circling my wrist like a bracelet of fingers, always surprised that he could reach.

Even if we don't touch, we're connected; I can tell I'm meant to follow as he veers away from the slides, which Chris and Steve have headed straight for, and over to the long, low main building. Hand-painted wooden signs hang above the doorways, big red carnival letters advertising hot dogs, ice cream, change rooms, and staff offices.

Everything's open now, crumbling, accessible. It still smells like wet grass and chlorine, or maybe that's me imagining.

We wander through rooms, stepping around glass and debris as we turn around to take it in, like it's a museum or an art gallery. Bryan takes out his phone to use as a flashlight after I trip and crash into him. Here, he says, offering me his arm as we make our way forward.

He leads me deeper, through storage rooms and down a hall to a doorway with a sign that says maintenance. It's a boiler room or something, dark pipes running along the ceiling and down the walls. An equation of initials is written on the wall:

AG + RD. Or half an equation, I guess, because there's no heart surrounding it, nothing to indicate what A and R equal when they add themselves up. Fuck me, I'm screwed, reads another wall, the letters chaotically sized and warbling. Mostly it's tags, names too overblown and exaggerated to make out by the light of Bryan's phone.

When I turn back to him after reading the walls, Bryan is busy with a baggie of powder. Here, he says, try some of this. A small mound of white powder is piled into the valley between his thumb and index finger.

I remember then that I am the one with prior knowledge of this place, that he's been leading me back here blind.

When I don't bend down to it right away, he pushes it in my face. Come on, you'll like it.

Easy, I say. What is it even?

I traded some of your pills to Leech for it. And some cash.

I wait several heartbeats and ask him how much.

Enough, he says.

What is it? I ask again.

He puts the powder up his own nose, angrily. Then not. It's something he just got in from out west. I like it, he says. Laughs.

I'm good, I say.

He laughs again, at me this time. Since when do you ever turn anything down?

Our eyes really and truly meet for a minute, and what passes between us is an arm wrestle of emotions, but before I can tell what we're fighting for, his gaze wanders, even as it's still meeting mine. He's too newly high to fight.

I smoked a joint with Steve, I say. Let that wear off a bit first. And before he can protest, I say soothingly, Come on, let's go find the guys.

I walk back the way we came, away from the light of his phone and towards the exit, then out into the paltry light of the moon.

Hey, I yell to Steve and Chris, who I can hear but cannot see. Where are you guys?

Up here! Steve calls back. I look up and see him waving from the staircase to the slides a couple flights above us, his pale face aglow from working night shifts all summer.

Bryan shuffles along, suddenly zombie-like, next to me. I grab his hand as we start to climb but drop it when I see how decrepit the stairs have become. I haven't been here since last summer and the seasons have taken their toll. I go first and Bryan follows, letting me set the pace for once. The stairs are concrete and winding, with platforms you could stop and catch your breath at on your way up.

We find the guys halfway to the top, at the entrance to the lower slides that were intended for the young and the afraid. Coming here when I was a kid, it seemed like half the day was spent climbing stairs and then waiting in the line at the top for your turn and for that sharp, clear *go* that meant you could launch yourself into the dark mouth of the slide. But it was worth the wait and the climb both to whip around those corners, catching glimpses of the sky during the longer straight-away stretches towards the bottom. Boys would try to propel themselves forward with their hands, but going fast was all about aerodynamics, lying down flat and letting yourself get swept down the slide like a leaf going over a waterfall. The squeak of skin on plastic when there wasn't enough water, the whoosh of coming around a corner hot and seeing the shadowy back of a slow poke up ahead, trying to stop in time to keep from slamming into them.

Steve is looking out at the view, while Chris leans against the wall where the go girls would have sat, smoking a cigarette. The platform is cement like everything else here, and after being able to see the ground through the holes in those stairs, I eye it warily. The last thing I want is another life-or-death situation. And yet they seem to find me.

Steve offers us beers from his backpack, and Bryan bums a cigarette from Chris. We're quiet for a minute, the boys blowing their smoke out into the open air. The moon and stars light enough of the landscape around Wet n' Wild that I can see the parcels of farmers' fields on the far side of the highway, a straight stand of trees blocking a house from the wind, and the loping strands of powerlines.

Let's keep going to the top, says Bryan.

Sure, says Steve, ever game. Chris doesn't answer so much as he grunts his consent. I can see now that Chris is on something too, something that's turned his eyes unfocused and feral. He tilts to one side when he leaves the wall, like it was doing most of the work of holding him upright. Steve seems to only be under the influence of weed and beer, and he heads up the next flight of stairs relatively nimbly. I follow behind Chris, but when I hesitate a moment to let him get a bit ahead of me, Bryan overtakes me, brushing past and letting his hand trail across my ass. Turns and says, Race ya.

I make no move to speed up. The weight of the three of them above me makes me aware that the entire structure that supports the slides is swaying slightly, bouncing almost, with the motion of our climb. Buildings are made to bend to make them strong, I tell myself, but I test my footing before moving to the next step.

Everyone is out of breath at the top, the boys having refused to put out their cigarettes. Up here there's more garbage on the ground: beer cans and bottles, a girl's sneaker, a pair of jeans flattened and hard from the weather, but there's more view to take in too. The dark bed of treetops down below, and the breeze moving steadily by, like it's determined to get somewhere else. I wish it would take me with it, but the boys are gathered at the entrance of the two slides, and I go over to them.

Do you think you can make it all the way down the slides? Steve asks me.

No way, I say.

I bet you could, says Chris, sticking his head into the slide on the right.

Don't, I say. It's probably full of raccoon nests and broken glass and shit.

I bet there's some weird fucking graffiti too, says Steve, sitting down in the slide opposite and looking in. He scoots forward, one hand on the upper edge of the tube, says, Whoa.

What is it? I ask.

His head reappears. I see something funny. I'm gonna check it out. He dips back into the slide and out of sight.

I look over at the other slide and find Chris is gone too. Idiots, I say.

You're not going to follow them? asks Bryan. He takes a sip of the beer, which he's finally cracked. The wind moves his hair, reminds me of some of why I liked him. Mostly I think it's that he demanded access to parts of me I've always kept to myself. And that seemed significant.

Personally, the last thing I want to do when I'm drunk and high is crawl through sketchy enclosed spaces, I say.

He laughs. The breeze blows harder, becomes wind, and bolsters me.

I like places like this when I'm fucked up, I say, throwing my arms above my head and spinning around, shaking out my new hair.

Wide open spaces, he says. Just that, like it's a poem and not a Dixie Chicks song.

My mom used to tell me that fairies wash their hair with the wind, I offer, knowing it's the kind of thing he likes me to say. It's the kind of thing I used to like to say too, before he started acting like he invented everything about me.

Oh yeah? He smiles.

Yep, I say, wandering to the other side of the platform, conscious of his eyes on me. She also said they do the dishes by licking them clean. She helped me leave snacks out for the fairies, a Cheerio in the corner of every room, until we got mice. I lean into the wall and look out over the landscape.

I liked your hair better before, he says.

Before any outrage can register, an object flies at me out of nowhere, veering away at the last second so it just barely brushes my naked shoulder. Rushing backwards, I bang into Bryan, grabbing onto his arm in fear before I realize—it's only wings flapping. I've disturbed a pigeon or something.

Sorry, I say to Bryan, letting him go. That startled me.

He runs his hands over my arms to warm them, though I'm not cold.

Hey, Steve, I shout at the slide. You guys okay?

Muffled yells return. I want to rifle around in my bag for a pill and a smoke but don't want him to see me wanting anything right now.

Bryan has stayed close since I grabbed onto him like an idiot, and now he says low to me, So, what do you say?

About what?

He snakes an arm around my waist. About selling your stash to Leech. We could make some real money, Bria. Maybe we could even move in together.

I pull away and look at him. Sorry, what?

That's what I was there to talk to him about tonight. We made a deal.

It finally hits me then, that I've got nothing left. They're basically gone. Panic grips me at the thought of my pills and what I'll do without them, runs rampant, and spills over into something else as he holds me close, his hands sliding down my body, breasts, waist, tummy, touching me like I'm his to touch at all times and I'm not in fact fucking freaking out right now.

I don't want to make any deals with you, I say. I'm out. It's over. I need some space.

He laughs, but I can hear the edge. Calm down, he says, grabbing my arms just above the elbows.

Unthinkingly, I shove him in the chest, but he's so fucked up, he bends like rubber, bouncing away and then back, hands even tighter now around my arms. I remember the self-defense moves we learned in gym last year, bringing my hands out, around, and down so wildly it breaks his hold on my arms.

For fuck's sake, Bria. He steps back, glaring at me while searching his pockets for a bump.

For an instant, I see it clearly. Dad and Steph. Tash and Rick. Me and everyone I've been with basically.

I open my mouth to tell him again that it's over, when someone starts to scream from down below. A man's voice, frantic and familiar, but I can't tell if it's Chris or Steve, yelling help, over and over.

My eyes snap to Bryan's and we run together to the stairs and down towards the sound. Careful, I say when I hit the missing stair, putting my weight onto the railing and using it to vault down a step, making better time than him.

Round the corner to the first platform, but there's nothing, no sign of them. The shouting has stopped. We keep going, down and down the short flights of stairs to the next platform, until finally, two stories down, just above the baby slides, there's Chris bent over Steve on the cement ground, doing chest compressions. Oh my god.

I come skidding to a stop over them, already reaching for my phone when Steve sits straight up and smiles.

Gotcha, says Chris, falling back on his heels and then onto his ass laughing.

You were right, Steve says to me, getting up and dusting himself off. It was a horror show in there. We both climbed out as soon as we could.

You guys were too distracted to notice I guess, eh, says Chris.

I look at all of them, seeing nothing in their faces except how little they care about me, and keep going down the stairs.

When I reach the bottom, I start to run, needing to put more space between them and me. I stop past the hot tub where parents would relax while their kids hit the slides and sit down on a relatively intact picnic table.

The guys come slowly after me, calling out various apologies. By the time they emerge at the bottom, Steve is ahead and Bryan and Chris drop back, sit down at the edge of the empty main pool, legs dangling. I hear fresh beers crack.

Steve says my name as he approaches. I don't answer. He sits beside me.

Listen, that was dumb. I didn't mean to freak you out. I was just drunk and went along with it.

That's okay, I say and mean it. It's the most automatic thing in the world. Forgiving men for scaring me without intending to, for hurting me by accident.

And that's when I know. It's just like Steph said, about how you'll know when something is over. It's the most obvious thing.

Steve and I sit, talking slow about coming here when we were younger. Eventually Bryan ambles over. How're you kids getting on? he asks.

Good, says Steve, standing up and walking back over to Chris.

One thing I love about that guy is he can really take a hint, says Bryan. When I don't respond, he goes, Aww, you're still mad. Tries to pull me towards him, romantically. He means it: he really does think I'm being cute. I shake him off.

I'm serious, you know, I say.

About what? he asks. All at once he can go from wanting me to not wanting anything to do with me. I can see him flip the nice off, like turning out the lights. It falls off him.

About Leech. And about us. It's over.

Reflected in his eyes, I can almost see myself, spinning. Try to gauge how fucked up he is, if anything I say right now matters, and if we should be getting into a car with him and Chris right now. Of course, we shouldn't, but I don't even know how to drive. Theoretically Steve could, but getting the keys out of these goons isn't going to be easy.

Stay here and calm down for a while, he says eventually, standing up to go back over to the guys. I follow, tired enough not to be afraid of him and wanting this to be over. Willing to let it go for now, even if it means I have to re-break up with him tomorrow.

Bryan drives because Chris is now truly fucked up, but not so fucked up that he doesn't ask Bryan for a bump before we get in the car.

Sorry, I'm out, says Bryan. But we can stop at Leech's on the way back, he says brightly, looking at me.

So, he is listening, at least well enough to know that would piss me off. I don't say anything; it would only make it worse. The radio comes on loud when Bryan starts the car, but he turns it off, and that makes me feel one modicum safer than I felt before. Same when he rolls down every window. I hold my breath for the first few moments we're on the road, but he seems to be doing a decent job at staying in between the lines. No one speaks until we get to the turnoff to Leech's.

Really? Steve asks. Can't it wait until tomorrow? He's probably sleeping by now.

He's not sleeping, says Bryan.

I don't know, man, says Steve, yawning. Even drug dealers have bedtimes.

In the front seat, Chris's head is resting against the window frame, but I can't tell from this angle if he's awake or not. Bryan turns, keeps driving.

This is the road everyone takes to drop off garbage at the dump. People who don't have trucks will just pile their bags of garbage on the hoods of their cars and drive over like that. The road is bumpy and sometimes a bag of trash or an item that hasn't been secured will fly off on the way, making the road feel like an extension of the dump itself. I do my best to direct all my attention outside the truck as we drive, watching the fields blur by and letting the wind wake me up and up.

Then a black blob interrupts the blur. Bryan swerves around it, a huge bag of garbage that almost resembles the round rump of a bear.

Oh my god! I say, brain tripping over itself because of what it thinks I saw.

What? asks Bryan.

Pull over! I yell and don't remember what I say next, but then he's swearing at me and pulling the truck onto the shoulder. Before anyone can tell me not to, I open the door and run back up the road.

15.

And it is a bear, because some things are exactly as they seem. Like Bryan, like me.

The bear is hit and dying, and I saw it because now I see.

Bria! What the fuck? Bryan screams at me out the truck window.

The bear lies on his side, half on the shoulder and half over the line. It's darker here than it was at the slides, but as I get closer it's bright enough to see his eyes are open, his breath shallow and intermittent. I can smell him too, a wet herbaceous smell, like kidneys and cut grass.

Bria get back in the fucking truck. Or I'm gonna leave you here.

I continue to ignore him, and he continues shouting my name like he can use it to control me.

Shut up! The words tear a hole in me. I turn around to face him as the wind picks up my hair and tosses it around. Scream them, one by one.

Shut!

Up!

Each word scrapes my throat coming out. I turn back to the bear. He's not moving except to breathe those short breaths. I'm about ten feet away, but it feels close, and I'm wary of what effort he might suddenly summon.

There's a song Dad loves with this line that asks, Do you know what blood looks like in a black and white video?

Shadows is the answer, and it's the same in the dark. Blood like shadows.

Right now, what is and isn't blood is unclear. I can't look at the bear's back legs—they're so broken.

I swear to god, Bria, Bryan says and gets out of the truck.

The bear's eyes are yellow-brown and beady. They fix on me, and I'm held in the hot light of their pain.

Shit, Bryan says, coming up behind me and seeing. And to his credit, he does stop and stare as the bear tries to turn towards us and lets out a sound like the beginnings of a moan, cut short. Foam gathers at the corners of his mouth. He doesn't try to move anymore. I want to scream again.

It wasn't me, says Bryan.

I have the feeling he'll deny everything, anything I say now he'll deny, but I try, for the bear, to convince him. We have to help it, Bryan.

He enjoys me this way: imploring. Doesn't understand, still, that we're done.

Come on, he says and gently tugs me by my shirt back towards the truck. Let's get out of here before someone sees us.

I yank away. No. You go, I say. I'm going to stay.

He goes off again immediately. Bria, I don't have fucking time for this. Just get back in the truck.

I meant it, you know, I say. It's over between us.

He laughs like I'm funny. Whatever, he says.

I'm staying with the bear.

We hate each other with our eyes, each trying to outlast the other, but I can't be moved.

Suit yourself then, he says.

I bend down to the bear's level, try to broadcast comfort at it. Behind me the truck door opens and shuts again. Hear voices arguing, calling my name. Then the sound of something thrown out the window, into the ditch.

When they leave, they take the light with them. Dark rushes in. I go retrieve my bag from the ditch. Then back to the bear.

There are no cars coming from either direction, but I try to get the bear to move off the road anyway. Come on, I say, slapping my thighs and speaking to it like it's a strange dog or something. Come on, over this way. It's not safe there, buddy.

Closer now, there's no mistaking the extent of his injuries. I take out my phone and go to my contacts. Remember I have none.

It's okay, I say, but the bear doesn't believe me. It lets out a sound like a whine, a sound that's not human and not animal but something else.

Pain reduces us, makes us all the same. The yearning in the bear's eyes grows wild, and I have to do something to make it stop.

Clutching my phone, I look to it again for an answer, but none are forthcoming. Fuck, fuck, fuck, I whisper-chant to myself.

Despair rolls in then like fog, thick and impenetrable, for me, for the bear. I look around for a worst-case scenario rock, a weapon to end its suffering, but there's nothing, just gravel and grass. I couldn't do that anyway, with these shaking hands.

Crouch down and watch the bear from the place I paced to. This time it doesn't watch me, doesn't move its eyes to follow.

And then it occurs to me: if it's pain that needs relieving, I am in a position to help.

In my purse: three of my last-chance pills, my better-figure-it-the-fuck-out-soon pills. End-of-an-era pills. Sacrificial birthday pills. I'm not well versed in the science behind opioid treatment for bears, but three seems like the minimum that would be required to have an impact on an animal of its size.

But how to deliver the dose.

Clutching the baggie that holds the pills, I return to the bear. He doesn't attempt to move as I approach, and up close I find I'm not so afraid anymore. Two things I know: it won't be long now, and if I can take away some of its fear, I have to try.

I empty three white pills into my hand. I could crumble them, sprinkle the dust onto his snout so that he licks it off, like we do with the hairball treatment for the cats. But the wind could carry it away and I sense that he can't move much now. Could pop them in his open mouth, in which I can see his tongue, the pink ridges of the top of his palate.

I test getting closer, closer still. Two feet from my hands to his mouth. Then one. Right beside him now. There's no warmth in the air, nothing that radiates off the bear but suffering. Panic flickers for a moment, then gone, even that untenable. His only reaction is to widen one eye at how close I am. I'm sorry, bear, I say and take a pill between my fingers. Reach out and touch the back of his head. Feels like running your hand over the bark of a tree; its fur has a roughness, but my fingers can imagine it sun-warm, sniffing for berries in the low bush, digging for meals at the dump. He doesn't react, so I move my hand towards his mouth, aiming for the far recesses, where tongue slopes towards throat, and drop the pill in.

It disappears from sight. The bear doesn't move, doesn't react to my touch. I drop the next one, again trying to get it far enough back that he'll swallow.

And it works, the instinct intact—the muscles contract and force what's in his mouth down. I'm bracing to drop the last pill when I hear another sound: not just the bear breathing, but the sound of someone else's lungs and footfalls.

In my surprise, my fingers release the pill. It falls onto the bear's snout, then to the ground right beside his mouth.

Steve runs up, red-faced and panting. Holy shit, he says.

I didn't know what to do, I offer in return, panicking now that there's someone to panic to and also at what I've done. My sacrifice. I had to try to help it, I say.

Steve takes in the scene, and I keep starting forward towards the bear, then stopping.

I don't know, Bria. I think it's beyond help.

Are you sure?

His eyes go to the bear's hind legs, where mine won't go again. I think it's dying, he says.

I wince to hear the words. What should we do?

I don't know, he says. Call animal control?

In the middle of the night? And tell them what?

Or I don't know, he says, searching. Do you know anybody with a gun?

I recoil at this, but then look at the bear and feel defeated. I take out my phone, the old burner of Dad's, and hit redial.

All Stars, Dave answers, on the first ring.

Hi, I say. It's Bria.

Bria? Where are you? Everyone's worried.

Everyone? I ask.

Are you okay? asks Dave.

Not exactly.

What's wrong?

I was wondering if you might have a gun?

Jesus, what's going on?

I tell him.

Call somebody! he says.

I did!

I mean the cops or animal control or something.

The bear's still breathing the same labored breaths. Resting his head on his shoulder, he watches me with one yellow eye, the final pill inches from his teeth. Look, I say, if you can't help, I'll call someone else.

You're out by the dump?

Yeah.

He pauses. I'll be right there.

I tell him where we are, to the best of my ability.

The turnoff to get to Leech's, he says with a sigh. Yeah, I know it.

I hang up and turn back to the bear. I need to get the pill I dropped before Dave arrives.

Steve checks the time on his phone, and I try to make my move while his attention is elsewhere, but he grabs me. Bria! he says, jerking me back. Don't get so close!

He keeps looking over in the direction Bryan drove. If they go to Leech's and then straight home, they won't pass us again.

What happened after you guys drove off? I ask.

Steve shakes his head. I told him to stop. I mean, obviously he can't just fucking leave you out here in the middle of the night.

He did though, I say.

Yeah, says Steve. Asshole. I'm sorry he treats you like that.

I shrug. Not anymore, I say.

Good, says Steve.

We broke up, I add.

Oh, he says.

It feels good to say it, exhilarating even, but then the bear snuffles, brings me back. His breathing now even more hard-earned.

We wait for headlights to appear. Steve stands back from the bear, watching it and me both.

Thirty minutes pass this way. I check the time on my phone constantly, so often it surely encourages the space-time continuum to slow. Adrenaline woke me up, sobered me up, and with a clear, uncomfortable mind, I try not to think of the fallen pill. I want to cry for the bear but cannot, because it's not over for it yet, nothing is, there is still all this pain, so I pace and hold onto anything I can, mostly my elbows, my breath.

Finally we see headlights speeding towards us. I panic for a moment, thinking it's Bryan.

But it's Dave's car, I see as he stops. The passenger door opens, and Dad steps out.

Jesus Christ, Bria, is the first thing he says. He comes straight over and looks me up and down as if checking for damage, then hugs me hard.

Did you do this? Dave demands of Steve.

No, Steve says, we were driving by and Bria saw.

Someone else hit it, I say. We found it this way.

What are you doing out here in the middle of the night? Dad demands. Dave has rushed over to the bear, slowing as he nears.

Please, I beg, just do something to help it. Though the commotion has alarmed the bear, it still doesn't move, but the look in its eyes escalates.

Go wait in the car, both of you, Dad orders.

We go, grateful to finally be told what to do. I climb into the second backseat I've shared with Steve tonight and watch through the windshield as Dave and Dad talk over the bear. To me, the pill on the gravel next to the bear screams out to be seen, heard.

Dave comes back to the car. Pops the trunk.

Don't look, says Steve.

Why? I ask, but Steve grabs my head and hides it in his shoulder. I try to pull away, but he doesn't let me go until there's a shot, then another. When he loosens his hold on me, I stay slumped against him. There'll be no looking now.

The driver's door opens, and Dave gets in, then Dad. I wait for them to say something about the prescription-grade fentanyl pill resting near the bear's muzzle. A pill that should be very familiar to them both.

Let's go home, Dave says, starting the car.

There's my favorite word again. I can't take it anymore; something in me tips from tragedy to comedy as Dad turns around and squeezes my knee. You okay? he asks.

Where did you even come from? I ask.

He glances at Dave and then says, Dave's been letting me stay at his place for a few nights. We'll talk later, okay? Then, to Steve, he says, Where can we drop you off, son?

I laugh, loud, and all of them look at me, even Dave, who is turning the car around, taking care not to back into the bear. The poor dead bear. I want to cry but laugh instead. Son, I say.

Uh, says Steve. I live in the townhouses over on Prior Road, but you can drop me off anywhere, sir.

Sir! It's all too much. I can't stop the laughter or the tears.

Take Steve home with us, I order, when I collect myself. We can call you a cab from there, I add, thinking of what might happen if we drop Steve off and Bryan is there.

I'm the cruise director of this night now. Maybe I always have been, orchestrating everything behind the scenes of my mind, unbeknownst even to me. What did Bryan say about me again? That I had some kind of masterplan. Do I? Am I doing everything on purpose, after all?

We drive on in silence. Dave steers the car carefully, driving below the speed limit all the way, pushing the button attached to his rear-view mirror to open the garage as we pull into his driveway.

Inside, Dave switches on the kitchen light, and we blink at it, Steve and I especially. His eyes are red, and I feel the full weight of how tired I am finally.

Dad gets us glasses of water, pulls out a chair, and sits down at the kitchen table. He touches my hair. Looks good, he says and then turns to Steve. You better call a cab, he says, or you'll be waiting until next week for it to show up.

Steve nods and takes out his phone, asks Dave for the address.

I'm starving, says Dave. Anyone else?

Dad and I shake our heads. Sorry, Dave adds. I was closing up when you called. I haven't eaten all night.

Eat, I say, and he begins rooting around in the freezer, taking out a pizza and tearing open the box. Steve joins us at the table, having ordered the cab.

They said fifteen minutes, he says.

That's code for two hours, Dad says. You better get comfortable, he adds, referencing how distinctly uncomfortable Steve looks. So, how long have you guys been going out? he asks me.

We're not, I rush to say. Steve is . . . my friend.

Dad nods, not believing. And what were you doing out by Leech's in the middle of the night?

I hedge. Uh, it wasn't the plan. We were out with some people, and they wanted to stop at Leech's . . .

Bria saw the bear as we were driving, Steve says. She insisted we stop, but the others didn't want to.

They left you out there? Dad asks.

Yeah, I say, annoyed at him of all people being mad at someone for abandoning me. Imagine that, I say.

Dave slides the pizza into the oven, though it hasn't had time to come to temp yet. Bria, he says, I'll pull the couch out for you, okay? and goes to get that set up.

I should keep an eye out for that cab, says Steve, following Dave into the living room, leaving me and Dad alone.

Don't you dare be rude to Steve, I say as low and angry as I can. He's the only nice guy I know. And we aren't dating. If it wasn't for him, I'd have been stuck out there alone.

Dad smiles. Okay, he says. I believe you.

And I hate you, I offer.

Easy, he says, serious now. I'm sorry, kiddo. You know I love you.

Dave comes back in. Bed is made up, whenever you want to hit the hay.

I'd like to now please, I say.

Good, says Dad. We can talk in the morning.

In the living room, Steve is at the front door, about to sneak out.

Is the cab here? I ask.

No, but I thought I'd wait on the front steps. Let you get to sleep.

I'll wait with you, I say and follow him out.

That same stupid wind is still blowing, making me cold out here in my summer clothes. I duck inside and pull one of the blankets Dave put on the couch for me around my shoulders, then sit next to Steve on the concrete steps. I swear it's like summer ended since we got back to Dave's. That's how our seasons go around here. Really throwing themselves in your face.

We fall silent. I cannot think of a thing to say. We just sit and watch the end of Dave's block for one of the green and orange cabs that serve our town to appear. Nothing moves at this hour. It's too early and too late for anything.

I'm gonna see if the cab will take me to my folks' place, says Steve.

They will, I say, for sure.

Good, says Steve. I don't want to go back to our place.

He means Bryan's. How come? I ask.

He's always been an asshole, but tonight, and you . . . He looks at me, his face angry, upset. The way he treats you, he says, trailing off again.

I feel it now. Shame. And I want out from under it. He's not all bad, I say. It's weak even to my ears.

It's fucked up, he says.

I guess it is, I say. I can't feel feelings any longer. I can't even think another thought. Underneath the blanket, I put my hand in my pocket, and my fingers find a pill.

You. I would know you anywhere.

And it beams through me like happiness. I'm not full out.

I see it then. I'll never be out, not fully. I'll always know where to find more in Dad or in Bryan, or in a guy like Bryan. Somewhere, somehow. I see all of it. All the lies I've lied for you. How, as shit as things are, there's so far still to fall. Even with tonight's finality with Bryan, it could all be reversed. The easiest thing in life is giving in.

You don't have to wait with me, says Steve, breaking into the prison of my thoughts.

No, no, I say. I don't mind. I don't think I can sleep yet.

Okay, he says. And we go back to sitting silent on the steps, Steve craning his neck trying to see around the corner for the cab, probably dying to get out of here, out of this, and never go near a mess like me again, and me fingering my pill. Turning, testing it. I wonder if I can taste it through my skin—I might have heard that from that nurse who gave the talk in the school gym last year.

Can you get this away from me? I don't care what you do with it.

I thrust it at him, holding out my open palm so he can see the pill.

Steve, for his part, stares. Stares for so long I pray I won't have to tell him what it is. And why.

Something moves behind us, inside the house, and Steve covers my palm with his as Dad opens the door and steps out. When Steve lets go of my hand, it's empty.

Sun's coming up, says Dad, and we all turn to look where he indicates. Indeed, in the few moments our attention has been on the pill, the night has receded. Now the predawn light casts the block in a pink hue that reflects off the windows of the houses, amplifying itself.

The cab appears as we all watch the light grow, and it creeps slowly up the block, as if the cabbie too, is in awe of the dawn.

Bye, Steve, I say as he stands.

Thanks for looking out for her back there, Dad says.

No problem, says Steve.

As he's shutting the cab door, he calls out, Happy birthday, Bria!

Thanks, I say and raise a hand in goodbye as the cab starts rolling down the block.

Dad and I go back inside the house. Dave is rinsing dishes in the kitchen, humming a tune.

I crawl straight into the couch bed Dave's made for me, wrap the blankets around myself, cocooning up tight.

I expect Dad to leave me here, go talk to Dave, go to bed, but he sits down in the armchair next to the couch and asks, Mind if I watch some TV?

Sure, I say and close my eyes. Listen to the sound of him breathing next to me, feet up on the far side of the couch, flipping through channels, finally stopping on an old sitcom, so the laugh track is the last thing I remember before falling asleep.

16.

A ins lies down, her weight familiar even before conscious-
ness fully finds me. Next come the bodies of Doug and
Emily with their soft kid smells.

Hi, I say, as Doug snugs in between us and Emily big spoons
me from behind, one of her little hands wrapping around to land
on mine. Ains must have told the kids to be good, because they
settle in like angels, all gentle and quiet.

I blink at Ains through sleep-crusted eyes, recognizing the
distinct metal rods of a pullout couch or a futon digging into my
back. Wonder, Where even am I?

Hi, says Ains, looking at me solemnly. You get some sleep?

I guess, I reply, though I'm still trying to figure out if I'm in
fact awake or dreaming—I'm not moving from the fetal position
she's found me in until I do. What is sleep with no rest, anyway?
I offer.

Is that some kind of Zen koan?

Yeah, I say, I'm Buddhist now, and am relieved when she smiles.

Ains? Tash's voice calls from somewhere. I hear a door open, and then her voice again, more clearly. Can I talk to you outside for a sec? she says.

Coming! Ains replies hurriedly. I'll be right back, she says to me.

Okay, I say.

I roll over, finally recognizing Dave's living room. But that small motion breaks some precarious peace treaty with my body. Excuse me, I manage to say to the kids as nausea urges me up off the couch I've somehow slept on. Suddenly it seems I'm reaping what I've sowed. Before another thought can be born in my mind, let alone last night's salient details—or the night before that, or the night before that—strange saliva fills my mouth, my heinous-feeling head. Moving isn't easy anymore: my feet keep fumbling the hallway floor and the doorway shifts as I pass through it, slamming its frame into mine. You'll regret that later, I warn.

In the bathroom, sweat blooms at my temples. Right, what about water? My cells sound their approval as it flows forth from the tap. But it's a trick—the first swallow triggers landslides in my belly, and I wretch over the open mouth of the toilet begging for relief. I'd say I don't know what I did to deserve this, but I do, and I'd do anything to get it to release me, this demon that's possessed me this morning.

Morning. Morning follows night follows information that assails me. Bears, boys, waterslides come back to me now. Dave and Dad come back to me now. Bad dye jobs come back to me now. Gunshot to the head comes back to me now. Pill in my pocket comes back to me now. Who I used to be comes back to me now.

Tear my shirt off to save it from the flash flood of sweat I'm swimming in. Yank a towel from the rack and stand up, mop up.

Hate the mirror more than me in it. Stupid flat fucking reflective surfaces.

Hear voices outside coming through the closed window. Them. My people.

Ride a nausea wave to the kitchen realizing on my way what I'm hearing and not hearing. Who I'm not hearing.

Watch them from the window like a ghost until all I am is angry now. Grab my backpack, shirt, shoes. Be right back, I say, avoiding looking at Emily or Doug as I close the front door.

Pavement, newly poured, exfoliates my bare feet as I walk up Dave's sun-strangled street cursing the light and my lack of sunglasses. Shoes hanging from one hand, shield my eyes with the other, and spot a pathetic little parkette at the end of the block. Seems as good a place as any to aim myself, so parkette ho.

Consider the facts at hand.

Dad gone. Drugs gone.

My mind traces a path back to Bryan. It's only a matter of ten, twelve blocks. Twenty, thirty minutes and I'd be back in his room. Wonder if he'd welcome me, or would I have to win him over, pay my penance. Could go either way, same as me: I can never tell if I'm going to hate him or want to submerge myself in him like he's an ocean and I'm a submarine.

I reach the entrance to the parkette—the path that cuts through it goes in the direction of his place—but before I can go any further someone slams into me from behind and then I'm skipping across the grass like a stone.

The impact knocks thoughts back out of my head. If I'm hurt, I don't feel it yet; this morning's misery has a claim on my body that will not be outbid.

When I regain the good sense to sit up and confront my attacker, I find Ains sprawled on the ground beside me. Look on her face like a slap. She's breathing hard, as if she's run a great distance to catch me, even though she's the athletic one among us.

Where the hell are you going, Bria? she demands.

That's a good question, actually. When I looked out Dave's kitchen window, he and Tash were deep in conversation, while Ains was standing nearby, not saying anything it seemed. As soon as I saw them out there without him, the lack of Dad was so obvious, the whole place screamed with how stupid I'd been for thinking he would stick around. So I left. Seemed logical at the time. But now I don't know how to defend myself as she kneels over me, sun making halos around her head.

Bria! Ains says again. Where were you going?

I put my hands up, palms green with grass stains, as if to say I'm unarmed. Because the way she's looking at me, it's like I'm causing her so much harm. I wasn't going anywhere, I tell her. I just needed a minute.

Do I believe myself? Does she? Who's to say.

I see Ains then like one of those slideshow albums your cell phone makes out of your camera roll without being asked to—you know, here's a collection of cat pics, beach day, Christmas with the family. Except I see all these images of her, sacrificing herself for us. For me. But what about me? I've sacrificed too. Hurt myself when I could've hurt someone else just as easily.

Get up, Ains says, having already done so herself.

I obey, brushing the grass from my knees and identifying new injuries on my way to standing.

She starts to speak, stops herself, looks so fed up with me I back away from her a little.

Are you going to tackle me again? I venture cautiously.

Not unless you try something stupid, she says, and it builds the slightest bridge between us.

The centerpiece of the parkette is a two-seater set of swings. Ains walks over to it, and I follow. The look she gave me when she caught up to me still stings, humming along above all my other aches. She's never looked at me like that before. I sit down next to her, trying not to swing too much in my state.

Mom kicked Rick out, Ains says, her voice weirdly high.

You told her? Glance at her, nervous.

Of course! I told her right after you took off. Bria, it's not that I didn't believe you . . . I just didn't know what to think. It was a lot to process. Anyway, I'm sorry.

I can feel her looking at me, and I evade hard, stare furiously at the ground, the sky, anything, everything but look her way.

Anyway, she says again, sad and low. Rick acted guilty as hell when Mom went for his phone. Long story short, Mark escorted him off the premises.

Imagine I barricaded myself inside a tin can. Imagine I built a fortress around me out of everything available here today, summoned the metal poles of the swing set, the boards of the bench, the bushes surrounding the park, and used them to camouflage and conceal me. Get thee to a bomb shelter, baby. That's what I feel, what it feels like to hear her talk about not believing me even for an instant. I throw years in the trash can, slam it shut. Throw myself into a black hole I can't back out of now. Or can I?

Ains is talking, her eyes welled up to the brim. I've been worried about you all summer, she says.

The word *worry* breaks her voice, and me along with it, but even as pitiful as I feel, I still try to put up a defense. I can explain, I begin.

And then my sweet cousin, who I do not deserve, who deserves better than this, delivers the killing blow.

You're addicted to them, aren't you? she asks. It isn't a question though, but a statement of fact.

Air rushes through my head, nothing but wind in between my ears. Certainly, no words in response to this. To be so known, so found out, freezes me, shines a light into my brain and exposes every corner.

I shake my head. No.

You are, she says, striking my no down with ease. I know you better than anybody. It's true. You've been acting like a fucking junkie.

A cat has been making its way across the park, its fur speckled and tawny, belly hanging low to the grass, and what occurs to me when she says this is, Oh shit, that cat heard Ains call me a junkie. It's such a ridiculous brand of embarrassment, I almost smile at the thought but stop short when I feel a knife of shame pressed into my gut, so close I can't breathe without it cutting.

I close my eyes to shut out the world, but the sound of traffic alone, cars driving places with people in them, is enough to break me. And there's more: the beep of a truck backing up somewhere, chains clanging into a tetherball pole at the school nearby, car doors slamming, and women chatting. Suddenly nothing in the world feels like it belongs to me.

How could you tell? I ask.

Her answer is ready. Lists off examples on her fingers. You seem out of it, all the time, she says. And, like, weird and cagey and . . . high.

She sways on the swing next to me, dragging the toes of her sneakers in the sand. I'm still barefoot, my shoes somewhere over there on the grass, and I bury my feet in the sand in search of something to save me. I don't know what. A trapdoor maybe. A time machine.

I mean, she goes on, I remember what Steph was like when she was high. But I wasn't sure, until the other night when I got . . . confirmation.

Her eyes flash, remembering our fight.

I was going to confront you about it a while ago, but then you seemed okay sometimes, you know? And then after that day at the beach, I barely saw you, and then your dad came back and it never seemed like the time . . .

I am silent, computing this. Even though we exist next to each other constantly, it feels like the first we've talked in months. In among everything else, there is that one good thing: her and I telling each other the truth. The balm of that makes it a little easier to hold my head up, heavy with guilt, and ask, Who else knows?

Ains started to pump her legs while I worked up the nerve to ask her, nudging herself higher and higher. When I turn to see if she heard me, she's paused like a pendulum at the top of the swing. Then her face goes grim, and she plants her feet in the sand on the downswing to come to a stop beside me.

Well, she says, Mom's back there at Dave's waiting to tell you they want you to go to rehab.

~~~~

The night of Steph's OD, the night of my first pill, no one knew what to do with me. I didn't know what to do with me.

It was too early to text Someboy. Not only in terms of the hour, but us, it was too early for us. We'd been on three dates I think, maybe four, if you could call them dates at all. I was playing games, but they were nothing compared to his. He'd had years to work his out. Being with him, around him, felt like . . . swimming out too deep? No. Like swallowing wrong, down the wrong pipe, and being held prisoner by your lungs for a while? Not quite. Felt like anytime you're moved by something too powerful to fight. Like airplane turbulence. Or trying to stop the sun from going down.

The first pill felt like that. Another thing I couldn't stop.

Just like I couldn't stop the night from dragging me along, to a party, to the bar, to his place. His hands, his bed, his face. Couldn't stop myself from doing dumb things. Certainly couldn't stop the night from turning, when I got home, into something more real than anything I'd ever encountered.

Her skin, a bit blue, but maybe that was just the TV's flickering light. My hand touching her blued skin, trying to wake her, pushing the needle through. The one thing I managed to stop.

They took me to Paradise Gardens, and we sat on the grass beyond the balcony. It was just starting to become summer. The shock of everything made me feel alive in an unhinged, exhilarated way. I needed to slow, to calm, to kill the thoughts. We sat out and watched the sun begin to pull up over the rooftops. A sleepy Mark emerged from his apartment opposite us and walked silently over to the pool to start dumping chemicals in for the day. Ursula stalked along the side of the building towards home, returning from a night of hunting and other mysteries. She slunk by us, rubbing the length of her body across Ains's back. Tash said that she was going to take a sick day. And that we could go see Steph in the hospital if I wanted.

I didn't know what I wanted, but my mind was turning, had turned, to the bag of pills in my backpack.

It should have been enough. Having them to swoop in, save me, surround me.

But there was a feeling in my belly that reminded me of shoveling snow, finally scraping down to concrete. Stomach empty, inside out. A feeling like I was sliding downhill on a fast toboggan, except standing still. Overwhelming, drowning feeling.

You should try to sleep, said Tash.

In the bathroom, I brushed my teeth, washed my face, and downed glasses of tap water, one after another, to bury the pill I'd swallowed so easily upon closing the door. Like medicine.

In bed, as Ains breathed beside me, I closed my eyes and scanned my body for a difference.

I felt something. Not better. Not exactly. Felt like . . . less. I felt less.

~~~

We go home to Paradise. Ains takes my loose ends, wraps me up. Puts underwear, socks, soft clothes in a bag. Whereas I can't imagine where I'm going, so I don't know what I'll need. Just like I don't know if I need to laugh or smoke or sleep or cry. I think of Dad and do. Cry. Puddle out in Tash's arms. She says the sort of things that should be a comfort to me. About how he'd be here if he could, and he loves me, and how he's finally facing up to his shit, and things will stabilize soon. She says it's not my fault, and it's tempting to believe she's not lying. Even says some of it's her fault, begs me of all people for forgiveness. But I see their love and raise them my failures. My fuckups. Half of which they don't even know about.

They nudge me along like a toy boat floating down a stream, keeping me from sinking to the bottom at any given time. And what can I do but let them.

~~~

Pam from next door is going to watch the kids while we're gone. Or while Ains and Tash are gone, I guess, since I don't know when I'll be back. When we're ready to leave, Emily gives me her stuffed polar bear and I wonder what they've told her. Try not to seem too serious as I bend down to hug and kiss her and Doug goodbye, holding on just a little longer than I normally would otherwise.

The deal, Tash said, is that her friend pulled some strings and got me to the top of the waiting list, but they can only hold the bed until the end of the day.

Hold the bed, I thought, what a weird way to put it. As if quitting drugs only involved having a bed to sleep in. I imagined my body, filling a bed, emptying of drugs and their aftermath, and then leaving so that the next drug-filled body could move in. I must have winced or looked otherwise ill, because Dave reassured me that they'll help me with that in treatment, give me meds and stuff for the withdrawals.

For the occasion of my first trip to rehab, they try to make me ride shotgun, but I insist the honor go to Dave. Elders first, I say, climbing into the backseat of Tash's truck with Ains. I wrap myself in a fuzzy blanket Ains provided, cold though my forehead is also sweating, and hope I don't need to use the bag she also pressed on me in case I need to puke again.

How about you tell us your doubts and fears and we'll refute them? Tash suggests from the driver's seat once we're on the road.

That sounds fun, I reply, not wanting her to know how good she is at guessing what I'm thinking, even now. How did she know? And how can I be expected to describe my fear when it's so gigantic?

It's important to get an outside perspective on your inner monologue sometimes, says Tash.

Just try it, Dave says.

Okay. My head rattles against the window as I close my eyes and let fear come to me. Fear like the dark when you're a kid. Fear that dwarfs all other fears, omni-fear, fear of everything at once. I open my eyes. Can we just listen to music? I ask.

Sure, says Tash, worried. Dave lunges for the radio controls, Ains squeezes my hand, and we all treat ourselves to pretending this isn't happening for a while.

Near the city's outer limits, they try to distract me with chatter again, each offering their own cautious kindnesses. Dave tells me things about treatment, and Tash chimes in with metaphors and analogies that are as uninspiring as ever. I'm a house mid-renovation, a work-in-progress fixer-upper that'll be flipped for millions in a couple of years with a little elbow grease. I'm trapped at the bottom of a deep well of intergenerational sadness. Rehab won't do the work of getting me out of the well for me, but it will drop down a rope I can use to climb out, if I'm willing to try.

Like a phoenix, I say.

What? asks Tash.

You forgot the part where, like a phoenix, I rise.

Right, says Tash, glancing over her shoulder at me. That too.

Just listen to what they tell you, says Dave. You won't feel better right away, but if you give it time, you won't believe how much better you can feel.

That would be nice, I say, pressing my face to the cool of the truck window.

〜〜〜

I had a vision once.

Don't get too excited. What I mean is it was like a picture someone put in my head. I don't know who. I didn't put it there. It just appeared.

It looks like this: a grown woman I don't exactly recognize, but I know it's me. And I'm sitting there at an outdoor table at a café or someplace like that. The details, like the fact it's a sunny day or what I'm wearing or if I've maintained my commanding physical presence, don't matter. This is what matters.

My fingers moving across the keyboard, pausing while I stare into the middle distance thinking something through. Lost in whatever I'm working on. And I know, somehow, that I live in a city, and I have a job and make enough money to pay for everything I need. I can buy a coffee at the corner, pick up takeout after work, maybe meet a man at a restaurant for a date I walk home from alone. Let myself into my own apartment, owing nothing to nobody. Take off my own clothes. Get into bed and fall asleep dreaming dreams I'll never tell.

I like thinking of myself that way. Even if it was just a hallucination, it's one I like to return to.

~~~~~

How does it end?

Like this: you and me against the world, ourselves, each other, or something.

Ains and I stand together outside the treatment center, where through some sliding doors Tash is talking to a person at a desk while Dave's off finding parking. Looks like I beat you to the city, I offer, just for something to say.

Yep, says Ains. You always were a competitive son of a bitch.

No one laughs.

It won't be for long, says Ains.

Long enough, I hope.

Tash comes back out the automatic doors, a stack of papers clutched in her hand. They gave me a list of acceptable personal belongings, she says. We'll go shopping and bring you some new pajamas and a bathrobe tomorrow. Maybe some books and magazines.

Okay, I say. Scared but glad for this promise of tomorrow. I'm good at storms. I know how to batten down, make blanket nests to hide in, how to pile the snow high into forts that insulate from the cold. Know how to light candles and gather everyone around and whisper stories in the dark while it rages. But I don't know how to handle this.

Tash is still rattling off words of advice. Drink lots of water and do whatever they tell you, even if it seems dumb, okay? You have to be open to this.

I'm open, I say.

The intake worker Tash was talking to is waiting for me inside the doors, letting us say goodbye. Ains takes a deep breath, and I can see the pep talk forming in her muscles, but before she can launch into it, I pull her into a hug. She hugs me back, equally hard.

I leave before she says go.

Acknowledgments

I'd like to extend my love and solidarity to all those impacted by addiction.

Thank you to Susan Scarf Merrell and Meg Wolitzer, founding directors of the BookEnds novel revision fellowship. Susie and Meg—you have taught me so much about writing, but also about how to lead with grace, generosity, and humor. Thank you, Susie for pulling me into your office to talk all those years ago. I'm also grateful to the larger BookEnds community, my Fellowship Four cohort, and especially Rachel León, whose brilliant mind benefited this book so much.

Ron Eckel is a dream of an agent: thank you for your belief in my book and your expert guidance.

Thank you to the entire marvelous ECW Press team for all the care and skill they showed me and my book throughout the publication process.

Thank you to my editor, Jen Knoch, for getting it. Your smart, sensitive editing made this novel so much better.

The Canada Council for the Arts, Manitoba Arts Council, Access Copyright Foundation, and Winnipeg Arts Council provided vital financial support that allowed me time to write while also keeping the lights on, which is a fine balance indeed.

I'm grateful to my family for cheering me on and putting things in perspective: My parents, Ian and Rebecca. Binesi, Sam, and Kristi. Ann, Richard, Maryam, Rosie, and all the Decters. (I'm related to all of them.) My grandmother Noreen and the Sanders family. Paul and Rita and the Lefebvre-Froklage families. Special thanks to Leah, Jeff, and Hazel for the location inspiration and floats down the river.

Nic, Frankie, and Lola gave me endless everyday support in the trenches. Thank you for loving me so well.

Jess, Jen, Ed, Emily, Alison, J.J., Anna, T., Dervla—thank you for your friendship while I was working on this thing. Thank you to Nicole Hebdon for her correspondence and eyes on early drafts.

Cate Le Bon is a musician whose work has inspired me for years. "What's Not Mine" is the title of a song from her 2016 album, *Crab Day*. I'm grateful to Cate for her art.

All love songs are for Nic Lefebvre.

Nora Decter is a writer from Treaty 1 Territory. She studied creative writing at York University and Stony Brook University, and in 2019 received the Kobo Emerging Writer Prize for literary fiction for her YA novel *How Far We Go and How Fast*. Nora lives in Winnipeg with her partner and their two cats, near the foot of Garbage Hill.